Requiem
for a
City

by
Anthony Hartnett

Michael Terence
Publishing

First published in paperback by
Michael Terence Publishing in 2021
www.mtp.agency

ISBN 9781800942486

Many of us recoil at the vulgar fest that is much of modern Ireland. The rampant, unrestrained drunkenness, the brutal, random violence that infects the smallest of our townlands and villages, the incontinent use of foul language... the debasement of our civic life... the fracturing of our community life...

Emily O Reilly (The Irish Times, November 6, 2004)

Cork is a mercantile port, ruled by merchant princes with pragmatic and philistine values. Having neither the metropolitan culture of a capital, nor the idiosyncratic identity of our smaller cities, the city seems consumed with resentment that its commercial prowess (now in severe decline in both cases) cannot buy it the pre-eminence it desires, and withdraws to the comforting prospect offered by the parochial mirror.

Paddy Woodworth
('Exile in the Second City' from The Cork Anthology)

Giles Norman
(with permission)

Adagio molto semplice e cantabile

Beethoven Piano Sonata No. 32 in C minor, Op. 111

Contents

CONTENTS

Part One

THE WEEKEND

The next generation of adults is likely to be the fattest, most mentally disturbed and least fertile in history, doctors warned yesterday...

Dr Vivienne Nathanson, Head of Sciences and Ethics at the BMA said teenagers' behaviour posed an extraordinary threat to an entire generation...

The (London) Independent December 9, 2003

Friday Night

Kearney was in The High C and he had attitude. He was already not in the best of humour as he and his fellow rake, Murphy, had just passed through a herd of trogs who were engaged in one of the many brawls that broke out in the city centre by night. They had barely got through the multitude without getting caught up in the simian skirmish which was in full flow on the nearby main street. Inside The High C Kearney was displeased to see that more of these trogs were scattered here and there amongst the more placid, if eccentric, clientele. This particular bar was one of the few 'character' bars left in the city, with a long marble counter and high windows through which shafts of sunlight occasionally shone by day. In winter time an ancient fireplace glowed in the cosiest corner, warming its mixed clientele - anyone from judges to hobos could be found in close proximity. At one end of the counter was Barnie Pilkington - a Lear in the storm scene type, with streaky long black hair and an austere demeanour to match his ferociously volatile temperament. In a far corner was the original Motley Crew – a clique of guys, all over forty, crumpled up, in varying stages of decrepitude. None of them had never touched a woman (except by accident) in the course of their collective lives and they spent much of their time looking at the bar floorboards or ceiling. Sitting at the other end of the counter was Doyle, an ugly, wife beating type with a drink problem. However, as well as this regular crew of misfits and deranged, arty types, there always seemed to be new people coming and going (including the occasional stunner).

Kearney was on about the city - always a touchy topic at the best of times but even more dangerous in this overcrowded den. Initially he was talking to Murphy about how the Irish were not such a good looking race. Then, as if in confirmation, a troupe of female trogs came in - attired in pink tops and skimpy mini skirts complete with flabby waists, plain to sheer ugly. When they got their pints of lager they lurched to a corner, inviting Kearney to really take off.

'Look at those trogs over there,' he said with a sigh of resignation. 'Am I right or am I right?'

'Moses O Reilly, you'll come to a really bad end,' Murphy replied, wincing at such non-pc pronouncements - it seemed that everyone in the bar was listening. He glanced around and ordered another round of drink.

'And it's not just physical appearance,' Kearney continued aloud, recounting his earlier meeting in a café with a teacher friend of his and some of her colleagues. He had just bought a stunning book on Vermeer as he was of late especially taken by the master's sublime *View of Delft*. This particular work held him in thrall with its pellucid evocation of a summer morning in 1660, its sheer brilliance in capturing a moment in time with such poetic insight, 'the light of fulfilled creation' as one critic put it. He had placed the book on the table as they all had coffee yet not one of the company passed a single comment or expressed even the remotest interest in Vermeer. Instead it was the usual banal conversation about mortgages, clothes, soccer and sprogs.

'And these were all bloody teachers,' Kearney ranted. 'What a crowd of total philistines. What a parochial waste land we live in.'

As he looked around him he saw that one of the female trogs was getting sick onto a table. He sighed, and asserted sarcastically that Ireland was originally inhabited by an especially rough Neolithic breed and so the natives couldn't very well be good looking after such a bad start. However, on Murphy's insistence, he did acknowledge that when Irish people were good looking they really were good looking. Then, as if to prove his point (these things happened in The High C) a tall, leggy brunette came in and sat down on the far sofa. 'Nine,' said Kearney promptly. 'At least,' agreed Murphy. The conversation resumed after these ritual remarks and Kearney repeated his observations on how some women behaved. The nymph behind the bar winced. 'Here we go again,' she thought and got ready for another round of perilous talk on the touchiest of topics.

'What gets me about so many women in this here city is the way they know you to see for ages and still can't even say hello,' Kearney orated. 'They dress to kill (some of them anyway), yet they come in, yap in groups, go to the toilet *en masse* and pay no attention at all to men around them. Not to mind the mixed signals brigade. Take that dame I met last week - all over me for a few nights and then what happens on Saturday night? I'm in The Beech and she turns up with some dipstick she calls her boyfriend? Why does she bother with all these mixed signals and not just go for whomever she fancies?'

Murphy had some sympathy for his fellow rake. Recently he himself had designs on this tall, lithe, glamorous redhead and he kept on getting these very positive signals. When he had finally got talking to her, he asked her to a symphony concert (a rare event for such a philistine city) but she declined, even though she had already put his phone number into her contacts list and had expressed a great interest in classical music. What really took the biscuit was that she continued to give him all these come on signals. No wonder he went round saying 'Give me a break' all the time.

Meanwhile the good looking brunette had been joined by an obese heap with dull, glazed eyes. This led Kearney to pronounce 'Second Law', with an air of exasperated despair. It was his contention that the Second Law of the universe determined that a very high percentage of attractive women had the most awful boyfriends (and vice versa according to some of his *amigas*). There might have been many reasons for this but it was a source of continuing annoyance to him.

'What could be worse than seeing a really classy woman come in with some trog?' Kearney moaned. 'Why do they do it?'

Murphy offered some nonchalant explanations. 'Maybe they're insecure? Maybe they are so attractive that guys assume they have someone even when they haven't? Maybe women like ugly guys? Maybe they look for different things?'

Whatever the reason there was evidence to confer a certain validity on the Second Law.

Just at this moment Bibi arrived into the tavern. That was what the two rakes had code named her. She was a very attractive blonde (though Murphy had reservations about her slightly common jaw), and she always dressed in the very best designer outfits - down to the fine leather handbag. She was well known by sight to the two and she must have known them in return. However there was a haughty disdain in her attitude - not for nothing was she classified as a Frosty. What was a bit peculiar was that she sometimes wore a wedding ring but not on the traditional finger, and she often played round with the ring as if she was playing mind games with nearby admiring males. This night she was dressed in a slinky black outfit but was totally indifferent to all men in the bar. This type of behaviour really vexed the rakes. Why bother going to all this trouble when she was seemingly not interested in meeting men? A stool became free and Kearney offered it to her, which she declined with a quick, glacial smile.

'Sorry for living, Ice Maiden,' he retorted, almost within her hearing.

'Forget about the wench - her loss,' said Murphy, controlling his annoyance. The night was quickly assuming its usual Friday night air.

Outside the main streets were full of the tattoo-tracksuit brigade - loud, rough, and drunk. Single women dared not walk alone after dark. People got beaten up and even killed for being in the wrong place at the wrong time. Murphy often asserted that you could walk around most European city centres at any time of the day or night and feel safe, but not in 'this zoo without a roof.' Looking out of a side window (with its view of two nearby bars) he mused wistfully on great cities he had lived in or visited.

'Your round or are we going to the next port of call'? Kearney interrupted. 'One more here and then onwards and upwards,' Murphy replied with an air of fatalism. So they stayed for one more as people kept coming and going. Things quietened down and the two took stools in the best part of the bar - near a window where they had a panoramic view of both the bar, the street outside and the two nearby bars.

In the furthest corner from the two rakes, the shapely brunette was seemingly getting into a row with the fatso she had come in with. This delighted them both and they were quite elated when he trundled off and didn't seem to be coming back. They were even more delighted when, sometime later, she approached the counter for another drink. She got her brandy and port (very impressive they thought) and sauntered back to her seat with a nonchalance that was very fetching. There was a sparkle in her eyes and a half smile on her lips. Their own sense of humour was not appreciated by all and sundry and often got them into trouble, especially with women. They were caught between two stools a lot of the time - if they talked about what really interested them (apart from women) people looked at them with scorn, and if they joked and wound people up, they were also met with a kind of disdain. They both acknowledged a keen interest in the woman. This was quite a rarity as most of the time they went for different kinds of women. Kearney (being the more forward of the two) ambled over to her and sat down next to her.

'Matt Kearney,' he said to her with a hand outstretched.

'Emma Reilly,' she replied with a confident ease.

'So how come we haven't seen you here before?' Kearney asked - the first question he always seemed to ask new women who ventured into The High C.

'Maybe you weren't looking. Maybe you were too busy grading women and looking down on the masses. Maybe I'm a new girl,' she replied with a warm glow and a look of intelligent amusement. And so the repartee went on.

'So who was the guy?'

'Oh it's a long story.'

'So he's not your beau?'

'Give me a break. Aren't you going to invite your friend to join us?'

'No.'

'So what makes you think I prefer you?'

'Why don't we meet women like this more often?' Kearney thought. Most local women were so indirect and full of insecurities.

'Dare I presume? My buddy can cope I'm sure. So what do you do?'

'CERN, Geneva believe it or not.'

'You CANNOT be serious,' said Kearney in a John McEnroe-ish tone.

'Indeed. I'm here for a seminar - I left here about five years ago and got a job in CERN.'

Kearney was fascinated... the world of neutrinos and muons, of ghost particles and leptons, Schrodinger's Cat and Einstein's faith in a comprehensible universe, light as a wave and as a particle, quarks and string theory. The chances of meeting a woman like Emma in The High C were about the same as the Motleys collectively losing their virginity at the same time. And yet here she was. But as soon as she had finished her drink she had to go, promising that she would try and make it back the next night - and bring a few of her female friends.

'I need a brandy,' Kearney said to Murphy. 'What a stunner. Would I or what!'

'She prefers me, you sleazebag. Did you see the way she was looking at *moi*?'

'Not a chance.'

The night was sheer anti-climax after this. The Frumpies came in and sat down (uninvited) with the rakes. Murphy was really annoyed. These were the female version of the Motleys - really boring, virginal, plain goody goodies. Frumpy One was slightly above plain but so utterly conservative and self-righteous. She was tall in a gangly kind of way and had spent a long time in Birmingham of all places. Second in command was an out and out brontosaurus with a shrewish personality to match. The other two were always in the background and were so non-descript that neither of the rakes could ever remember their names. After Emma, Kearney saw even more clearly how wan, drab, staid and utterly grey they were and so the two rakes left after a few minutes and headed on to the next port of call. Meanwhile the night turned raw and cold, with an easterly wind picking up and the prospect of even bleaker weather. It had been quite some time since Kearney had been smitten, but tonight he certainly had been by the beautiful Emma, and he walked to The Short Hill in a kind of daze.

'Well what would you do if the ambulance came to get you now?' Murphy asked him with a degree of sarcasm. (Kearney was a pessimist and once said that if he was in an accident and the ambulance came to get him he would tell them to leave him where he was).

'Okay, okay,' Kearney growled. 'Point taken.'

The Short Hill was once <u>the</u> bar in Cork, full of dishy women who went there before going to the clubs. These days it was not such a hot place. Physically it remained one of the more atmospheric pubs though it seemed to be increasingly inhabited by urbanised rustics, hill walking types and worst of all, primary teachers. The first person they encountered was none other than Satan, who was seated down along the counter, slunk over his usual pint of lager. He was originally from Belfast and had a grating accent. He had been nicknamed Satan for a number of reasons. A lot of people found him sinister on first impressions and took an instinctive dislike to him. He was about forty and had a slightly hunched gait. He was lecherous, uneducated, sly, untrustworthy, insincere and he inflicted all kinds of psychological and physical abuse on past and present girlfriends. In short he was the ultimate Mr. Nasty. He had a very annoying habit of turning up at the wrong time and was brazenness in its worst manifestation. What was exasperating was how so many women seemed to go for him. He was involved with a fat and fairly stupid woman who worked in an auctioneer's agency and he usually came to talk to the rakes for a few minutes before going back to her. However at this particular time he had had some falling out with her so he was around all the time. This was a real drag as his company was overbearing. He certainly had a sinister side. He was utterly without scruples and he had a very irritating habit of butting in if or when he saw one of the rakes with a new woman. He'd sidle up and sit next to them, vulture-like. After a lot of drink one night, much to Kearney's horror, he confided that he 'hated women', despite having regular sexual congress with a whole host of women when his self-deluding girlfriend was out of town.

All three were just about to start another round of drink when the Frumpies trundled in. Murphy groaned and said he had to go upstairs and do a scan. Satan smiled his lecherous smile. Frumpy One and the Bront were milling about while the other two seemed to have vanished into thin air. Murphy came back after a few minutes and the Bront immediately started on in her usual nosey parker, disdainful way.

'So who are you chasing tonight?'

Normally Murphy put up with her by ignoring her but he was becoming a bit fed up of her constant prying into his forays and so he said with more than a touch of acid sarcasm, 'Why don't we talk about your romantic life for a change? That should keep us going for a few seconds.'

A frosty silence descended on the company for a tense lingering time until Murphy announced that it was time to escape to another port of call. Spending Friday night with the Bront was a no no. Life was short enough. Kearney was stuck with her dull friend but was equally interested in getting away.

As it happened, Satan had designs on Frumpy One (some chance he had) so the two rakes managed to bid them all goodbye and sidle out of the back door with considerable relief. They headed off, with a deeper sense of fatalism than usual, to the bar next door which symbolically had no name on its frontage.

As Emma seemed to have put all other women in the background (temporarily at least) the rakes had an even lower opinion than usual of what was on offer. At the far end of the counter there were two women who they had known for years but who had never acknowledged their existence. One was quite fetching with very impressive celestial orbs but she was the ultimate small town snob and so there was no point even thinking about her orbs not to mind anything else. Through an arch on the far side was a group of women who tended to hang round *en masse* and were usually accompanied by a swarthy little know-all runt who was as ugly to listen to as he was to look at.

These women had definite notions about themselves. One was a primary teacher who was separated and had two young sons. She was typical of those insecure types in that as soon as she heard bells telling her to get married she went for whoever happened to be on the conveyor belt at the time. In her case it was alas an even more disastrous union than usual in that it lasted for less than a year. The guy she married was a simple rustic interested in farming and rugby and that was that. She had this silly notion of a superior 'social status' and was permanently dazzled by her own reflection. She lived outside the city but on no account would she ever lower herself to get a bus into town. The mere idea of doing something so common was beneath her. She had absolutely no intellectual interests apart from a persistent preoccupation with her hair and appearance. She in particular drove Murphy off his trolley.

Meanwhile Kearney started going on about CERN and one thing led to another until he declared that if the Motleys met the Frumpies it would be like matter meeting anti-matter - they would just annihilate one other. Wishful thinking indeed. It was only a matter of time before the two groups of losers would arrive in and the only thing that would be destroyed would be the rakes' chance of meeting more diverting company. The bar was getting quite full so they went further towards the back in the hope that they would not be seen by the undesirables. Here there was a large collection from a hill walking club, including a high percentage of female primary teachers drinking (in the main) mineral water, and steadfastly ignoring all men, despite the fact that men were the reason they were there that night. Some were actually quite attractively done up, but they were really a bunch of gold diggers looking for security in the form of some 'nice' guy who could give them material comforts and a few sprogs to boot, someone their respective mummies would approve of. There was something about teachery types which got on the nerves of the two rakes - they were in general so boring and uninteresting, so conventional and conservative.

After a while came one of those lulls when the bar temporarily lost a large group of customers who had wandered on to some other watering hole. The conversation by now had modulated to the late Beethoven piano sonatas, and to Murphy's ongoing attempts to relate such works to the divine. One of the ongoing arguments the rakes had concerned the relationship between religious experience (in the broadest sense) and art. For Kearney (a Richard Dawkins man through and through) science would explain everything. We were just machines. It would only be a matter of time before computers created music that would be superior to Beethoven's. Murphy vehemently disagreed with this while Kearney insisted that in any case he didn't want a life after death - this world was enough to put up with without having to face another one. So vehement was this conviction that he made Samuel Beckett seem an optimistic kind of chap. He had a bleakness about him that allowed for no possibility of hope or redemption in any shape or form whatsoever. No wonder his motto was 'One door closes and another slams shut'. Despite rare numinous experiences that Murphy experienced, he was in fact almost as pessimistic as his fellow rake. He too saw the world in quite desolate terms and had little faith in human nature, which he often characterized as 'non-league football'.

The colloquy on Beethoven did not last long as the bar was filling up again and it became very noisy as some tedious boom-boom music started blaring from all corners. A few female trogs appeared alongside the counter. One was a tall, leggy blonde with an outrageously sexy cleavage and a curvaceous body to go with it. She was dressed in a cheap pink outfit and, as she passed, they could hear her rough hoarse voice declaiming 'I was fuckin scarlet when she told him I fuckin fancied him in front of him.' 'What a waste of a body,' they thought, as they moved towards the front of the bar where they saw a number of women who were as attractive as they were unavailable. The notion of equating sex with entertainment had never even remotely occurred to them Kearney had observed on more than one occasion. At best sex was a bargaining chip they used for marital conquest and beyond.

One of the women was an acquaintance of theirs who always dressed to kill and wore outfits that were both tasteful and slinky - no mean feat in the eyes of the rakes. She once spent hours talking to Murphy, sending out all the 'right' signals and giving him her phone number, but when he phoned the next day she made up some excuse that she was busy that night. Later he came across her in town sitting in a bar sipping wine with one of her female friends. What a waste of time. Her name was Susan and she was a receptionist in some upmarket medical clinic, though the way she behaved gave the impression that she was some Monte Carlo heiress. Her friends were equally attractive but aloof and disdainful most of the time. They were of course very attentive to the bar owner's son - in the best gold digger's tradition. 'They'll come to a bad end,' Kearney often asserted. Murphy gave Susan a knowing half smile as he brushed past her pert orbs while Kearney just walked past them (the girls) as if they did not exist.

The rakes were just about to move on to another watering hole when two very fetching girls in their mid-twenties came in and made a bee line for Kearney. These were German, and worked in a café he frequented so much that he called it his office. They came and had a few words in the friendliest of fashions. They had a natural confidence about them and an engaging intelligence which allowed them to commune with men without any of the silly game playing the Frosties and others indulged in. They shot the breeze for a few minutes with the rakes and then moved on. A bit later, the rakes headed for The Wild Geese with a fatalistic attitude - it was not exactly a place full of interesting, beautiful women at the best of times.

Here, inside the door, was a semi-anorexic arty type called Joanne who was always broke, always scrounging drink and always smoking. Luckily she was facing away from them, talking to some Crusty and so they passed her with alacrity. They steadfastly moved further down along the bar, hoping that the social minefield would not get worse. But it did. Satan and his blubbery sidekick, Fatima, were at the counter. They were engaged in one of their many arguments which on this occasion seemed to have a more than usual ferocity. It was not often that Satan's slick exterior betrayed his truly exceptional viciousness. In any case it was impossible to avoid the happy couple and Satan seemed happy to see the rakes as a kind of way out of an argument he seemed to be losing. Fatima glared at the two and there was a strained atmosphere as small talk was exchanged. 'Moses! The night can hardly get worse than this,' Kearney thought. 'What next?'

Only a few nights before Murphy had bumped into Satan in this very bar and the evil one recounted in gross and graphic detail a liaison he had had the night before with an fb (faded beauty). Murphy knew the woman in question to see and thought her to be a low and vulgar type and more an ffb (former faded beauty) than an fb. How Satan was not riddled with a collection of sexual diseases was a mystery. Murphy wondered what Fatima would have said if she had known about her beloved's lecherous and lascivious adventures. Amazing that she didn't find out as it was such a small town socially.

Between avoiding the Frumpies and musing on Emma the rakes looked a bit out of sorts. They were at the very end of the bar with no escape route and they were sitting ducks for all sorts of undesirables who could enter the bar at any time. Murphy was in one of his self-indulgent moods (the Black Dog was temporarily out of sight) and so he decided to treat himself to a Canadian Club - his favourite kind of whisky that he occasionally indulged in. This always instilled a warm and mellow feeling in him and put him in a mood whereby he almost tolerated the Frumpies and the Frosties. Kearney was talking to some acquaintance and so Murphy sat in temporary contentment, where he could enjoy a panoramic view of proceedings from the best stool at the very end of the bar counter.

'You'll get nowhere unless you are willing to compromise,' Kearney's gnomic friend pronounced.

'You know very well that there are certain C words that are not to our liking - as in commitment, castration, compromise to name but a few,' Kearney responded.

Murphy agreed. He knew of too many people who spent their lives compromising and ending up getting nothing they really wanted. Life was too short for compromise. Imagine ending up with one of the Frumpies or the Frosties - life wouldn't be worth living. On the other hand it certainly was no joke heading all alone towards the inevitable abyss.

Across from the counter sat a married couple who were both staring into space. Such a scene was common enough but always got on Murphy's nerves - the silence between the two was not a natural one. It was just that they had simply nothing to say to each other about anything. How boring. They had gone through the ritual of romance, marriage and breeding, and so nature didn't need them for anything more.

Just then Molloy came in and sauntered down to the rakes. He always took his time so that he could scan the bar for attractive women but on this particular night this did not take very long. He was Welsh and was for certain one of the most rakish of rakes. The other two looked on him with a certain awe. He had had hundreds of liaisons with women and despite being significantly older than the other two he seemed to have a magnetism that women could not resist. He had won the lottery a few years previously and had bought a house in West Cork. He divided his time between Middle Earth (as Murphy called Wales) and Ireland. Apart from being an out and out philanderer he was a writer (in the Welsh language) and a historian. There was always much hilarity when he appeared and an added air of expectation. Things seemed to take on a heightened sense of drama with him on the prowl.

He, as usual, had a few women 'on the go'. He was involved (rather dangerously) with a married woman in Schull whose husband was a farmer. West Cork towns being such small places Murphy had warned him that it was only a matter of time before he got into serious and irreversible trouble. Added to this, he had started a romance with a German girl in her early twenties - he was over fifty himself! This girl was a waitress in one of the more upmarket cafés in the city and she was in town for a year brushing up on her English (among other things). She was tall, lithe, intelligent, sparkling and witty and had fallen completely for his dubious charms. How he did it was beyond the comprehension of the other two rakes. It didn't seem fair for him to have so many liaisons and for them to have so relatively few. The German girl was called Isolde and was very finely attuned to the nuances and subtleties of Cork English. She was to drop in a bit later and meet Molloy. Meanwhile in Middle Earth he had ended one relationship with a married arty type and started another - this time with a wealthy banker's wife who was alone too often and sexually starved (that is until she met Molloy). He regaled his two buddies with intimate details of his adventures. The woman in Middle Earth he informed them had great taste in black lace lingerie which made her even more alluring. She bordered on nymphomania and certainly made up for lost time with Molloy. He had had sex with her in every room in her house including the utility room. The first time he had visited her in her house (the husband was in Frankfurt) she had worn a slinky black number and had slid onto the pine kitchen table before he could get his coat off not to mind anything else. It got so steamy that they were lucky the table didn't collapse completely.

'There should be some rules about hobbits from Middle Earth coming over here and stealing our women,' Kearney added.

'Our women? Isolde is from the Fatherland,' Molloy pointed out with unquestioned correctness.

'Yeah, but in general,' Murphy added. 'Why all these women go for an outdated rake like yourself is beyond comprehension. You are not even tall - hobbits have been known to be taller. You are unprincipled, ruthless, insincere, unfaithful and prey especially on vulnerable women.'

'Exactly Murphy ol' chap,' Molloy retorted smugly.

'We'll have to start going to completely new bars if this goes on,' Kearney exclaimed. 'I can only take so much of goody goodies and past the sell by date virgins on a Friday night when we are supposed to be having a good time.'

'Let's get out of here,' Murphy said with the tone of one going to an execution.

The three rakes slowly made their way through the crowded bar towards the exit.

'Ok let's try The Beech for one,' Murphy said unenthusiastically, intoning those favourite lines of his:

'Nothing to be done... I'm beginning to come round to that opinion. All my life I've tried to put it from me, saying Molloy, be reasonable, you haven't yet tried everything.'

'Waiting for Godot is just about what we're doing,' Molloy agreed.

'Three characters in search of an author,' murmured Kearney.

Murphy always got depressed as soon as he entered The Beech. He said on more than one occasion that there should be a sign put over the entrance saying, 'Abandon hope all ye who enter here.' It was always a compromise and a sure indication of how awful the choice of pubs was in the city centre. The first thing he saw was a trogette with one of those tank tops exposing her blubbery stomach, protruding from the gap above her jeans. They went down to the back part of the bar where there was some band playing imitation Christy Moore songs. Molloy as usual had wandered off to do some scanning. Kearney seemed to be in some kind of daze while Murphy roamed round aimlessly. They soon decided to leave without having a drink as the place was just too rough and full of uncouth types.

They walked outside and wandered down the street in the bleak cold. Outside The High C there was a group of people they knew vaguely - students in their early twenties, several of whom had worked in that bar at various stages in the past. The leader of the gang was a girl called Kate who was a School of Music post-grad student. She was an out and out stunner - tall, lithe, busty and with the most beautiful, intelligent face. For once her fat, inane slob of a boyfriend didn't seem to be present. Murphy was completely perplexed when he first found out about this particular coupling. It was indeed an extreme case of the Second Law.

The gang was going off to The Fiddler's Curse - a student bar at the end of the street and they invited the rakes along with them. They wandered down the street stepping over trog vomit and avoiding small gangs of scantily clad trogettes and loud yobs. The Fiddler's Curse was spacious with lots of nooks and crannies. It was full of people who thought it cool not to wash according to Kearney, but this was not completely true. The music was heavy rock but never outrageously loud and the place always seemed to be crowded. What Murphy really liked was that it was a great den for just floating round and losing oneself. There was the occasional academic there as well, who tended to be the arty, alternative type which was a rarity in the city. In Murphy's experience most academics were dry, boring and most of all frugal, living in paper empires and spending their lives in a kind of second hand existence.

He got his vitamin M and intended talking to Kate but as she was talking to some nerdy type he went walkabout. If half the clientele in The High C was permanently deranged then here half the clientele was temporarily so. The smell of cannabis wafted all over the place and the low ceiling made it even more pungent. Most people in the bar were certainly quite drunk at this stage but there was no air of threat like there was in so many other watering holes. Murphy winced as he saw Kate in the distance greeting the guy she was living with. The Big G must have had a really black sense of humour. What juxtaposition. What a combination. All three rakes at various stages expressed the gravest disbelief that such an articulate and dishy girl could talk to that orangutan, not to mind have sexual congress with him. He was fat, ugly, boring, mean and inarticulate. 'Bloody hell, he isn't even rich,' Murphy pointed out with total exasperation. And yet there they were... Romeo and Juliet, Anthony and Cleopatra, Abelard and Heloise!

Murphy let them be and continued his walkabout while Kearney talked to a nymph called Anne. Groups of students and arty types stood around tables which were overloaded with glasses of beer and spirits. Some women smiled with a kind of bemusement at Murphy. He always returned the smile much to the chagrin of their boyfriends. He tried to chat up one good looking blonde in her thirties. When she told him coyly that she was married he replied with his usual retort reserved for married women, 'That's a pity, not a problem.' He quickly wandered off as her husband made his way back from the counter, leaving her smiling and more than amused. In one obscure corner around a big table there was a group of people who were actually not much younger than Murphy so he went in that direction in a kind of zig-zag way. When he got to the edge of the group he leaned against a wall and gradually pieced together that they had been at some seminar in the local university earlier in the day. One lady was about thirty and was, as Kearney would have put it, 'a fine woman'. This was not a compliment used often by the three rakes so when it was used it was meant as fine praise indeed. She was in physical terms close to Murphy's ideal - tall, lithe, intelligent looking, fine bone structure and even better looking than Kate. A mere glance told Murphy that she had a sparkling personality and the thought occurred to him that she might have been part of the same seminar as Emma, the beauty they had met earlier in The High C. 'Two new beauties in the one night - must be some kind of record,' thought Murphy. 'What would Kearney say about this one?' He got talking to one of the other women in the group after a while and it transpired that they were all from English departments of various universities and had indeed spent the day in the local university discussing Chaucer. He was gradually weaving his way towards the stunner and finally managed to stand next to her.

'So are you into Chaucer?' he asked her, amused at this novel chat up line.

It transpired that she was working in Aberdeen University. When she told him that her name was Emily he spontaneously quoted a line from the 'Knight's Tale':

'Up rose the sun and up rose Emily.'

This amused her and the conversation soon took on a momentum of its own. They shot the breeze about Geoffrey for a while and then the conversation broadened out. She was, he was relieved to see, one of those rare academics who was interested in lots of things and not just her own field of study. She adored music and she spent a good few minutes talking quite passionately about Monteverdi's *Marian Vespers of 1610.*

'Real Sunday morning music,' she enthused. 'You open the curtains and let the light blaze into the room. So much dazzling colour and energy.'

He had wanted to ask her about her marital status - he could not get a clear look at her fingers as they were covered by long sleeves. In any case he soon found out. Along came a gangly, cross looking and cross eyed, grey haired guy in his late forties who told her in no uncertain terms that it was time to go. Murphy had no idea whether he had been in the bar for a while or whether he had just come in. When Emily introduced him as her husband Murphy was ready to throw up. He gave her a bewildered look and she had just time to say that she would probably be back later in the year for another seminar at the university. The others all seemed ready to leave as well and before Murphy could say anything they had vanished into the night. He did catch sight of Emily as she left - she looked back with a glance that he was to remember longingly. Meeting attractive and interesting women fleetingly seemed to be his inevitable destiny he mused.

He then wandered about losing himself among the Crusties and the drunken good humoured students. The place was fairly jointed at this stage and had more than a touch of a medieval tavern about it, with its large number of unkempt and roughly attired denizens, and its raucous revelry, not to mind the elemental feeling created by the big blazing fire at the far end of the bar and the comfort of being in a safe place in contrast to the cold, dark night outside. Murphy recounted his meeting with Emily to Kearney and his fellow rake was amazed that such a thing could have happened so soon after their earlier encounter with Emma in The High C. He sympathized with Murphy about her marital status but pointed out wryly that marital status had never stopped Murphy from pursuing women before. However, as she lived in Scotland, Kearney thought it best if Murphy was to forget about her at once as it was obviously all a waste of time. There was no arguing with Kearney, so Murphy changed his drink and ordered himself a Canadian

Club to round off such an unsuccessful night.

'For certain the Big G has a black sense of humour,' Murphy muttered as he swallowed the last of his whiskey. Kearney just raised his eyes to heaven and moved towards a nook where there was room for two people. Murphy stayed by the bar counter and let him off. Near the end of the counter he noticed a student type who had been with the Emily group earlier. She was tall, pale and good looking in a kind of offbeat way. He gradually made his way through the crowd thronging the counter area and when he got to her he was delighted to find that she was happy to speak to him.

'I know what you are going to ask me,' she said as soon as he was next to her.

'Do you really?' he retorted. 'So tell me, what am I about to ask you?'

'You're going to ask me about that lady you are smitten with. Emily Cardew, lecturer in Middle English at Aberdeen University. And to save you a lot of time and grief forget about her. She's married to a complete pillock and will never leave him.'

'That's all a bit abrupt,' Murphy replied.

'Tough.'

'And so who are you - her little sister?' Murphy asked.

'You can call me Jane. I'm doing post-grad stuff in Middle English. I've come across Cardew a few times at seminars and let me tell you that you are not the first to be taken by her.'

'So what about the drip - hubbie?' Murphy asked, warming to the intrigue.

'Well, he's a very rich engineer who is very possessive and treats her very badly as far as I can make out.'

'So why doesn't she leave him?' Murphy probed. 'Bloody hell. Half the unhappily women on the planet seem to be married to engineers. She seems strong enough to lead her own life.'

'Not a chance. He seems to have some hold over her. Everyone is dismayed when they are told all this but that is the way it is,' she explained patiently. 'She'll be back after Christmas sometime, so why don't you wait until then to shoot him and do everyone a favour?'

'Well I just might do that,' Murphy said enthusiastically.

'And after all that info I reckon you can buy me a drink,' she demanded with a smile. 'Make it a Powers with ice and ginger ale.'

'Anything you want,' Murphy replied, being more than happy to treat her.

Kearney was now at the bar counter as well. He was alone - Anne had gone off with some of her friends (who were a lot younger than Kearney). Murphy was always telling him that she only hung around with him because he bought her drink. Kearney half-agreed and asked about Jane.

'Just don't tell me you are interested in her,' Murphy whispered with exasperation.

'Well she does seem to have a certain attractiveness about her in a strange kind of way don't you think?' Kearney answered rakishly.

Murphy then introduced the two and they retreated to a nook that had just been vacated. They were quite near the blazing fire and Murphy temporarily put earlier events out of his head. Jane was turning out to be the new star of the evening after the earlier disappointments with Emma and Emily. She was doing a doctorate on the identity of the anonymous poet who wrote the medieval romance *Sir Gawain and the Green Knight*. It seemed that some new sources had come to light about his identity and she was lucky enough to get an inside track with some contacts in high places. She was obviously extremely bright and seemed a bit on the solitary side despite being in a wild student bar in the middle of the night. She warmed to Murphy especially when he expressed his enthusiasm for the Gawain poet. He even remembered some lines from his college days - the poem was full of an elemental vigour which appealed to him:

'Ferly fayre was the folde, for the forest clanged,
In rede rudede upon rak rises the sunne,
And ful clere castes the clowdes of the welkin.
Hunteres unhardled bi a holt side...'

'The right place to be reciting medieval poetry no doubt,' Kearney said.

The conversation went on and the two rakes were certainly going to put this new girl on their social list at the very least. They returned to the nook near the fire with their drinks when Molloy reappeared. After being introduced to Jane he started on about Welsh poetry and had her undivided attention for a few minutes. However as the incorrigible tomcat realised that she didn't show any romantic interest in him he wandered off towards the counter to continue his endless prowling. The more Murphy talked to her, the more perplexed he felt - she had a charming and natural openness about her but at the same time she was not easy to get an angle on. She exuded an air of self-confidence but he detected a certain vulnerability, even fragility about her as well. Inevitably the conversation turned to higher matters as Kearney made his usual pronouncements on the accidental universe and the impossibility of a divinity. In turn both rakes were surprised to discover that the Renaissance nymph (as they were to call her) was a Catholic, though not an admirer of the institutional church. What Murphy most liked was that she had an ethereal air about her, a lightness of being which made her poetic in a way no one else could match even remotely. She reminded him of one of those beautiful women in a Chagall painting who floated effortlessly over village houses. At the same time he had no romantic designs on her.

'I have to go,' she announced rather suddenly as she finished her whiskey, scribbling her mobile number on a beer mat. 'We'll discuss these matters of import another time,' she promised and so once more the two rakes were back to square one.

They got another drink and sat near the fire. The bar was quietening down a bit though it was still fairly busy. Most of the students were blotto at this stage and the rakes seemed to be the only ones not totally the worse for drink. Murphy started on about Emily Cardew. He seemed quite intent on meeting her again - that last look left an impression that was not going to fade easily.

'Forget about her right now,' Kearney advised. 'What a waste of time. Get real.'

Now it really was closing time so the two rakes drank up and went off to their respective homes with mixed feelings about the night's events and shenanigans. It was raining sleet and the cold was bitter. Murphy hated this part of the night as he often could not get a taxi and the walk home took him along streets littered with strewn paper from chip shops and ossified trogs crawling back to their caves. 'Human nature reduced to the Caliban state,' he mused, 'but that wasn't fair to

Caliban.'

***

Some hours earlier in a rich suburb a few miles away Jennifer Kiely shut the garage door to her big five bedroomed house that overlooked the city and was the envy of many. She was a single, good looking woman in her mid-thirties and generally regarded as a 'high flier'. Outwardly she was the quintessentially successful modern woman. No one would have guessed that she had been profoundly unhappy for months (she had lots of acquaintances but no close friends). She had left the house in an immaculate state, and her last will and testament on the kitchen table. She sank into the leather seat of her 7 series BMW and turned on the ignition. On the radio Beethoven's Fourth Symphony was playing. She heard the two great chords that heralded the *Allegro Molto* of the first movement. The windows of the car were open and she was unconscious in a matter of minutes.

***

Father Gillhouley - or Father Gillfuckinghouley (GFH) as he was familiarly known among his intimates - was not having a good Friday night. He had intended staying overnight with his favourite mistress, Mrs Olivia Nye, whose husband was away on business a lot at weekends. However, he was no sooner in her lascivious arms than the phone rang with his fellow parish pastor asking him to see after some suicide as he himself was already dealing with one as they spoke. The reverend father GFH had already wearily spent the day presiding over one of those long, tedious weddings where he had to endure the full menu: the monotonous talk, the endless, banal speeches and the tedium of the lull between the end of the meal and the start of the musical shenanigans. He was always good on wedding sermons, on the great sanctity and mystery of marriage, and was a popular choice among couples opting for the sacred ceremony of Mother Church. He was, however, to use Murphy's phrase, 'a bacon and cabbage' priest - a functional minister who did his share of baptisms and weddings and funerals much as an auctioneer bought and sold houses. It was a job and, like many of his fellow priests, there was not a religious bone in his body, but that was hardly an obstacle to functioning effectively in an organization that required little more than an outward show of devotion.

'Some silly bitch topped herself,' he complained to the semi-naked Mrs Nye as he made for the door. 'See you anon,' he said and was gone.

***

Emily Cardew's husband was the bane of her life. He didn't get on with any of her family and so whenever they came to Cork he insisted on staying in a guest house - and a rather down market one at that. His frugality was quite overbearing but then again he was Scottish. Emily had arranged to meet her sister the next day in the city centre for an early lunch. At least she still had this to look forward to before she flew back to her unhappy home. Why she had endured such a disastrous marriage no one understood. True he was away a lot on business and so she did have quite a lot of time without his menacing presence. But she was one of those women who was just not strong enough to walk away from disaster. And even if she did break free would she, like many fellow sufferers, end up with another of his kind?

She and Uriah (her circle's name for the stingy Scot) got back to the guest house and slept in separate beds. In the morning she did a tour of the two bookshops in the city centre before heading off to the family home where her father and brother still lived. It was a bleak raw day with a bitterly cold easterly wind. Emily didn't mind this, as she was free of Uriah for a few hours and could enjoy the time she had to herself. She walked the twenty minutes to her family home, enjoying the sharp, cleansing bite of the breeze but was a bit puzzled to see a priest on the doorstep talking to a stranger. They turned and looked at her apprehensively, and she froze with a sense of dread as she approached them.

Saturday Night

After the comings and goings of the night before the Irish rakes felt a bit ragged and depressed - though they would not openly admit it. The same routine faced them - they were always talking about trying new places but there was such limited choice in this city of trogs. Crossing Patrick's Bridge they had to skip over drunks sprawled on the pavement and avoid gangs of simian types heading towards gloomy taverns.

Saturday night found them gathering in their usual 'starting off' haunt where they frequently met before wandering off to other bars in their quest for women and engaging company. Kearney was convinced that he was going to meet the beautiful, erudite Emma in the course of the night, while Molloy was hunting afresh. The bar they were in had an upstairs which was reminiscent of a pre-war Berlin café, complete with candles on the tables and a touch of decadence in the clientele.

Sitting at a table about halfway down the bar was Debbie Wright - one of the city's biggest dweebs. She was a silly, superficial, snobbish and utterly materialistic woman with endlessly silly prattle, and an obsession with what other people thought of her. She had married a fairly uncomplicated guy who owned a very lucrative pharmacy - the pharmacy being the only reason for the marriage. She was an out and out gossip, utterly obsessed by social status and the need to have money and security above all else. But as time passed by even she began to realise the folly of marrying for material gain. She had no sex life and her social life was beginning to fall apart as most of her friends were marrying and drifting away into the exigencies of their own separate lives. Whenever she was in town socially she loved the buzz of the busy pubs but she was coming to realise that there was little prospect of romance left in her life though she was still only in her thirties. She inwardly envied some of the people she knew who were still single, footloose and fancy free. She got drunk quite easily, and in her inebriated state would flirt with various guys and often banish her long suffering husband to another bar, saying that he bored her.

He was a passive sort of guy and was often more happy than not to go and have a pint in more pacific surroundings with some of his old university buddies. He had no real sex drive in contrast to his frustrated wife who went through vibrators as swiftly as she went through his money. She fancied Kearney and had told him so on more than one occasion. Kearney saw through her though and had little time for her. On that particular night she was with an unusually large number of female friends because one of them was celebrating a birthday.

'All we need,' Kearney groaned as he spotted the gang of women and saw Debbie waving at him enthusiastically. There was a time when Kearney would have 'had' her but that was out of the question at this stage. There would be too much small town fallout. He returned the wave and indicated that he would join them shortly as soon as Murphy had got his vitamin M. The barman was taking his time and Murphy was in no mood for small talk with those silly dweebs.

'Let's get out of here after this drink,' he suggested, though Kearney didn't need this superfluous advice. They ambled down to the coven of sillies. Debbie immediately made towards Kearney and had her hand on his knee almost before he sat down. Murphy was amused by this and could barely control himself. He wondered which of the three sillies was the thickest - and he concluded that it had to be Debbie. The others were at least less obsessed with themselves and could actually listen as well as talk. They were quintessentially 'nice girls' who wanted husbands and children and a life like the rest of their peers - at least like those who weren't yet divorced.

Murphy mused that the peer pressure to get married affected impressionable women like these the most. They had no real independence of mind and were utterly conventional. Debbie of course would have loved to have had a liaison with Kearney but the presence of her friends kept her restrained. They were going on and on about Christmas and upcoming parties.

A large Klimt poster above Debbie reminded Murphy of the closing bars of Mahler's Ninth, which drifted into his consciousness. Those final pages were as close anyone had ever come to evoking the coming of death and the experience of letting go serenely and with resignation. What a fool Mahler was to have taken such a treasure as Alma for granted. There certainly wasn't much chance of meeting an Alma round here, Murphy almost said aloud, as he was forced to take notice of the company once more.

'You're far away Murph,' Debbie said with an over familiar air that always grated on Murphy's nerves. He knew very well that she absolutely detested him but he pretended otherwise out of indifference.

'Oh yes, I'm just thinking of what to get you for Christmas,' he replied acidly. 'Maybe an extra-large vibrator with my picture on it,' he thought wryly.

'Well time to move on,' Kearney eventually said with an air of false sincerity. She wanted to know where the two rakes were going next so Kearney mentioned two bars he and his fellow rake were certainly not going to visit and so a minute later both rakes were on the street feeling relieved. Molloy had temporarily disappeared.

'Maybe we're dead already and this is for all our misdeeds in the last life?' Murphy suggested.

'Hell, we must have been really bad to deserve all this,' Kearney growled and off.

They went to The High C hoping to see Emma there. Murphy repeated his theory of the universe as they walked along the trog infested street. His theory was one not previously heard by Kearney. Murphy claimed that if God existed, perhaps he was in the middle of making the universe when he got diverted for a second - kind of like getting locked out of the house - and he couldn't return to finish what he was doing. Hence the mess! It made as much sense as a lot of other theories Kearney allowed.

'At least the theory of evolution is sound enough,' Murphy scoffed as they passed a particularly uncouth horde of trogs.

'Not really fair to the apes though,' Kearney replied sardonically as they headed upstairs to the usual crew of deranged and misplaced inmates. There was a raucous din coming from within which was much louder than the usual Saturday night 'fever'. They inched their way inside and it seemed that there was some kind of birthday party in motion. A Hollywood director could not have come up with as perfect a cast of misfits: trogs, uglies, brutes, drunks, losers and vulgar types. It was definitely like being in a medieval tavern on some holy day. There were inmates wolfing down food as if there was no tomorrow. Doyle the wife beater was spewing bits of a sandwich in all directions, while a fat and utterly filthy brute at the counter was eating with his mouth open and was about as good a reason as any for not believing in God. In another corner there was an overweight, brutally ugly wench who had three or four sandwiches stacked on her wobbly knees - she was obviously storing as much as she could in case there wasn't enough for her flabby body.

In contrast, behind the bar there was a very curvaceous bar maid, who though not exactly an intellectual, exuded formidable feminine charms. She was very sexy but had little self-esteem and went for the wrong type of guy all the time, despite Murphy's admonitions. There was a certain chemistry between the two but it was always just an undercurrent. There was something quite elemental about her womanliness that appealed to him even though he knew he would never have a skirmish with her.

Kearney got talking to two brunettes who seemed to be primary teachers but were actually nurses. His hopes of meeting Emma were ebbing away on a minute to minute basis. Earl, another libertine, was there too - in the corner talking to an fb about music. This particular fb was often in the tavern and she loved being the centre of attention. She was still quite good looking and flaunted herself as if she owned the place. Murphy however ignored her consistently as the first time he tried to engage her in conversation she showed Frosty tendencies.

A trog came back from the toilet to find that his seat at the bar was occupied by some equally brutal female. He thumped her in the back and grunted something incomprehensible, making her get up and wander off without any reaction at all. Maybe she was used to cavemen. At the end of the counter there was a man who looked like Woody Allen in a rumpled and ruffled sort of way. He was laughing away to himself and seemed to find the whole experience of sitting at the bar very diverting. Even when Doyle, the wife beater, spewed some sandwich in his direction he didn't seem to mind.

Murphy looked around at the other denizens and could only smile at the sheer baseness of the scene: humanity's lowest common denominator all communing in Neolithic Xmas revelry. Kearney by contrast was disgusted with the sheer brutality and vulgarity of what he was watching. There was a group just next to him so drunk as to be on the verge of complete paralysis. One was an out and out zygote - a bloated, vulgar, nefarious type who inspired instant loathing. He slugged his beer back in long uncouth slurps that slobbered over his mouldy face, making him look even more moronic than normal. He was of course one of Doyle's gang - Kearney had never seen any of them sober, as they generally tended to arrive in the den about seven in the evening and so were well sozzled by ten. They actually considered themselves to be quite intellectual. They were the archetypal also rans who spent their time solving the world's problems when they couldn't even tie their own shoe laces. Earl proposed on more than one occasion that these types be eliminated. Murphy thought this a bit extreme - though as he watched one ape drain another glass he tended to take his point.

What art thou that dust grumble there in the straw? Murphy echoed to the amusement of his fellow wolves and to the bewilderment of nearby trogs. The bar was now so full that Murphy's elbow was pressed up against the impressive bust of some woman at the counter. She was good looking he noticed and he was more than amused as she half-smiled complicitly.

'That's a sin,' Earl muttered to Murphy but the latter just smiled and asked if he wanted to swap places.

By now Kearney had given up any hope of meeting Emma - another once off appearance at The High C. It happened intermittently that they met some really interesting woman there only never to see her again. Gradually the crowd diminished and there was breathing space. The rakes even got three prime seats in a corner by the window where they could see all that was going on in comfort.

Time passed. The crowd began to thin out more - there were these mysterious ways in which the clientele seemed to ebb and flow as if by some preordained force. In the absence of any female diversions Kearney and Murphy were having their ongoing colloquy about the God question. Kearney's insistence that the universe (no less) was an entire accident didn't convince Murphy, but Kearney acted as if he had an absolute knowledge of such matters. On the cosmic level he saw only chaos and a universe running out of energy.

It was now time for them to move to a bar called The Shack. This was like an enlarged hobbit's emporium with all sorts of nooks and crannies and with a very mixed clientele - though happily it was not really a place for Frumpies or Motleys. Murphy had a bet with Molloy (who had reappeared) that they would not see more than one attractive woman there and had promised to give him a euro for each good looker they espied. They stood just inside the door for a while and groaned at the litany of women who were coming and going. Some were merely plain but overall it was a rake's nightmare. They moved into the bar and found themselves in one of the bigger recesses which was mainly lit by candles and was very atmospheric. There was a group in the distance playing traditional Irish music with some tangos thrown in for good measure. All the rakes needed now was for a bunch of busty, leggy and obliging wenches to arrive. Kearney spotted a woman he knew who worked in a pharmacy and who was extremely attractive in a glamorous kind of way. She was blonde and curvaceous and oozed sex appeal. However her beauty tended to belie her personality which was shrewish and of the gold digging variety. Despite knowing the rakes for a long time she wouldn't deign to salute them - after all why should she when she had never been formally introduced? Murphy still had hopes of seducing her at some vague time in the future but the others were turned off completely by her small town snobbery.

Murphy looked admiringly at a fresh pint of Murphy's that had just appeared in front of him. 'You can't beat a perfect, creamy pint of vitamin M,' he mused and rounded on Kearney.

'Kearney, how can you drink those insipid bottles of Yankee beer when you could be drinking vitamin M?' he asked rhetorically. The three of them were now seriously scanning for wenches but there was not much hope of Molloy getting a lot of euros. Instead a big and ominous looking rustic came in their direction and asked Molloy very abruptly, 'Are you the Welsh whoor?'

The rustic was not really threatening and was actually well dressed - for a rustic that is. He was wearing a tweed jacket and gave the impression of being educated, even if a bit on the abrupt side.

'Am I what?' Molloy countered, stifling his surprise at such an unexpected question.

'You're knocking off McMicheal's wife, aren't you, down in Schull?' the rustic continued.

'Well, maybe I am and maybe I'm not,' Molloy mustered.

'You are or you aren't?'

'Who are you to be asking such dangerous questions and we out trying to have a good time?'

'Don't worry. Most locals think McMicheal is an out and out thug so you have nothing to worry about - except of course McMicheal. They say he is on to you and has been practising with his new shotgun waiting for your arrival.'

Molloy was not at all pleased with this news though the other two were in stitches, not often witnessing such scenes that would not have been out of place in Dodge City in the days of the Wild West.

'So you'd better introduce yourself - I suppose your name is hardly Billy the Kid?' Kearney intervened, stifling a laugh.

It transpired that the interloper's name was actually William and that he was living in Schull with his partner who was some kind of artist. She was due to arrive at any time and so they all introduced themselves and Molloy bought William a pint of vitamin G. It seemed that everyone in Schull knew about the antics of Molloy and McMicheal's wife since it had not been unusual for Molloy to occasionally exit via the bedroom window, across a field onto a road to his parked car. McMicheal's wife was usually sure when the coast was clear but then again when a shotgun was put into the equation things began to take on a new perspective.

As they were talking about life down in West Cork and lauding the place for its character and scenic beauty a drop dead gorgeous woman, dressed in a simple but alluring black dress, came in and put her arms around William from behind. Molloy was shell shocked - she and William - another example of divine injustice! She had the most sumptuous Jane Russell bust, was tall and lithe, and as it transpired, had a personality to match such sublunary beauty. Her name was Sadie and it seemed that she was not one of those artists who made silly earrings from bits of safety pins, but quite an established lady who was widely known for her artefacts (among other things). First impressions of William as some kind of rustic oaf were rapidly revised, and the rakes all silently acknowledged that their judgements had been rash. Sadie had been much amused by the antics of Molloy down in Schull. He was of course absolutely enthralled by her beauty but even he knew that she was out of bounds. Murphy really liked people like Sadie - natural and intelligent with no false airs and graces. They were such a breath of fresh air compared to the endless tedium of the Frosties and the Frumpies.

'Maybe she has a sister,' Murphy whispered to Molloy while the others were talking about some bookshop in Schull.

'Some chance,' Molloy sighed. 'Anyway I'm a dead man if I ever go down west again.'

'Think of the great funeral we could have old chap,' Murphy laughed.

As the conversation went on into the night, and turned towards McMicheal, it soon became clear that he was generally regarded as a bully who treated his wife, Rose, with a roughness that amounted to physical abuse. It was another example of the 'victim complex' Murphy thought - some women would never leave their obnoxious partners no matter what transpired. McMicheal had been going for the priesthood earlier in his life, it emerged, but decided against it after five years enclosed in the seminary. Like many of his kind, he had a dark and sinister nature with a sadistic streak hidden beneath his public respectability. Most people were sympathetic towards Rose - a refined but unintellectual woman. It transpired from the conversation that she would be alone next weekend as McMicheal was definitely going to be in England. Out of the blue Sadie suggested that the three rakes come down to Schull for the weekend. Molloy was far from enthusiastic - the possibility of being shot by an irate husband was not a thrilling prospect but how could anyone refuse an invite from such a heavenly creature (even if she was permanently out of bounds)? They agreed to meet the following Friday in Schull in a tavern called The Black Bull and they were all invited to stay in Sadie's place. Murphy got Sadie to repeat that McMicheal would definitely be away - the more he thought about it the more he pictured the three of them being blasted with a shotgun if they were anywhere near Molloy when the shooting started.

As William and Sadie were about to leave Jane arrived in and said a few things to Sadie - they were obviously friends of some sort. Jane then managed to persuade the barman to get her a late drink even though serving time was definitely over. She seemed to be one of those people who glided effortlessly through life and who had a kind of magnetic attraction for all sorts of people. She was a seasoned drinker who rarely if ever left her guard down and it was very difficult to know what she really thought or felt. She conveyed the impression of great familiarity but this was offset by an inscrutable quality which made it impossible to divine her inner life. None of this bothered Kearney or Murphy as they both instinctively guessed that she was cast for a transient role in the overall scheme of things.

Sometime later Molloy went off with some acquaintances to a club and Kearney simply disappeared, as he often did. Jane and Murphy were last to leave the pub. Outside they were delightfully surprised to see that it was snowing. This was indeed a rare event and it gave an enhanced atmospheric quality to the night. It seemed that Jane lived in the same part of the city as Murphy and so they headed home together along the whitening streets. Across the street a bit up from the pub a trog had fallen through a shop window - Murphy's sympathy was definitely with the window and they passed by as the brute was attempting to get on his feet muttering incoherent trog curses. Two policemen walked by and kept going, not wanting the hassle of having to deal with yet another trog in a night full of casual and meaningless violence. Murphy and Jane walked on as the snow began to fall more heavily. The contrast between the beautiful scene created by the snow falling on an old church they passed by and the rough brutality of the denizens of the streets was quite stark.

By the time they got to Jane's home it was snowing almost like a blizzard. The house itself was at the top of a long series of steps which had gardens on either side. They walked to the top and then looked at the sweeping view of the city below them. It was so unreal to see the city in a snowstorm. They stood in silence for a while and then all of a sudden she said a quick goodnight and was gone.

Murphy was not really tired when he arrived home so he poured himself a Canadian Club and put on Mozart's *Requiem*, letting the ethereal music fill the room while he watched the snow at a big window. There was an added transparency and otherworldliness about the music as the beginning of the *Recordare* fashioned magical spirals of sound that seemed to float downwards in harmony with the falling snow outside.

Part Two

LOVE AND DEATH

Who knows if the moon's
a balloon, coming out of a keen city
In the sky - filled with pretty people?

E. E. Cummings

If grief could burn out
Like a sunken coal,
The heart would rest quiet.

Philip Larkin

Whatever about the drawbacks of sex in the city, sex in the provinces was even more of a disheartening experience for discerning philanderers. Rural Ireland was a deeply desolate place for many who lived there. There was the terrible isolation of those who lived outside villages; the relentless monotony of everyday life; the claustrophobic gossip; the ever increasing suicide rate and the numbing sense of futility for any thinking person. Then there were characters who for one reason or another were very wealthy but who still lived in squalor as if doomed to inevitable impoverishment.

Romance in this context was generally a fairly basic and rough affair. In Schull, to where the rakes were to head shortly, there was a distant relation of Kearney - admittedly from the rough side of his family - who recently told him about one of his recent sexual encounters. He was in a nearby village and met this wench in a bar. She had been drinking for a long time but like many rustic women she could take her drink. She had slightly protruding teeth and a jaw to match but she was tall and well built. She wore a long, loose skirt which became shorter as the drinking session gathered momentum. It was one of those bars full of lonely and desperate types, with men sitting along the counter in various stages of drunkenness and the TV blaring in a corner with no one looking at it. Kearney's cousin, Tom, started talking to the wench and they had a few whiskeys together. When closing time arrived the buxom temptress led Tom by the hand to a large and empty car park where her car was parked. She caught him around the waist as they walked slowly across the dreary open space and kissed him hungrily. Her 'car' actually turned out to be a Hiace van and instead of opening the doors at the front she opened the two back doors with a certain air of bravado and climbed inside. There was some kind of rough carpet on the floor of this love mobile which exuded a strange mixture of odours, of oil and vegetables and dog. She lay down on this love bed, and as she opened her legs towards the lucky Tom, she bellowed 'Horse it into me.' She had amazing breasts with very erect nipples into which she buried his face. The van swayed in the deserted car park and the two rutted for a good hour before he had to leave the love mobile and face home.

Then in the same village there was a wizened old farmer who, in his seventies, had regular sexual encounters with the most vocal of local gossips, after his consumption of copious amount of porter. They coupled with extraordinary indiscretion in the back of his ancient, rusty

Morris Riley. In contrast, there were the married couples who arrived into the local village pub and sat there in stony silence for endless hours, the man invariably downing pints and his partner more often than not drinking some insipid soft drink. Only after these intervals was there occasion for sex, which was a sordid and brutal affair at the best of times.

Murphy was often appalled at the amazing wealth of some of the people who lived in these villages. He knew one yokel who was worth millions because of various inheritances he had received, yet this uncouth rustic rarely left the village, consorted with a moron (who was 'technically female') and spent most of his time looking at soap operas, football matches and porn videos (which certainly didn't do much for his sex life). Murphy often wondered futilely what he could have done with all that wasted money.

The snow that fell over the weekend continued to fall during the following week, but along the south west coast it only stayed on the higher ground, making the rugged scenery around Schull even more enthralling. The rakes had slightly changed their plans as Rose had persuaded Molloy that her husband would not be in the vicinity that weekend. Molloy accepted her assurance and agreed to meet at her place, though he still went along looking over his shoulder at the grim prospect of an irate McMicheal bearing down on him with a gleaming shotgun.

William and Sadie had a spectacular house, almost a mansion, overlooking the entire bay. It had eight or nine bedrooms and was full of old timber and beamed ceilings with roaring fires in both the huge kitchen and the living room. There was an impressive collection of paintings to be viewed, with an original Chagall as the highlight. They later found out that Sadie came from a rich English family who actually visited her from time to time, unlike those hippy types who made up most of the arty set in the area and who were forever abandoned by their families. The three rakes had arrived on Friday evening at about nine. Molloy had decided to stay at Sadie's as his own newly acquired house was being decorated. After a quick Irish coffee to settle the Welsh tomcat's nerves William took him off to Rose's house which was just a short drive away. The other two luxuriated by the fire and spoke to Sadie about art matters. She had quite strong views about modern art and thought a lot of it was an enormous con job. She also was one of those very rare arty people who was seriously interested in science, though she had no formal education in this discipline. Her awareness of quantum physics impressed Kearney no end as she talked about her attempts to convey in some (obviously abstract) form the topsy turvy world of sub-atomic particles and the weird quantum world.

The phone rang as William came back from his trip to Rose's - it was one of Sadie's friends arranging to meet later in their favourite pub. As time passed there were a few more calls - all seemingly from women - and the rakes gathered that Sadie was gathering a bevy of her female friends to meet them. 'Why couldn't things always be like this?' Murphy mused. This sort of weekend made up for all the hassle they had to put up with in the city - the world of the trogs seemed for once to be far away. Just before they left for the pub there was an animated debate between Kearney and Sadie on the meaning of the word 'soul'. Sadie was irked by his irritating absolutism and what she considered to be his overbearing smugness while the others just looked on in bemusement. Eventually they walked down the long driveway with the harbour lights in the distance and moonlight glistening off the snow-capped hills.

The Black Bull was one of those all too rare survivors of days long gone with its big log fire, its authentic ancient furniture and antique prints, its old world atmosphere enhanced by the lack of a TV and gaming machines. There were all kinds of nooks and crannies with big windows looking out towards the sea. The clientele was a mixture of locals and foreigners (who had moved here for all sorts of reasons). By the time the rakes had arrived it was getting busy but they managed to get a table in a corner near the fire. They were soon joined by three women who were part of Sadie's set. One was English and married - tall, slightly pale but attractive in a quiet sort of way. Her name was Georgina but most people called her George. She was actually happily married and her husband was due to arrive later. The second woman was in her mid-thirties and was in Murphy's eyes the most attractive of the three - she was slim but had quite an impressive bust and wore a long, light textured black dress. Her nipples seemed erect as he cast lingering glances at her curvy body. Her name was Claire and it turned out that she was a quite well known potter. Karen, the last of the trio, was smaller than Claire, blonde and with the most amazing red lips, though there wasn't a trace of make-up on her. She was, from Kearney's point of view, the dishiest of the three, and was definitely the most attractive librarian he had ever seen.

As it happened, Kearney was sitting between William and Karen while Murphy was on the other side of the table between Sadie and Claire. Sadie had a mischievous sparkle in her eyes and looked conspiratorially at Murphy more than once. Murphy wondered how Molloy was getting on - he was probably having a table job with Rose before venturing forth. He had told Murphy that she had a penchant for sex on the big pine kitchen table. It seemed that when it came to sex she was nothing if not sophisticated. She teased Molloy by wearing black slinky silk stockings and not much else on under her skirt. As it happened, Molloy was in no mood for any kind of amorous activity, even when Rose reiterated that her obnoxious husband was in London and that Molloy could relax. He even jumped nervously when the phone rang, but to add to the suspense it was only a wrong number.

'Fine for you but I didn't happen to bring a bullet proof vest,' he said to her morosely.

'A bullet proof vest would be useless against that gun of his,' she joked and laughed, while he could only manage a wan smile. They got ready and headed off to The Black Bull, down a lane with the moon shining on the sea and the snowy mountains half-glimpsed in the distance. Rose mentioned the sad story of a girl from nearby who had died the week before and whose funeral would be taking place in the local cemetery on the following day. The actual removal was that evening in Cork and there was a big crowd expected in Schull for the burial. Rose knew the woman only to see but seemingly she had been a regular visitor to the town of her childhood. A sudden noise made Molloy jump as they got to the end of the lane - it was only a door slamming in the wind but he was not at one with himself at all.

They got to the pub, and after surviving a few inquiring glances from the locals, joined the company and everyone was introduced. The women with Sadie only vaguely knew Rose but they definitely knew what was going on. Molloy made for the inside of the table with his back to the wall, and near a quick exit to the left towards the toilets. Meanwhile the other two rakes were getting quite friendly with the two available women in the group - Sadie's 'conspiracy' was going to plan nicely. Rose mentioned the death of the woman who was due to be buried the next day and Sadie indicated that she too knew her to see but no more than that. Kearney and Murphy were giving all their attention to Claire and Karen. It seemed a bit hard to believe that the two of them could be successful on the same evening with women from the same company. The atmosphere in the bar was conducive to sapient colloquies and there was an elemental quality about the whole ambience with the blazing fire, the sea in the distance and the wind beginning to pick up, creating strange noises in the beamed ceilings. It reminded Murphy of the great hall in Anglo-Saxon times with the outside dark contrasting with the inner light of the hall where people communed and, for a few short hours, forgot about demons abroad.

Towards closing time it seemed certain that Claire would end up with Murphy while Karen seemed sure to be leaving with Kearney. Both rakes weren't certain whether they would be staying in Sadie's house or whether they would be taken back to their respective new catches' houses. As it happened closing time was still a long way off as there seemed to be little heed taken of the law. Murphy was getting closer to Claire as time passed, becoming quite excited at the prospect of touching her very fetching breasts. She was quite diverting and like Sadie had her own original opinions on matters artistic. He was quite interested in hearing her view of Picasso as a failure and a charlatan, someone whose life ended in despair, loneliness and self-parody. He mentioned the Chagall that he had seen in Sadie's house and Claire said that there was a very long story behind Sadie's acquisition of that masterpiece and it would have to wait for another time. This reference to 'another time' was not lost on Murphy and his sexual excitement went up a gear when Claire told him that he would be staying at her place which was a few minutes outside the town. Here there was not much notice taken at the possibility of being stopped by a police roadblock and so most people seemed to drink and drive without any fuss. As they left the pub the company broke up into almost predictable couplings - Molloy went off with Rose, not at all at ease with himself, despite the prospect of a very steamy sexual romp, while Murphy remained with Claire. Poor Kearney had to go back to Sadie's as his potential conquest had decided to go home alone much to his annoyance and frustration.

Claire's house, like so many of those owned by the arty set in the locality, was at the end of a winding lane and its ordinary exterior gave no sign of the stylish nature of the interior. She led Murphy to a large bedroom which had a spectacular view of the sea still lit up by a brilliant moon. After sharing another glass of wine they began to kiss passionately and in a moment she had revealed those firm, delicious breasts that had so tantalized him earlier. As they got more entangled in each other's bodies he heard her say 'Talk to me' and he couldn't help but reply 'What do you want, a running commentary?' Her passion made it a very memorable encounter, and as they drifted off to sleep, the wind was picking up outside, while the moon was now covered by fast moving clouds coming from the east.

Meanwhile Molloy was having a less entertaining time as his sexual performance - usually five star - was hampered by his unease at imagining McMicheal arriving out of the blue. The incessant wind added to his nervousness and the night passed for him in fitful sleep.

The next day he went to Sadie's about ten where he found Kearney and Murphy feasting on an impressive looking breakfast. William had gone to Bantry and Kearney was enduring some banter about his failure to seduce the librarian, but it seemed that there was some 'subtext' which had inhibited her and which he had not yet figured out. Outside there were flurries of snow and the wind, coming from Siberian regions, was bitterly cold. A fire was a great luxury at breakfast time Murphy thought, and he was in his element joking with the company and recalling past adventures in Mid Wales with Molloy. He had not been long acquainted with the Welsh rake when he himself developed 'rakish tendencies'. He was indeed surprised at what went on in small Welsh villages. They joked about one particular night, at a time when Molloy was having a liaison with a married woman (what else?). They had all been in a bar, with the woman's sister in tow as it happened, when after some time Molloy and his 'beloved' decided to leave. So the incorrigible rake gave Murphy his car keys (and his lover's sister so it seemed) and told him to meet him about an hour later. So there was Murphy, driving round aimlessly with this woman he had never met before. He decided to leave the initiative with her. After a few minutes she saw a lay-by and asked him to pull in and stop. She finished a cigarette and rolled down the window a little and flicked the butt out. 'Give me a kiss then,' she said in a matter of fact voice, and in a jiffy the car windows were steamed up as she kissed Murphy with lusty abandon. She then ordered him in no uncertain terms to 'take' her and what could the surprised rake do but dutifully oblige? Life was indeed full of surprises where all could be gained with nothing ventured, and nothing won when all was risked.

***

After breakfast the rakes wandered round the outside of Sadie's house and took in the spectacular scenery with the added attraction of the snow-capped mountains. There was one building at the back of the house which looked like a stable. It was made of the most beautiful stone and they thought they would find a few horses inside. However, they were surprised to find it locked and not just with a standard lock but with several padlocks. Kearney tried to see inside from one of the windows but it was too dark to make out the outline of anything. Back at the house the plan was for the rakes to go on a drive around the locality while Sadie did some chores. They were due to regroup later for lunch in The Black Bull - the rakes intended to treat the happy couple to lunch in return for all the hospitality. They had reserved a table in the pub as they had been told that there would be a lot of people there later because of the funeral. It seemed that the funeral crowd was to be catered for in a room at the back of the pub but there would be lots of people milling round elsewhere as well. So the rakes headed off on a mini-tour, heading towards Bantry and exchanging notes on the night before. Molloy was in the back seat by request and had an ominous feeling that it was not going to be a trouble free day.

Meanwhile the funeral was the usual Irish affair - a big social gathering made sadder than usual because of the youth and beauty of the woman who had died and the manner of her death. Fr GFH did his usual routine, while occasionally thinking to himself that the dead woman was 'one hell of a waste of a good ride'. He was immune to death and all the hassle that went with funerals. All he looked forward to was a good (free) lunch in the local tavern and a few hot whiskeys, before he could leave and maybe liaise briefly with one of his network of unhappily married women before Confession later that night. He thought he did a good job conveying sincerity and it did work with most people, though some did see through him and his smooth, silky talk. The burial was the most stressful part of the ritual as the stark, windswept beauty of the day and the rugged landscape added to its poignancy. When the dead woman's sister read the closing lines from Eliot's *Four Quartets* at the graveside Fr GFH grew very impatient as he had little time for anything remotely aesthetic. He was indeed a practical man with no poetry in his soul. There was a sharp east wind cutting across from the mountains and the sky seemed a deeper than normal shade of azure. A solitary windswept hawthorn tree stood out against the cemetery wall where the burial was taking place. The funeral crowd gradually made its way back to the town and while some went to various taverns the immediate mourners headed for The Black Bull.

The rakes meanwhile were looking at some archaeological sites as they toured round before heading back towards Schull. Molloy was well versed in archaeology while the other two expressed a keen interest. Molloy in particular was fascinated by a dolmen they came across and he would have stayed there longer but for their lunch appointment. They eventually got back to the house, freshened up and then went off for lunch to The Black Bull - without William who was delayed and wouldn't be making it after all. Claire was to meet them there while Kearney's librarian was expected to turn up at some stage. Sadie had hinted to him that all might work out and that last night's turn of events had nothing to do with him. When they got to the pub the funeral party had already started its lunch in the back room and so they all sat round the same table as the night before and ordered a round of drinks while waiting for the food to arrive. Murphy was a bit uneasy about Claire - he liked her and she was a 'ten' sexually but he didn't want to fall into the usual trap of trying to extricate himself from a 'relationship' with someone he merely liked. Karen huddled together with Kearney as soon as she arrived and she seemed to be telling him why she had left him 'in the lurch' the evening before. The scene seemed set for a longish afternoon of conviviality.

Molloy had again placed himself with his back to the wall and at the side of the table nearest to the toilets. Murphy went to the bar to get a round of drinks, and, as he was returning to his seat, he was taken aback to see the mercurial Jane, news bringer and breaker, seated at the far end of the counter. She gave him a strange kind of salute and, having put his round of drinks on the table, he wandered down to her and waited for her to finish talking with some people who seemed to be part of the funeral contingent.

'So you obviously haven't any idea why we're all here?' she said and quickly told him about the suicide of Jennifer Kiely, Emily Cardew's sister, and of the events of the previous week. Murphy was really shocked but, despite all this bad news, felt a certain exuberance knowing that Emily was not far away. He didn't know what to do if he should see her - Jane told him that he could only wait and see what transpired. She also added that her creepy husband was there as well. Murphy didn't even know if Emily would remember him.

'Oh she remembers you alright,' Jane assured him. 'But you may have to ignore her at the moment. Let's see whether she wants to talk to you or not.'

Murphy wanted to sympathise with the bereaved woman at least but it was difficult to know what to do as their acquaintance was so tenuous. He went back to the others and told them the news. The mourners would be inside in the back part of the pub for about another half hour. Then they would probably come out to the main bar before dispersing.

Claire was not at all pleased that Murphy seemed to be ignoring her completely, as he was really on edge waiting for the chief mourners to make their appearance. He had no idea whether or not he was going to talk to Emily or indeed what he was going to say - he would have to rely on his instinct which was usually sound enough. After a seemingly interminable period people began to come out of the back in twos and threes and, finally, there she was. She was dressed completely in black and, despite being pale and worn, still looked extremely attractive. She passed their table but didn't notice Murphy or any of his company. She walked along the side of the bar counter occasionally stopping to talk to sympathisers. When she reached the end of the counter she talked with Jane and the small circle that had gathered there. Then she went out the door - Murphy was suddenly plunged into despair. 'There she goes again, gone again, twice in the space of a week,' he mused. He suddenly became aware of Jane, who was now standing next to him.

'Her odious husband will be back in about fifteen minutes,' she said. 'She's across the road looking at the harbour before it gets too dark to see anything. Go and talk to her if you want.'

He did not need to hear any more, so he put on his long overcoat and went out the door. Across the road was a long low wall and the wide circular expanse of sea and mountains beyond it. He sympathised with her, acknowledging that they were more or less strangers, but adding that he had to say something. She was quite in control of herself considering the situation, though she did keep looking round as if expecting the terrible Uriah to appear at any moment. 'What the hell do I do now?' Murphy thought. He could hardly ask a married woman for a date on the day she had buried her sister? And on the other hand, if he didn't say something he'd probably never come across her again.

'Look, I know this is an awful time to say this but as I am not likely to see you again I'd just like to say that...'

'It's okay,' she interrupted. 'There's no real need to say anything just now. Don't worry, we'll meet some other time.'

With that she shook his hands and she was gone before he could even reply. He was filled with a lightness at her words but this was counterbalanced by his sorrow at her grief. He went back to the pub and made for a place next to Sadie who, by now, was talking to Rose who had in the meantime appeared. Claire had left as she had to go to meet some customers and this really suited Murphy. Sadie soon learned what had been going on and was full of empathy for Murphy. Molloy had meantime decided that he would not be coming back to this town for a while and was not paying much attention to anyone as twilight arrived, filling him with even greater unease. Sometime later Murphy went to the bar to get another order in, only to see Fr GFH sitting at the counter with a few locals he seemed to know. As Murphy was about to go back to the table he saw a rough and dim looking rustic come in with copies of the IRA's *An Phoblacht*. He would normally have ignored this as the people sent out to sell this rag were in his view close to sub-normal in all respects. However, when he saw the reverend father buy a copy he could not contain himself. He had never seen a priest do this before, though he was aware that many of them had a secret admiration for Sinn Fein and its former army of bombers and psychopaths. But this was too blatant to be ignored.

'You are some bloody disgrace buying that rubbish,' he almost hissed at Fr GFH.

The priest looked surprised that anyone would challenge him in such a public place and muttered back, 'I'll buy whatever I like so why don't you push off my man.'

Murphy could see the priest and his crew of ill-bred yokels in a huddle, as if they were trying to decide on whether or not to have an out and out encounter. Luckily, as it happened, William arrived in and his presence tilted the balance against the possibility of a bar brawl. Shortly afterwards, Fr GFH left with a final glare at Murphy, as if to say that he would be seeing him again. More drinks were ordered. Murphy was certainly having a dramatic day but it was far from over yet. As they were getting over this encounter, the door opened and some woman came over and whispered something to Rose.

'Oh God, he's back and may be here any minute,' Rose exclaimed.

At this Molloy shot up like a scalded cat and without waiting for any confirmation headed for the toilets. Indeed McMicheal was back, inexplicably but definitely back. The door opened and in he came. He was dressed in a casual rain jacket and, much to the relief of the company, he was not carrying a gun. He was with some big oaf and they both went to the counter and ordered a round of drinks. Rose walked over very casually and used the excuse of the funeral to explain her presence. McMicheal was suspicious but could not argue with what she was saying. He cast a sinister look in the direction of Kearney and Murphy, then strode over and asked the rakes angrily, 'Where's your Welsh friend?'

'Oh, he had to catch a bus,' Kearney replied unflustered.

'Smart alec,' McMicheal growled. 'You tell your Welsh buddy if he comes anywhere near this town again he's dead.'

'Did you all hear that?' Kearney asked the others as McMicheal marched off.

It was still only six o clock though to the rakes it felt more like being in Dodge City on a busy weekend in 1880. In any case, they were now back in Sadie's house along with Jane and Claire. Sometime later, Rose sent Molloy a text saying that her 'beloved' had indeed taken his newest shotgun and was gone out. 'Well, at least you're safe here,' Sadie assured Molloy who looked less than convinced.

The rakes now had to consider what to do as there was a long interlude before it was time to go back to the pub for the Saturday night session. Claire seemed to be paying a lot of attention to Molloy and Murphy wasn't sure if it was because of his recent ordeal or a way of getting back at him for his ignoring her the previous day. He didn't really care and for once he actually hoped that Molloy would do one over on him and take her off somewhere. As it happened this is what transpired. Claire announced that as it would be unsafe for Molloy to go out that night with the rest of the crew she would take him back to her place for 'safe keeping'. Murphy and Molloy exchanged knowing glances when she came out with this meaningful phrase.

William was gone off again on one of his mysterious tours and Sadie had some work to do so Kearney sat by the fire by himself looking over some of Sadie's eclectic book collection. Murphy decided to go for a walk with Jane who always seemed to be in with everyone and in the know about all kinds of things. She was completely likeable and her formidable academic intelligence was unusually mixed with an unassuming naturalness. The rakes were amazed at how she seemed to be so well acquainted with Emily Cardew and William's set as well. She kept turning up like some ubiquitous genie.

'What happens if we meet Buffalo Bill?' Murphy asked as he left the house with her. 'I mean, Rose did say he had gone out with that gun of his.'

'Well, he's hardly going to shoot you because you know Molloy,' Jane joked.

'Suppose so,' Murphy agreed and off they went down towards the harbour and then along a path which ran parallel to the coastline. It was near dusk and it was quite exhilarating to see the moonlight on the sea against the backdrop of snow-capped mountains. As they walked along they had to climb over a kind of stile so he helped her over by the hand and, as they continued along the path, she kept hold of his hand so naturally he felt no awkwardness with her. He still had no designs on her romantically though he did like her company a lot. He wondered why he didn't want to get involved with her romantically. He mused at possible reasons for this. Maybe she was a bit too good to be true and he lacked the confidence to take her on. There was also the age difference to be considered, not to mind the fact that they were not going to be living anywhere near each other in the future. As well, there was her perfected ability to keep people at a distance emotionally as if she had some kind of invisible shield around her. It seemed his role was to be that of protector, though against what he wasn't so sure. Then again he had had some very spicy relationships with women who were initially just friends.

At the end of the path there was a small promontory which they climbed to look at the seascape. He noticed that she was holding his hand a little tighter than before. He gradually started a conversation about past romances but she was very evasive. He increasingly got the impression that there was a darkness at the heart of her emotional life, as if something really terrible has befallen her in the past. She did confide that her father (an eminent professor of classics) died young and that her brother had later committed suicide by plunging into a stormy sea (the body never to be found). However he was sure that there was something even darker lurking inside her but she was completely inscrutable. Counterpointing all this was her irrepressible lightness of being that dominated her personality. She confessed as they looked at the sea beneath them that she was a kind of mystic.

'Whenever I mention epiphanies to most people they either don't know what I'm talking about or else change the subject,' she declared in an almost childlike way.

Murphy empathised with her but still felt her aloofness despite the intimate nature of their walk and talk. He wondered if being near a cliff overlooking the sea was painful for her, given her brother's fate. In any case the wind was now near gale force and so they turned back along the path towards the town.

On the way back Murphy got a text from the Welsh rake saying 'Congress imminent boy,' so he replied by saying that McMicheal was on the prowl and was likely to visit Claire's place looking for target practice. They were all aware that an unfortunate German woman living in the area had been brutally murdered a few years before, and that the brute who murdered her had never been caught. So talk about another killing was no joke. Indeed some of the locals were convinced that the murderer of the beautiful German woman was still living amongst them.

As they ambled back Murphy mentioned the locked building back at Sadie's place. He added that William went on a lot of mysterious trips and seemed to be constantly on his mobile. Mysteriously Jane told him never to mention the locked building to anyone and never to bring up the topic in the company of either Sadie or William. This made Murphy even more bewildered but he gave her his word and they got back to the house just in time for a sumptuous high tea that Sadie had been preparing.

William was still away so the company around the great pine table was made up of Sadie, Kearney, Murphy, Jane and George. The main topics of conversation were the suicide of Emily Cardew's sister and the antics of McMicheal. Jane seemed to know most about the suicide and told them all she knew. There had been no outward sign that Jennifer was in any way even depressed, not to mind suicidal, so the talk drifted into a general discussion of the cases they had known and the unfathomable reasons why people chose such a lamentable end. Then the conversation wandered on to the topic of Emily and her awful, soulless husband. Murphy was keen to find out as he could without showing too much interest. He was quite surprised to hear Jane suggest that she half-expected them to separate sometime in the not too distant future.

However all were aware that it was not in good taste to talk too much about Emily given current circumstances so they let the conversation turn to other matters. Murphy found himself in a colloquy with George about what made a painting 'a work of art'. This led them into all kinds of intellectual paths and byways and the conversation got quite animated without ever being acrimonious. Kearney was talking to Sadie and Jane about the murdered German woman. There seemed no doubt in Sadie's mind that the thug who perpetrated this foul deed was still in the locality. At the same time she didn't feel any great fear for herself. She even hinted that there were more dangerous things to worry about - a remark which puzzled Kearney no end. Between the locked building, William's mysterious trips and a few other vague impressions, he got the feeling that there was more to William and Sadie than met the eye. At this point his phone vibrated with a text from Molloy which read, 'Someone keeps ringing and then putting the phone down.' Kearney told the others what the text said but they didn't seem to be too worried. No doubt Molloy thought he was going to be shot before dawn.

At about nine they got ready to go on the Saturday night walkabout and, as William had not yet come back, Sadie locked up and the company wandered down the lane towards the town. The first pub they visited was one of those dreary pubs built or renovated in the sixties. It was a big, cold empty space with awful, cheap metallic tables and all sorts of gaudy memorabilia displayed behind the counter and on the walls. However, it did have one saving grace - a small snug which seemed to be a remnant of the distant past. The company took refuge there, leaving the rough looking rustics at the counter. Murphy noticed that at least one of the rough types lurching at the counter was one of Fr GFH's cronies from the earlier part of the day.

To the surprise of Kearney the sexy, if enigmatic, librarian arrived in as they were in the middle of their first round of drinks. She acted as if nothing out of the way had happened the night before. If there was one thing that gave the three rakes attitude it was to be given the certain impression that they were about to have sexual congress with some attractive woman only to be thwarted at the last minute. Experience had taught them not to make the same mistake over.

'I suppose you're going to do your disappearing act again tonight?' Kearney asked Karen.

He was especially hoping she would be more accommodating as she was dressed to kill - a loose black dress (what else?) just covering the knees with tasteful fish net stockings (a great weakness of his). As well she showed a hint of cleavage which was very enticing to such a sexual animal as Kearney.

'No, tonight,' she whispered to him, 'you will certainly be kidnapped.'

Meanwhile Murphy was annoyed that Molloy was with Claire. Even though he had fallen for Emily, he was such a serial womaniser he would have indulged himself with her if he now had had the chance again. On the other hand, as Jane seemed to be some kind of inner circle friend of Emily, perhaps it was better if he laid low for the time being. At this moment Molloy and Claire arrived in out of the blue, Molloy saying that he felt safer in a public place than in some lonely house in the middle of nowhere. He also missed the revelry of a good Saturday night session. Murphy smiled wanly at Claire and was surprised to find her choosing to sit next to him. There seemed to be a greater kind of freedom socially and even sexually in these parts Murphy thought but then there was a kind of holiday atmosphere and, added to this, arty types were always more liberal than the goody goodies they came across in the city. As well, perhaps women living locally preferred having liaisons with outsiders. Meanwhile the irrepressible Molloy was no sooner back from the bar than he was engaged in some colloquy with Jane about literary matters.

George had been talking to Murphy and Claire about the afterlife and told them casually that she was a medium. As nothing really surprising the rakes, Murphy took her at her word. He knew this was one conversation Kearney would have liked to get in on if he hadn't been getting so cosy with Karen. Molloy, on the other hand, seemed to be having an engaging conversation with Jane rather than trying to allure her. Their conversation had modulated onto abandoned copper mines further south-west in Allihies where seemingly there was a strong Welsh connection. No doubt, though, he still hoped to seduce the young student, programmed as he was to have as many unrelenting conquests as possible.

Murphy was getting the feeling that Claire was still interested in him and he wondered how discreet Jane would be in talking about Emily. What dominated his feelings most at this stage of the evening was an edgy kind of tension - or rather tensions. There was a heightened sexual tension between him and Claire not to mind his ongoing desire for Emily. Then there was the palpable tension among the locals as their awareness of a murderer in their midst permeated their whole lives. McMicheal's threatening and volatile nature unsettled his peace of mind, not to mind the moronic Provo contingent which seemed to be scattered throughout the area. And then above all, was the recent suicide of Jennifer Kiely and the fact that she was Emily's sister. Jane meanwhile was casting amused glances at Murphy while Molloy was trying all his well-oiled charm on her. They eventually finished their drinks and headed to The Black Bull. The wind was raw and coming from the east. And still the moon shone down from a clear sky.

'Look out for Buffalo Bill,' Kearney joked to Molloy who was walking as close as could venture to Jane. They got to The Black Bull and were lucky to find a table by the window which faced out onto the harbour. The big blazing fire pleased Murphy - it made the atmosphere and he liked nothing better on a Saturday night than to have a few creamy pints of vitamin M in engaging company with the prospect of a steamy sexual encounter afterwards. While Jane and Molloy continued their earlier conversation, the unavoidable topic of suicide was brought up by Murphy and he, Claire and George gave various opinions about why there were so many suicides in Ireland. In Cork city a fire brigade contact of Murphy had once told him that the public didn't know half of what went on - the daily dragging of the river for bodies and the numbers found being were much larger than people realised. On one occasion, when a guy jumped in the river it was said that the rescue people looking for him had found twelve more bodies along a narrow stretch of water nearby. Murphy knew several people who had killed themselves in Cork and he had his own theory. It was a clannish and parochial place so he reckoned a lot of highly intelligent, cultivated people killed themselves out of a sense of alienation and displacement. Outside academic circles, many of these people lived in a kind of intellectual vacuum having few if anyone to share their thoughts with. Then there was the visual dreariness and mediocrity of the city itself, its overall medieval roughness combined with an overwhelmingly philistine population. Occasional lights in the darkness like the annual film festival brought a body of really interesting people under the one roof but in general there was no forum where thinking people could gather. The pub and club scene was a disaster and so people like Jennifer Kiely drifted along with an increasingly growing sense of desolation and futility until the time came to end it all.

Meanwhile Murphy got a few more fleeting glances from Jane as if intimating that she was just playing around with the chief rake. Kearney was so immersed in conversation with Karen that he was outside the general company for the time being. As George and Claire were talking Murphy looked towards the counter at Sadie while she was getting a round of drinks. He had programmed himself not to consider her as a possible conquest but he had to admit that she was exceptionally gorgeous. Her sparkling and natural personality was combined with a body in the Kim Novak mode. She was fairly close to his ideal in many ways - a kind of Renaissance woman who had an in-depth knowledge of the literary and music canons, who created beautiful artefacts and who could talk on the Higgs field and string theory with great lucidity. He could almost admire her in an objective way. He tried to dismiss all lustful thoughts as she made her way back to the table, but this was easier said than done.

Nevertheless, he realised the spark between himself and Emily Cardew was far more charged, though he tried as much as possible to put her out of mind as she was seemingly unattainable. He knew being smitten was nature's way of getting two people together for the sake of procreation. It seemed completely anathema to him to be expected to spend the rest of one's life with only one partner. It just wasn't what men were cut out to do. They were wolves, hunters, rakes - and to think of the many women he knew who thought their partners were so faithful!

The pub was now comfortably full without being overcrowded. Kearney was back in the conversation having been fully absorbed by the librarian for a second night in succession. He was now having a very intense argument with George who couldn't cope at all with his attitude towards death, not to mind his bleak and desolate philosophy. She was shocked when he claimed that it was only a matter of time before computers produced music which would be as good, if not better, than Mozart's. His usual theme of 'we're just machines' was reiterated with intensity. That was not to say that George did not give as good as she got - unlike many who debated these matters with Kearney she had an impressive grasp of modern science and was particularly scathing of Kearney's 'fellow travellers' like Richard Dawkins. Much to Murphy's relief their argument temporarily ended on a note of levity:

'*There are more things in heaven and earth/Than are dreamt of in your philosophy*,' George reminded the nihilistic Kearney.

'*Why wouldst thou be a breeder of sinners… myself I am indifferent honest*,' Kearney retorted.

George rallied with '*the paragon of animals*,' and Kearney replied '*this quintessence of dust.*'

The conversation ended for the time being as they didn't want to spend the whole night in a one to one argument with so many others present. Besides, Kearney was getting a bit heated at her resistance to the absolutes of science, not to mind his scorn when she claimed to be a medium. In exasperation, George extended Kearney an invitation to her next scéance, while the usual free Saturday night plates of finger food were being handed round. The rakes appreciated this as the pub owners they came across in the city were the meanest shower of stingy gazebos they were ever likely to meet, with the exception of one generous mogul, nicknamed BMW, who knew the meaning of the word largesse. Murphy was a regular customer in one pub since his student days and, even though the same people still ran it, they never so much as knew his name or offered him a Christmas drink. These publicans were on the lowest rung of the ladder of the 'merchant prince' brigade, and had a niggardly shopkeeper mentality down to the last cent.

Murphy resolved that he would definitely buy a house in the locality just as soon as he won the lottery. Some of the locals at the next table started talking to Kearney while he was equally engaged with some friendly people on his side. The rakes liked nothing better (well almost) than speaking to new people. In the city they were so fed up of the Frosty mentality, of not even being acknowledged by people they knew so well to see. As they finished their snacks Murphy went to the counter to get some drinks. Next to him was one of the Provo scumbags he had seen earlier with the 'bacon and cabbage' priest. He steadfastly ignored the Pre-Cambrian looking rat but he was not to escape being noticed in return.

'You'd want to watch what you're saying about the national struggle sonny,' Rat grunted, as Murphy was about to pick up his creamy pints of vitamin M and G.

'The national struggle? Sonny? What a scream,' Murphy thought, but knowing how futile it was to engage in conversation with such types, he just looked straight past Rat and made his way back to the table. The bar was now getting very full - lots of locals coming out for the last hour of the evening and some frugal types coming in late to avoid spending too much. As he sat back down Murphy half-glanced at the crew of incomers. He thought he recognised one woman but she had his back to him and was far down at the other end of the counter. However when she turned around there she was - none other than Bibi, frostiest of Frosties. What she was doing here he had no idea but then again this was a very popular area so overall it was not such a great coincidence. He alerted Kearney to her presence and then the two of them regaled the company about the Frosties, and specifically about that snooty madam's small town snobbery. Karen was taking Bibi in with a certain degree of disdain, tempered with admiration for her good looks. Both she and Claire thought that Bibi had to be on rakes' list of potential conquests.

'The only man for her is Molloy - bring on the heavy guns,' Murphy quipped to Kearney. Whatever about these two rakes Molloy had fewer scruples and would gladly go off with any Frosty if he could get one. Bibi was with a group of women and was indeed looking rather fetching. She wore a shortish red dress with a slightly low cut top set off by pearls which were no doubt real. She had that haughty look of disdain she always wore and there didn't seem to be much point in approaching her.

'So do you still think she has a common jaw?' Kearney asked Murphy as the others were talking.

'Ok. I admit she does look fetching but what's the point?' Murphy replied with exasperation.

'She's beyond touching. She's hardly a different babe down here,' Kearney mused as she half-looked over but avoided their glances. 'Still, nothing ventured. If you're not going to have congress with Claire why not try her just to see?'

'Ok. I'll give her a few minutes but if she gives me the iceberg treatment that's it,' Murphy conceded.

Sometime later Bibi and her crew were still milling around at the far counter so Murphy went up and ordered a few drinks, and, as he waited for the pints to be filled, he gradually sidled towards the frozen one. So there he was yet again - next to the gorgeous Bibi, almost touching her back as she was talking to people he did not recognize. When he finally caught her glance he volunteered, 'I seem to be coming across you in all kinds of unexpected places. Are ye here for the weekend or just passing through?'

'I'm from here,' she replied tartly, 'so I'm here a lot.'

She turned back and continued her talk with the others. 'What a dweeb! That's the last chance she's getting,' Murphy thought, as he lingered at the counter waiting for the pints. One of her friends gave him a friendly look as he sauntered back to the table. Kearney agreed that they should just ignore Bibi in future and prophesied that she would certainly come to a bad end - and the sooner the better. The possibility of her being shy didn't really come into the discussion, and even if she had been so, there was no excuse for blatant bad manners, even towards rakes. However, Sadie, always one to be positive, suggested that indeed Bibi may have been insecure and lacking in the carefree confidence that characterized the rakes in their social encounters, and offered to test her theory if she got the chance.

Meanwhile, Molloy and some of the others were talking about Russia, the Welsh tomcat taking the viewpoint that the Russians were the unfriendliest lot of people he had ever come across in all his extensive travels. Murphy agreed and they both swapped stories on how dour and downright unfriendly the Ruskies were. Murphy had actually stayed with some Russians during his time in St Petersburg and so had got the 'inside track'. He recounted numerous tales of the many beautiful but cold Russian women he had come across, not to mind the everyday Russians he had met on the street when asking for directions and who didn't even show a hint of friendliness. The conversation was beginning to spiral downwards, and so between Bibi and the Ruskies they decided to move on to other matters of more positive import.

In the interim Molloy got a text from Rose, who told him she was housebound with her ugly hubbie, informing him that he was probably safe 'for the time being', a piece of news which cheered him up no end. Though it was now officially closing time there was at least another hour of drinking and carousing to be done before the company would have to leave. Outside flurries of snow started to appear. At this stage Jane was sitting next to Murphy while Molloy was further away talking to Kearney about the merits of Welsh poetry and the future of the

Welsh language. Jane was talking about relationships between older men and younger women and Murphy told her that all the goody goodies he knew, not to mind the Frumpies, poured scorn on men who had relationships with considerably younger women. Some types thought that a big age difference in a relationship bordered on the immoral and was not to be contemplated under any circumstances. The rakes, on the other hand, knew several women in their early twenties who they far preferred to socialise with, rather than some older women they knew who were so boring and illiberal. Murphy mused that whoever got Jane would be very lucky indeed, and he hoped that she wouldn't fall victim to the Second Law. It perplexed him how even the brightest of women often fell for the most odious and boring of men. On paper she was an ideal match for himself, but that was not how nature worked. In any case she would probably want to procreate at some stage and that was one road he wouldn't go down under any circumstances. At this Sadie came back and told Murphy and Kearney that she had a new theory on the Bibi 'enigma' - she said that she was fairly sure that she was lesbian.

'Charming,' Murphy announced. 'I don't know which is worse, a dishy looking lesbian who is out of bounds or a dishy looking Frosty with attitude.'

'So where does that leave us?' Murphy asked Kearney.

'Suppose you could get a sex change and then she might notice you,' Kearney replied in his usual sardonic manner.

'Ye are so obsessed with women. Talk about maniacs!' Jane suddenly erupted in exasperation before heading to the shelter of the toilets. While she was there Bibi came in and a conversation started between the two as the Frosty was doing her make-up. She seemed more than friendly and said that she recognized Jane from somewhere. Jane played along with her to see if Sadie's theory was correct but she couldn't decipher whether Bibi was just being friendly or if there was something more to the conversation. In any case, Bibi left saying that Jane should join them for a drink if she got tired of 'those guys' she was with. Jane told her that she would probably have to stay with her company and at that Bibi handed her a card with her phone number and disappeared before Jane could say anymore. Jane went back to the rakes feeling a bit flushed but decided to say nothing about this unexpected encounter. She did feel an undercurrent of excitement when talking to Bibi as she was not at all the unfriendly Frosty that the rakes had portrayed her to be. In truth Jane had very occasionally thought of experimenting with another woman but this always remained nothing more than a whimsical notion.

When she got back to the group Sadie was inviting people back to the house, and it seemed that the night was indeed far from over. Molloy was more relaxed at this stage, and again picked up on his conversation with Jane with his usual smarminess and 'eyes only for you' attention. William came in as the last round was being served and he hurriedly ordered two pints of vitamin G while the going was good.

The landlord finally called time and so the rakes, along with some others, were invited by Sadie back to the cosiest and most inviting house in the town. All that is except Jane, who said she'd follow on later, and then made her way over to engage Bibi in conversation. Kearney and Murphy exchanged glances at this development but said nothing as they headed off for Sadie's, Kearney escorting Karen and a surprised Murphy taking Claire, while Molloy was left to ponder the amazing fact that he was not going to bed with a woman with whom he had invested more than half an hour's conversation.

As Sadie's circle milled about outside the pub, Bibi was talking to Jane and the conversation was warming rapidly, with a very animated Bibi revealing that she had the parental home all to herself while her group was staying nearby with some friends. Jane found herself more and more taken with Bibi and that vulnerable air she combined with an overt sexual sparkle, although she tried not to think on these lines. When they were all outside The Black Bull Jane initially thought that she would say goodbye to Bibi and rejoin Sadie's gang for the last part of the night. However things developed differently and at a pace she could barely keep up with.

Bibi managed to offload her friends by saying she would catch up with them a bit later. Both she and Jane had had a fair share of drink though Jane did not feel really drunk in an 'out of control' kind of way. She found herself agreeing to walk back to Bibi's family home for a night cap. As they left the lights of the town behind they walked up a dark lane leading to the house - it seemed that everyone Jane knew in this town lived up a dark and desolate lane. As they walked along the lane it suddenly became almost completely dark. Bibi took Jane by the hand. Jane thought this might have been a natural thing to do, given the lack of light and the scariness of walking up a long windswept lane in the small hours of the morning, so she didn't read much into the gesture. As they got nearer the house she felt Bibi's hand kneading hers in a light but sensual way. Bibi didn't say much on their way but when they got to the impressive two storey building she led Jane into a large, warm living room with huge arm chairs while she made the excuse of having to go to the bathroom. She told Jane to help herself to a drink so Jane poured herself a Baileys and sank into one of the comfortable chairs.

Bibi seemed to be gone for an eternity but she finally returned to find Jane had been looking at some art books which lined one wall of the room. Bibi was now wearing a fluffy white dressing gown and beckoned Jane to sit on the large leather sofa. Jane did so, surprised that Bibi was sitting so close to her. Bibi gradually put her arm over the top of the sofa onto Jane's shoulder and let her dressing gown open to reveal a red and black set of lingerie which was slinky and alluring. What happened next was a bit of a blur in Jane's mind but Bibi was very direct and impossible to resist - she kissed Jane in a voracious fashion and had Jane's clothes off in a matter of seconds. Bibi was truly passionate and a very good lover. Jane was in a kind of daze and was only beginning to take in the import of what was happening when she realised that they had now moved to a large and comfortable bed at the other end of the house. Bibi was only just beginning her sexual romp and Jane was just carried along by Bibi's experience and passion. There seemed to be no limit to her lust but finally she stopped and just moaned for a while before looking into Jane's eyes and saying, 'Well, that was not bad at all.'

As Jane was rendered more or less speechless by all this sudden and unexpected new sexual experience she let Bibi do the talking. Bibi complained for a few minutes about how hard it was being a lesbian and then fell asleep, her head lying across Jane's bust with an innocent and beautiful look on her face. Jane was uneasy in herself, and as she looked down at the gorgeous body of Bibi, she thought wryly what a story this would be for the rakes, if only they knew what one of their favourite Frosties was really like!

Jane woke later and couldn't go back to sleep while Bibi seemed to be out for the count. She decided that it were best to leave - it was about two thirty in the morning and she would probably catch the end of the party back at Sadie's. As she was about to sneak out of the bed she felt a hand on her thigh and the feeling was electric. She turned back into the bed and was completely wrapped round Bibi once more as the latter mumbled, 'You weren't going to leave me were you?' When Jane awoke about seven in the morning she took some time to realise that the whole adventure had not been a dream.

Back at Sadie's people teemed about in the kitchen and in the big living room having drinks and animated conversation in a convivial atmosphere. Molloy was morosely resigned to the prospect of going to bed alone, while Murphy had once again given up on Claire who, he concluded, was too moody and temperamental and who seemed to be piqued, in any case, because of the interest he had shown in Emily. That left Kearney who was certainly getting on quite well with the librarian. Murphy milled round the house talking to interesting people from all sorts of places. There was a retired sea captain and his much younger wife, a tall, intelligent looking blonde who worked in a nearby language school. There was also a foreign looking brunette but, alas for the rakes, she was deep in conversation with some farmer who was regaling her with tales about local history.

Molloy got one final text from Rose saying that her husband had gone out and she had no idea where he was bound. For once in his life this put sex second on the list and he was quite content to go to bed in safety and not have to worry about being hunted down. With William again nowhere to be seen, Sadie sat near the fire and talked to Murphy. The fire was the 'icing on the cake' (so to speak) for Murphy and he didn't mind not 'having' Claire as he talked to Sadie about Emily and Jane and some of the other women he either knew or had been involved with. Sadie promised to find out more about Emily and also invited him back to Schull to stay with her whenever he wanted. He agreed to return again soon and added mordantly that Molloy would certainly not be coming back for a long time. Kearney then came over and told Sadie that he would be going to Karen's and that he would see them all in the morning. He gave Murphy one of his knowing wolfish looks as he left. By this stage the sea captain was absolutely blotto, and it took a lot of persuading by Sadie and his wife to get him to leave and head home.

Finally the house was empty of all the guests except for Molloy and Murphy. Molloy went off to bed and Sadie offered Murphy one last whiskey as they sat by the fire. Murphy didn't dare entertain the idea of trying anything with Sadie, but she was indeed so alluring by the fire, with the snow flurries drifting past the window and the room lit so subtly. He did get an inkling that she and William were not totally happy together even if there wasn't any hard evidence on show. Unexpectedly, she asked him to describe his ideal type of woman, so trying not to be too obvious, he more or less described herself!

'Well, if Emily is really out of bounds and impossible to pursue, then we'll have to find someone else like that for you,' she said with a sparkle in her eyes. A spark from the fire fell on the rug as she was talking and when she bent down to put it out Murphy couldn't help noting how sumptuous and firm her breasts were. However, she started talking about Emily again as if to lure him away from her own charms. She told him that if Emily was as unhappily married as Jane had intimated then there was some hope. Murphy reiterated his theory about women and the 'victim complex' and though Sadie agreed with him she said that there was always a chance that Emily would leave Uriah, especially after her sister's death.

'Why after her sister's death?' Murphy asked.

'Well, sometimes when something really traumatic happens, people can really have a deep look at their lives and make some dramatic changes,' Sadie theorised.

'Well maybe, but it seems a bit tenuous all the same,' Murphy said without much enthusiasm.

At this Molloy (in a dressing gown) came into the room with his mobile exclaiming, 'I've got a death threat! He texted me and told me it was only a matter of time before he would shoot me beyond recognition!'

He showed them the text message and there indeed were the very words. The text had been sent from Rose's phone so the conclusion was obvious. Murphy didn't know whether to laugh or not - it seemed so unreal and once again it looked like something out of the days of Jesse James and Wyatt Earp.

'Shouldn't I show the cops this?' the Welsh rake asked Sadie.

'I think you should delete it right now and forget about the whole thing,' she replied. 'William will deal with that idiot in the next few days and I can guarantee you that there will be no more threats.' Both rakes were a bit taken aback at the force of her reply. After all William didn't give the impression that he was some sort of local Mafia don.

The time finally arrived for them all to go to their respective rooms, welcome after such a long day. Murphy was in a room facing out on to the sea and the enclosing mountains. He read a few pages from John Fowles' *The Magus* which he found on his bedside table. The passage he read mentioned JS Bach's sublime *Goldberg Variations* and he fell asleep with some of these playing in his head interspersed with images of Sadie's seductive curves and Emily's forlorn countenance. At the other side of the house Molloy was once again having a very fitful night's sleep, determined to avoid Rose for the immediate future. He was also equally set on having a liaison with Jane soon. After all, he wasn't the number one rake for nothing.

***

About two miles from Sadie's house Emily Cardew was in her old family home - an old style, refurbished farmhouse used by her family regularly at weekends and during holidays. Her husband had flown back to Scotland earlier in the evening, more or less straight after the funeral, while she was going to stay in Ireland for a few more days. At this time she couldn't bear her husband anywhere near her, and was relieved that he was gone. The funeral had been one long blur and only now was she remembering various people who had come from far and near to sympathize. Among these she remembered Murphy and how thoughtful and considerate he was given her circumstances. She knew he had designs on her, and though she would not admit it, she had taken to him after that seminar on their first meeting in The Fiddler's Curse. Between her sister's death, though, and her increasing intolerance of her husband, she didn't feel free to indulge in freedom and romance. Besides, it was unlikely that she would be meeting Murphy again, though there was the tenuous connection through Jane who she saw occasionally. She tried to blot out the picture of her younger sister in a cold coffin in a deep dark grave a few minutes' walk away. She would stay with her family until Sunday and then they would all leave and start the long grieving and mourning which would never really end.

***

In the cold darkness outside the snow flurries had relented though

59

there was still a stiff easterly breeze. McMicheal had been on the prowl and had walked up the lane to Sadie's house where he noted the car registrations and tried to see inside to where they were having drinks. He was a brutal individual with known links to the IRA - there were even rumours that there were arms dumps on his land. He was fearless in a kind of animal way and usually acted on impulse, worrying about the consequences later. Though he had no great regard for Rose he was furious that anyone else should be interested in her. She was too scared of him to ever consider leaving him - he would track her down like a wild animal and drag her back to their loveless house. Her affair with Molloy was the first time she'd had any kind of physical liaison for ages - and even that hadn't lasted very long. She was aware that Molloy was a serial womaniser but she still liked the roguish side of his personality.

The next morning the three rakes headed back to the city having had the usual impressive breakfast at Sadie's. Jane turned up at the last moment and asked them for a drive back. She was much quieter than usual and no one said anything to her about her absence the night before. Kearney expected Karen to visit him in the city the following weekend - Jane scowled at him when this came up but he only smiled in return.

Despite her encounter with Bibi she still preferred men and couldn't think of any woman sexually (apart from Bibi). She didn't expect to meet Bibi again though why she thought this she couldn't say. The roads back to the city were a bit iffy with occasional stretches of snow but they cruised along smoothly in Murphy's old Saab and arrived back with a great feeling of anti-climax and disappointment, back to the trogs and to the bars full of dipsticks and philistines, back to the city without a symphony season, back to the suicide filled river and tabloid reading yobs, back to the mediocrity and the provincialism.

Part Three

THE BATTLE

OF THE SEXES

What do women really want?

They want a lovely, faithful, complex, sensitive bloke who has emerged from a really, really unspeakably roguish past wiser and reformed. He'd still have that twinkle so he could dip into his rogue mode in an emergency, but he no longer needs to go there so he can now enjoy long walks.

What do men really want?

A really wise, funny, patient, worldly woman who has emerged from a past of dull, ugly and sexually inadequate men. They want her to be very, very at home with her sexuality with no hang-ups, but also very, very few previous sexual partners.

The Independent Review 20 January 2004

Earl was fed up of the 'scene' and was spending a morning in his favourite café, mulling over his lack of a romantic life. One of his (unhappily) married friends joined him while he was starting his third coffee. She was a tall and attractive woman called Natasha who had married in haste and was repenting at leisure. She had a better life than many unhappily married women, as she had a lot of freedom and got on with her husband, even though the love thing between them was history. She listened to Earl's ongoing rant about the dearth of eligible women in the city and then advised him that there was one possibility he hadn't tried.

'The answer to your problem is quite simple - internet dating,' she told him authoritatively.

'You cannot be serious,' Earl could only muster.

She then went on to inform him of the successes many of her friends had had in recent months with this way of dating. As the conversation went on she made a bet with him that he would find a really suitable candidate within a month of trying a dating site she recommended. As he always had a weak spot for a bet they agreed on a fifty euros wager and she gave him the site address, wishing him happy hunting.

His most recent romance had certainly not been a success. He had met this fairly attractive woman called Celine in The Fiddler's Curse - she worked in a café and seemed promising enough at the beginning. However it soon emerged that she was dangerously Frumpy in many ways and her apparently liberal talk veiled a repressed and unbalanced psyche. On their second meeting she had joined him and the other rakes in drinking a few Bacardis and she initially seemed to be good fun and not at all like the Frosty/Frumpy brigade. She was wearing black (always a weak spot with the rakes) and was quite alluring. He asked her if she was a 'goody goody' and she gave him a mischievous look, clearly indicating that she was anything but. His hopes were raised despite a reluctance to feel even a glimmer of optimism (based on past experiences). Murphy and Kearney thought that he was onto a 'good thing' and tactfully moved off to another part of the bar.

Later that night Earl got an invite back to Celine's apartment and it was then that things began to go downhill. It did not take him long to realise that despite all her 'come on' verbiage she was of the Frumpy class - as soon as he tried to kiss her she backed off and froze like an iceberg. It transpired that she was still virginal and likely to remain that way until she was properly engaged to some 'gentleman' as she so quaintly put it. What annoyed Earl was all the time wasting and the silly games that led nowhere. 'Give me a break,' he muttered as she went into the kitchen to make some tea and tidy her ruffled blouse. 'What a waste of a body,' he heard himself say out loud as she shuffled round in the kitchen. He decided that the best strategy was exit stage left as soon as possible and to forget the whole thing had ever happened.

This latest experience was the final straw and so led Earl to sign up to a website called 'Yournewfriend', without any expectations. His next few adventures led him to quest in a new way, even if it meant paying Natasha the fifty euros. So he delved into the site looking for samples of women he wouldn't meet in his usual haunts, while deciding not to tell his fellow rakes of this latest twist in his romantic career. Some descriptions put him off a profile completely. 'Genuine' was an occasional word used by some women - he was really put off by this as it reeked of goody goodiness. The same went for 'sincere', 'nice', 'considered attractive', 'never drinks' and 'caring'. In any case he had soon compiled a list of possibilities from the site - women who seemed to fit his criteria and geographical range.

Top of his tentative list was a woman from Kinsale who had described herself as 'adventurous, outgoing, pretty, well-travelled', as well as 'tall and with a little extra padding'. Notwithstanding the 'extra padding' bit the overall impression Earl got was positive, and so he decided to make a date to meet her in a small wine bar in Kinsale, at lunchtime one Saturday. As he walked towards the wine bar on the appointed day he saw a woman approach from the other direction. She was wearing a red jacket (as she had promised) but surely not her... she was a blubbery, small Neolithic type. He started to perspire and was about to do a runner when Baby Elephant waved at him enthusiastically, and so he had no option but to go through with the whole episode. She barely fitted through the door of the chic wine bar and he was mortified in case anyone he knew spotted him. He got her a large glass of wine, and as he sheepishly tried to make conversation, she deftly moved closer and closer to him. She was wolfing down the wine and had four glasses while he was still on his first one. Time passed excruciatingly slowly and he could only contemplate one thing - the freedom he would feel when he could exit the bar and run for his life. She went on and on about sailing in Kinsale and her boring job in the bank and her family and so on and on. He wasn't really listening to her but she didn't seem to notice much in any case. She was pushing for him to come back and 'see' her apartment which was not too far away. He declined and so she forced him to make another date for the following night in the same bar. He agreed - he would have agreed to a lot at this stage - and finally, his shirt wet with perspiration, he managed to leave her and shoot out the door with a new sense of purpose and relief. All women who used the 'little extra padding' euphemism were to be given a wide berth from then on!

A few days later he got an e mail from someone code named Stunner69. He looked at her profile and was a bit wary when he saw the following:

'Attractive, sexy, fun loving, tall woman looking for a no strings attached liaison with an adventurous guy. Every woman's nightmare.'

Seemingly she was a divorcee and lived in the city. It was all a bit hard to believe but, nothing ventured, he banged off a standard reply and thought no more of her, until a few days later, he got another mail from the temptress. And so followed an exchange of increasingly promising messages until finally she gave him her phone number. They were subsequently to meet in one of the city's more exclusive hotels and so, one Friday night he was quite excited at the prospect of meeting a woman who seemed to be a kind of sexually advanced Pamela Andersen with a brain. She had told him that her best 'attributes' were her 'lips, legs and boobs' - not necessarily in that order - and this really got him going. When he reached the hotel he ordered himself a soda water, deciding to leave alcohol until later. He sat down in a large, comfortable arm chair in the lounge where he had a good view of the entrance, though in a discreet kind of way. The appointed time passed. 'Women are always late, especially so in the case of blind dates,' he mused. However forty five minutes later there was still no show from the so called stunner. And so there it was - a complete waste of a night, not to mind the disappointment of not having a steamy encounter.

When he got home he blasted off a text message to the missing woman but she never contacted him again and had vanished from the site the following day. At the back of his mind he had this inkling that Baby Elephant in Kinsale may have had something to do with the whole business - some nasty kind of revenge perhaps. In any case, there was nothing he could do except laugh and put the whole thing down to experience.

After these encounters he more or less lost interest in internet dating, and despite occasional visits to the site, he never met anyone even remotely interesting. He got a bit fed up of all the euphemisms and downright self-delusion which characterised so many of the women's profiles. His final encounter was with a woman who had given herself the code name Aphrodite and who gave the impression of being an extremely cultured and promising type - yet when he contacted her she turned out to be a complete philistine. She had never heard of Bruckner and thought the *Night Watch* was the name of a race horse. She was in the Frosty mould and he thought that if they had met by chance in a bar she would have acted as icily as Bibi. Their first encounter was fairly excruciating - they met in the Central Park Hotel and it was clear from even the way she walked that she was a small town snob with an empty head and an underused, beautiful body. After some small talk, she mentioned that she had been to Covent Garden the week before to see the *Magic Flute.*

'So you like opera?' Earl asked innocently enough after a few minutes of small talk.

'Oh yes, I just adore Mozart,' she replied with just a hint of unease.

'Which recording do you have of *The Magic Flute?*' Earl probed.

'Well I don't actually have any recording,' she muttered, and as the conversation lurched forward it became clear that for her it was very the idea of being in Covent Garden at the opera that was important. It made her feel quite superior to be able to tell people where she had been, along with elaborate fashion details about the opera set. Earl had a short fuse and didn't suffer fools gladly.

'So what you are really saying is that you know damn all about Mozart?' he growled at her.

He didn't really care what kind of music she liked but the pretentiousness of it all got on his gimp.

'Is this an interrogation or what?' she whimpered uncomfortably and went off to powder her nose and ring one of her equally vacuous friends. He muttered his standard 'Beam me up!' and left the hotel while Ms Opera (as he named her) was still touching herself up (as in face). When she arrived back she was incredulous to find him gone. What would she tell her bimbo friends now about her hot date? She paid the bill (he had decided to leave it unpaid out of annoyance) and then she drove home in her sleek BMW. It was a Friday night and most of her friends were in the centre or at some dinner party having a good time. She sprawled on a sofa and considered using one of her impressive collection of vibrators but instead, out of impulse and frustration, decided to head for the centre and meet up with one of her crew of superficial socialites and sexually frustrated gold diggers. She would of course change the story of her blind date and spin some yarn about Earl being 'sooo uncouth' or whatever. He, meantime, was also heading for town via home, deciding to dress down a bit before going to places like The Fiddler's Curse, where it would be most unlikely to meet Ms Opera and her bimbo crew, and where he could float around and lose himself in the atmosphere and music.

***

As it was very near Christmas, the bars were busier than usual. Murphy and Kearney were in The Short Hill sitting on their favourite stools, at the end of the counter where they had a panoramic view of the entire bar. Murphy was not at all amused. He had been to one of those rare Cork events - a symphony concert that had taken place in St Fin Barre's cathedral with a German chamber orchestra playing to a half empty audience. He had the misfortune to sit behind a young couple who talked their way through most of the first movement of Mozart's Twenty Ninth symphony. He hissed at them to shut up when this movement was over but to little avail. When the orchestra finished the second movement the leader had to signal to the audience to quieten down and not to clap until the work was over. 'All very embarrassing,' Murphy winced. After the interval the orchestra played Beethoven's Second symphony. This time the first movement went well enough, but then a dog began to howl outside and continued to howl right throughout the graceful and elegant *Larghetto* second movement. Murphy could only hold his head in shame. And then the final straw… as the orchestra was nearing the end of the bustling and happy music of the fourth movement there was a pause, and some sections of the audience started clapping only to realise that the movement wasn't over. 'What a disaster,' thought Murphy. He almost felt like apologising to the orchestra but instead made a dash for the exit and headed for a much needed drink. If the Second was Beethoven's graceful farewell to the eighteenth century, then this concert was Murphy's farewell to the music scene in this city. As if to rub salt in his wounds, he passed several signs on his way to the centre, proclaiming Cork to be the next European Capital of Culture.

In The Short Hill he was beginning to feel less stressed after a pint of vitamin M and, as there were no women on the scene worth considering, he got involved in an ongoing colloquy with Kearney about Sibelius and the issue of the Finnish government giving the musical genius a grant so that he was free to devote his time to composing. Kearney claimed that it wasn't right to give such a grant. The argument went on and on.

'Why not give a carpenter a grant so that he can make classy furniture in that case?' Kearney remarked sardonically.

'Because of course lots of people can make classy furniture but only a rare genius like Sibelius can create great symphonies,' Murphy retorted.

'Well if a carpenter has to make his way without any state handouts then Sibelius should have been given the same treatment. In any case who is to judge Sibelius' work?' Kearney sermonised. 'Sibelius makes symphonies and a carpenter makes chairs. A matter of taste, no?'

'It's not a matter of taste, it's a matter of perception,' Murphy growled while simultaneously scanning the bar.

'The trouble with you is that you regard art as some kind of quasi-mystical experience which leads to some kind of connection to the divine,' Kearney went on. 'It's just not like that. You are deluding yourself. And get me another bottle while you're being put right.'

'But art transmutes ordinary experience into something numinous,' Murphy persisted. 'Sibelius' Fourth, for example, is a work that touches on another world. All great art is religious in the widest sense of the word.'

'You just CANNOT be serious,' Kearney said loudly enough to get the attention of the porcine, shabbily dressed women next to him.

As the rakes continued their animated discussion Jane arrived in. They were relieved to see her - she had an easy-goingness about her which put people at their ease and they both valued her judgement.

'Ok, let's start with some news,' she said. 'Listen up Murphy. Guess who is coming to Cork on the 24th? Guess who is tipped for a job in the English Department in UCC? Guess who is rumoured to be leaving her hubbie?'

Murphy was suddenly extremely excited and even vaguely happy. Jane had his undivided attention.

'You cannot be serious?' he said to her.

'Hey, that's my line,' Kearney joked.

'So are we going to meet her or what?' Murphy wanted to know.

'The only certainty is that she will be in town on the 24th and in Schull from the 25th. Don't ask me how I got the info. Anyway I guess all this means that I am owed several drinks. Right?'

Murphy was once again more than happy to buy her a double Power's and ginger ale. He didn't want to labour the conversation by going on and on about Emily but he found himself emerging from the bleak desolation he normally felt at this time of year by the prospect of seeing her again. Meanwhile Kearney was asking Jane about her ongoing thesis and she became absorbed in telling him that she was onto something really big. If what she was researching proved to be authentic she would be a star in academia forever. When Kearney left to visit the toilet Murphy asked her how her romantic life was.

'Oh nothing serious,' she answered a little coyly. 'A few liaisons and no more. And what about your buddy - dare I ask now that he isn't here?'

'Oh, he's like you. Impossible to please!' Murphy responded. 'Nothing happening in particular.'

'Is he still seeing that librarian we met in Schull?'

'Don't really know. Don't think that was serious in any case. Rakes are hard to please.'

She was about to give him a dig but she saw Kearney returning and so she refrained.

'So why don't you ask Jane about the Sibelius grant?' Kearney demanded of Murphy.

'What grant?' Jane inquired and so Kearney gave her the gist of what they had been arguing about.

'Of course he should have been given that grant,' Jane announced. 'Kearney, how could you possibly deny such a genius free time to compose? You disappoint me,' she added. 'You think computers will soon surpass Mozart, you think we are all mere machines. You would have had Sibelius teach crumby music lessons while he could have been composing.'

'Agh! You are as bad as Murphy,' Kearney retorted. 'You put artists up on pedestals as if they are some kind of high priests above everyone else.'

'Exactly what they are in a way,' Jane replied.

'Look. Take his Fourth Symphony,' Kearney said in exasperation. 'It's obviously a great piece of music etc. etc. No one is denying that. But you think it is also a work of art in the sense of elevating it to some spiritual sphere beyond this existence? Like Murphy wrongly says - a religious experience.'

'Well I agree with Murphy in the broadest sense,' Jane confirmed.

Kearney threw his eyes to heaven, and with an exaggerated sigh, took a long draft from the American beer he favoured. They were clearly poles apart. Where he saw nothing but extinction and unrelenting bleakness in the face of human kind that was weak and largely despicable, she experienced the numinous and that lightness of being that attended those whose lives were to all intents and purposes lived in a parallel universe. She was as absolute in her mysticism as Kearney was in his nihilism. And yet, despite her ethereal air, there she was, unassailably down to earth, knocking back whiskeys and shooting the breeze with all and sundry.

Murphy took a drink of his creamy pint of vitamin M and looked down the bar at a gang of new arrivals, all dressed to kill. They were new to him. Two of them were tall blondes in their mid-thirties, and the third was a brunette in her late twenties. One was a real stunner with a sleek, long, navy overcoat, and an equally svelte body to match.

Jane saw Murphy scanning the scene and sighed wearily, 'Here we go again. End of the Sibelius conversation.'

'Well, it is the weekend,' Murphy replied to Kearney's disapproving stare.

Just then, with perfect timing, Kearney got a text from Karen the librarian saying that she would be in the city on the following day, Christmas Eve, asking if he could meet her in the early pm. As Kearney was replying to the text Murphy told Jane about the concert. They then started on about Beethoven's Second and Murphy sermonised about how underestimated the early music of Beethoven was.

'You do realise that at one of the first performances of the Second in Vienna the audience was so captivated by the *Larghetto* that they started to applaud and had it encored before the orchestra got to the third movement?' Jane asked him.

'Yes of course I know,' Murphy replied. 'I'm not against spontaneity, but the philistines at today's concert were *not* that Viennese audience!'

'So have you a date tomorrow or what?' Jane then asked Kearney as he put away his phone.

'No I don't. I'm just meeting someone for coffee,' he replied gruffly.

As the banter went on another round of drinks arrived. Murphy got a text from Earl asking them to come down to The Fiddler's Curse but Murphy replied telling him to hurry on down to their bar instead as there was a bevy of stunners all waiting to be charmed. A few minutes later Earl shot into the bar with unusual haste and a degree of unease.

'Knew I should have stayed in the other place,' he muttered to the others as he realized that Ms Opera was the stunner the other two rakes had been admiring. There she was half- scowling at Earl, and of course not saying anything about him to her retinue. Earl didn't say anything either, making his discomfort all the greater.

'We were thinking about going and talking to that coven down there,' Murphy told him.

'No! Bad idea. They're bimbos,' Earl spluttered nervously.

'And how would you know sleazebag?' Jane volunteered humorously.

In any case they stayed where they were and let the bar fill up some more. Kearney started paying more attention to Jane, further quizzing her on the scholarly breakthrough she was expecting. It seemed that part of a second copy of *Sir Gawain and the Green Knight* had turned up -

at least half the poem in fact, with a few pages at the end which indicated the poet's identity and a lot of other things about his history and milieu. If this was authenticated Jane would be catapulted to academic stardom.

'At least you won't have to sleep your way to the top like some academics,' Kearney scoffed.

'Lovely thing to say to an innocent nymph,' Murphy intervened.

The thing about this time of year that the rakes liked was that there was a continuous coming and going of all sorts of exiles who were home for the festive season, as well as a larger local attendance than usual. So they met people who they had known from their university days and who they only met at this time of year.

Just as Murphy and Kearney were thinking about approaching Ms Opera and her friends, a woman called Grace arrived into the bar and made straight for the rakes, much to the relief of Earl who was getting hostile stares from Ms Opera. Grace was a young academic and shared Jane's trait of not residing in the 'ivory tower'. Murphy had had a brief liaison with her some time back but that was well and truly history at this stage. He had been amazed to learn that she was engaged to someone she had only known for three months - and, he was even more amazed when he realised that she was not exactly a hundred percent enthusiastic about the whole thing. However, she gave the impression that she was resigned to her fate and that no one could do anything about it, least of all herself. Her husband to be was a small, boring rustic interested only in pastoral farming, fishing and being left alone. He didn't socialise much and Murphy immediately christened him Lance the Rustic, much to Grace's annoyance. While the rakes did not want to cause her undue distress they could not help making their feelings known about the absurdity of marrying someone after a three month acquaintanceship. The Second Law seemed to be universal without any doubt - there seemed to be so many mismatches that Kearney often joked that maybe they were already in the afterlife, in a kind of Purgatorial twilight zone. In any case as there was no sign of Lance they were treated to the rarest of occasions - the company of Grace for an entire evening with no rushing off as was her usual wont.

And so the bar filled until there was a real festive atmosphere with even the occasional Frosty condescending to say hello. The rakes and their company had the best seats in the bar and were soon surrounded by acquaintances from their college days who came and went as the drinks flowed. Kearney was paying attention to Grace who was far less inhibited than usual - Lance kept her on a tight rein and so she took full advantage of her rare window of freedom. She and Kearney got involved in a conversation about Schull that was full of sub-texts and undercurrents. Meanwhile Murphy and Jane were equally engrossed in a conversation about relationships. Jane asked him if he would consider ending up with a woman with whom there was no meeting of minds but at the same time a natural kind of empathy.

'You know what kind of woman I mean,' she said. 'Someone who is intelligent without being intellectual, someone natural and sensitive, someone who may not share your interests but at the same time acknowledges them, someone who is of course sexually brill.'

Murphy mused. 'Yes I suppose so. But then again I think that in the end I am going for the jackpot and nothing else. I could end up with someone as you describe but knowing my luck I would meet a woman soon afterwards who is everything you have described but more... a woman where there would be a meeting of true minds as well.'

He really liked this girl - she was a breath of fresh air compared to the silliness and goody goodiness of the Frumpies. She seemed so sexually secure and confident in herself, so intellectually independent and witty, so unselfconsciousness. He was indeed noticing her more than he had done in the past - she was indeed lithe and attractive in a kind of off-centre arty yet natural way. Ironically, even though he was normally fairly perceptive about peoples' inner lives, with her he wasn't to find out until much later that at the centre of her emotional life was a perpetual sense of betrayal, brought about by a disastrous relationship she'd had with a caddish Oxford smoothie. She remained wary of romantic relationships, and became aloof, even cold, when pressed about her romantic life.

'You will fall between two stools and end up a broken and lonely old man if you don't take heed Murphy dear,' she declared in between sips of her whiskey and ginger ale.

He was really impressed – the natural rapport between them belied the significant age difference between them. She put a lot of older women he knew to shame. At the same time, he knew that she was one of those transient figures who would disappear from his circle sooner rather than later, as her career took her along a different path. This conditioned him to think that there could be nothing romantic between them and his ongoing fatalism had already placed her outside his emotional compass.

Earl meanwhile was casting furtive glances down the counter in the direction of Ms Opera and her company. Was it his imagination or were they gradually approaching him? He felt slightly guilty about doing a runner earlier in the evening but he was nothing if not impetuous and spontaneous. She would hardly have the nerve to restart their acquaintanceship he mused, as he knocked back another pint of vitamin G. Then, as he again looked in her direction there she was - walking nonchalantly in his direction. As she passed him she whispered very lowly but clearly 'You're dead' and walked on in the direction the toilets. He was a bit taken aback by this turn as it was not what he had expected, but at least she had a bit of spirit. Maybe he had written her off too hastily!

Meanwhile Grace was drinking at a fast pace - as if she was making up for lost or future time. She was not really a drinker and it was not long before all her inhibitions were almost gone and her guard was down. She was paying Kearney more and more attention. He tried to steer her away from saying anything she would regret but then he decided that life was short and to hell with her pathetic engagement.

'So when are the nuptials?' he asked her as he poured another bottle of insipid American beer into his glass.

'I told you, in September,' she replied petulantly.

'So will it be a big funer… I mean wedding?' Kearney pressed.

'More than two hundred. It's all arranged, down to the flowers.'

'And when do we get to meet Sir Lancelot?'

'After the wedding of course. I'm not introducing him to you desperadoes before the wedding. I don't trust you lot at all, at all,' she blurted out without thinking.

'Oh come on - we want to meet this paragon of manhood. He can't be that brittle.'

'Never mind,' she retorted fatalistically. 'The whole thing is all arranged and that is that.'

Kearney decided to go for broke.

'So if you were not engaged to Lance you wouldn't go down that road again, would you?' he declared emphatically.

At this she seemed about to cry and made a dash for the toilets. Everyone looked at Kearney disapprovingly but he just shrugged and returned to his drink. Jane went after Grace and it was some time before they returned. Kearney did not expect her to cave in so easily he confided to Murphy. It seemed such a waste of a woman marrying like that, but if she was determined to self-destruct, then so be it.

'First of all you make Sibelius turn in his grave and then you make an innocent weep,' Murphy quipped.

'Well looks like we can't do much to save Grace, whatever about Sibelius and the grant,' came the usual sardonic reply.

'I don't know about you guys but I could do with a table job... what about those women down there,' Murphy said, nodding discreetly in the direction of Ms Opera.

He associated different women with different sexual proclivities and Ms Opera was definitely the table job type. This brought a confession out of Earl and they were much taken by his treatment of such a striking looking woman, even if she was a 'rice crispy' - empty inside but plenty of 'snap, crackle and pop'.

'So much for high standards in low places,' Earl countered.

'Yes of course but she would be a seriously good skirmish you must admit?' Kearney volunteered. His intention of joining Ms Opera's set was thwarted by the return of Jane and Grace. The latter had recovered somewhat and soon was drinking another Carlsberg with a vengeance.

Time passed. As usual Jane showed her flair at getting on with total strangers and she talked to Grace as if they were long lost friends. This even impressed Kearney but he still didn't really have any designs on her. By now the bar was really full and it was not a time for serious discourse. Earl was drinking twice as fast as his fellow rakes and out of the blue he got an impulse to speak to Ms Opera. So he began to sidle his way through the heaving crowd to where she and her friends were, and as the rakes looked on with bemusement, he made straight for her. She had her back to him as he approached.

'So I'm dead am I?' he asked as she turned around in surprise.

'Look who's here,' she taunted. 'The man who ran away.'

'Okay, okay, let me buy you a drink,' Earl said a bit wanly, without much of his famed confidence and off-hand charm.

'I already have a drink,' Ms Opera declared with more than a touch of irritation. 'So why don't you go back to your gang and we'll forget about the whole thing.'

'What's the rush?' Earl countered. 'I didn't do you any mortal harm did I?'

At this point one of Ms Opera's equally attractive friends intervened and gradually Earl wheedled his way into their company without feeling like a complete fool. He slowly came to the conclusion that when Ms Opera dropped her pretentious notions, she was good enough company, and she actually began to have a certain hold over him, defying all his expectations. He was attracted by her body language which gave the illusion of a comfortable sexuality. He was even beginning to wonder what kind of lingerie she was wearing - very tasty indeed judging by her designer clothes.

At the back of the bar Kearney was listening to an intoxicated Grace ramble on about the forthcoming nuptials. She wanted offspring and that it seemed was why she was getting married to Lance the rustic. Kearney didn't comprehend the baby gene and it was beyond him why people often so badly wanted something that ruined one's social life, cost a fortune (which could be better spent on trips to South America and carousing), and was a never ending encroachment on one's personal freedom and advancement. There she would be in a year's time, living in a boring semi-detached in a dreary north Cork town, with only Lance for company, and a complete lack of a social life or the prospect of meeting interesting people. She was not the housewife type. She liked the stimulation of meeting new people and being out and about. Added to this, her career in academia would end in a brutal cul-de-sac as it had no future in the city – potential advancement only came by getting up the ladder abroad before trying anything closer to home. Kearney was surprised and perplexed by her fatalism. She seemed so resigned to things. It was clear that there was no point in saying anything and so he moved on to other topics. He was only too aware of the many people he knew who were trapped in dead end marriages with partners who had nothing to say, and where sexual congress was either a distant memory or an occasional chore.

While Kearney talked to Grace, Jane and Murphy were discussing the Second Law in depth. This turn in the conversation was initiated by the arrival in the bar of a very attractive blonde who was accompanied by a large male who looked quite similar to a silverback gorilla. Murphy expressed perplexity at such frequent examples of the Second Law whereas Jane said wearily, 'We are repeating ourselves, aren't we? Are we always to have this conversation? Men and women go for different things overall. Women don't go for looks as much as most men do.'

'Are you right or what? So what does she see in Ape over there?' Murphy wanted to know definitively.

'Not speaking personally,' Jane replied, 'but a lot of women go for security and personality, and maybe money on occasion.'

'I'm disappointed in you,' Murphy said plaintively. 'Not enough to explain such bizarre couplings though you are probably right about the money!'

'Your expectations are too high,' she interjected with spirit. 'Nature wants procreation. People in general just live and don't think very much and that's how it is. You and your like may aspire to be more Ariel than Caliban but brute nature rules and that is that!'

Then, still animated, she intoned:

'The time of the seasons and the constellations
The time of milking and the time of harvest
The time of the coupling of man and woman
And that of beasts. Feet rising and falling.
Eating and drinking. Dung and death…'

'And so that is that,' Murphy rallied. 'In any case I think the gold diggers come to a sorry end going for rich gorillas. You have only to consider Debbie Wright and you see how her life has unfolded.'

The crowd was now heaving and so the group decided to go to The Beech where there would be more space. As the rakes left with Jane and Grace they passed Earl and Ms Opera and told him where they were heading for. Ms Opera and co seemed quite interested in joining them, although Jane and Grace did not share their enthusiasm.

When they got to The Beech Murphy was surprised to see a local politician sitting at the counter with a few companions. Like many of his ilk he was uneducated, ignorant, ineloquent and unprincipled.

Murphy regarded him as the archetypal gombeen man, the wheeler and dealer of parish pump politics, all nods and winks, all strokes and deals. Murphy winced whenever he saw him and his Dáil cronies on TV: the sheer embarrassment of it all - the provincialism, the mediocrity, the lack of coherent debate, the petty squabbles, the lack of any intellectual content to the speeches, the false posturing by the front men who went to communication schools to learn how to stand and hold themselves. This particular politician, despised by Murphy, had actually considered putting himself forward as a leader of his party at one stage - that would have been some laugh, a gombeen prime minister. The fact that he was actually serious about putting his name forward showed how blind he was. And there he was, with his circle of sycophants paying court to him, just a few yards away. Murphy's first impulse was to approach him but then he decided that there would be no point in saying anything to the idiot. So they walked past the gaggle of politicos and found a nook to sit in and continue the Christmas revelry.

'That's another difference between men and women,' Murphy said to Jane as they were sitting down. 'Women in general seem to have no interest in politics.'

'Well, you'd hardly expect any intelligent woman to take an interest in the politics of this country?' she retorted. 'But now I have to talk to someone over there so mind my seat and don't go away.'

'You're getting on very well with the Renaissance nymph,' Kearney queried Murphy.

'I'm keeping her in the company until you see the light. Why you don't fancy her beats me. She's a ten, she's a nymph, she's diverting, God, she's close to the ideal. She doesn't even smoke. And her handwriting - such style.'

'Well in that case what the hell are you doing yourself?'

'Don't forget <u>my</u> Emily C all by herself in cold Aberdeen. She's probably looking out her window now at the black North Sea night and thinking about me,' Murphy joked.

'Who's Emily?' a very tipsy Grace asked.

'We'll tell you when you grow up child,' Kearney told her imperiously.

***

As it happened Emily was indeed looking out at the dark, cold night from her third floor window. Uriah was somewhere in southern England. At least she wouldn't have to put up with him in future. She had the house to herself and she had already packed for her journey to Cork on the following day. She was expecting friends to call a little later. Meanwhile she was in her cosy study which had a panoramic view of the town and the sea beyond. She had been listening to a lot of music of late. It didn't console her in any way about the death of her sister but it made her feel less alone. This night she had chosen the Beethoven Thirteenth String Quartet in Bb major – the quartet with the *Grosse Fuge* ending. Or at least that was always the ending she listened to. It always annoyed her that so many string quartets played the alternative conclusion which Beethoven had uncharacteristically agreed to write as a compromise.

She gave herself completely to the music while she listened, the experience being a kind of spiritual journey at once uplifting and emotionally draining. It was music which made her weep. Composed in a world of infinite silence, from the sad, remote opening bars followed by the amazing, strange sounding *Presto,* to the serene resignation of the *Andante* and the wistful *Danza alla tedesca,* it was music from another world. She found the *Cavatina* impossible to listen to without a feeling of communion, of being aware of a cosmos that had meaning no matter what logic demanded. Ultimately there was the feeling of stillness she mused:

> '*The release from action and suffering, release from the inner*
> *And the outer compulsion, yet surrounded*
> *By a sense of grace, a white light still and moving…*'

The *Grosse Fuge* finale was indeed unrelenting in its assertion of the will, nurturing her formidable inner resource.

As she listened to the closing bars she felt strangely at peace despite the raw grief of her sister's extinction and all the other turmoil she had recently endured. She had had her long dark nights of the soul with no sense of any light or hope or relief but when she listened to this music she felt a lightness of being, a sense of inexpressible transcendence. She stayed in the silence of her room for a long time and only left it when she saw two of her friends coming up the driveway in the swirling snow.

She felt lucky to have a circle of such bright and articulate friends. There was also a fire down in the drawing room - she had begun to indulge herself the moment the frugal Uriah had left, and so she and her company drank cognac while the snow flurries pluffed against the window, all feeling relief at his absence. By the time they departed she was for once able to sleep for the first time for ages. She fell into the futon bed in her study while the fire still flickered and she vaguely recalled that tenuous encounter with Murphy in Schull.

***

Back in The Beech, Earl and the Ms Opera set had come in and were standing near Earl's fellow rakes, though still slightly out of range for introductions. Kearney was getting a bit uneasy about Grace's inebriated, almost amorous attentions, while Jane was giving Murphy an update on her ongoing academic adventures. Seemingly, if incredibly, she had made the acquaintance of this elderly Old and Middle English scholar at an Oxford seminar and he had become quite impressed with her. One thing led to another until he generously shared in his great discovery concerning the Gawain poet. He was past the glory seeking stage he told her, and he wanted her to do what was left to be done.

As Jane was coming near the end of her tale Murphy happened to notice a slightly agitated, gnomish looking pooka type wandering round the bar as if looking for someone. He suddenly realised it could be Lance the Rustic and was about to warn Kearney when they were spotted. It was indeed Lance who shot up towards them, undaunted by the crowd present. He was obviously not at all pleased to see his fiancé in such suspicious company.

'I've been looking all over the place for you,' he growled at the intoxicated Grace. 'Why the hell didn't you answer the phone?'

'Now don't be cross. I didn't hear the phone,' she replied honestly enough.

She was about to try and introduce her hirsute knight to the company but he made it fairly obvious that all he wanted to do was grab her and exit stage left. Before anyone could say much more the two of them were gone and the rakes were left to ponder the hapless

Grace's lack of a future.

'What a complete dweeb. What a throwback to the Neanderthal. What a dipstick,' Murphy finally managed.

'As if more proof was needed of the Second Law,' Kearney reminded Jane.

'Well it seems ye do have a point. Ye can be right occasionally I suppose,' she allowed.

Earl at this stage was on surprisingly good terms with Ms Opera but his attempts to introduce her set to the rakes were confounded by the heaving crowd. With Grace gone Jane also was about to leave for reasons unknown. There was a large trog count in the bar at this stage - the usual mixture of lowlifes and dweebs, tattoo types and rat faced skinheads, and separated ffbs with attitude. The rakes decided to move on as well and so headed for The Shack, telling Earl where to find them on the way out. They did manage to salute the Ms Opera set, both agreeing that they were not their type - there was something too affected about the whole lot of them, as if they were holding up placards saying 'Look at us, we're beautiful.' There was no accounting for Earl's taste, and like everything else, he was unpredictable to the end. When they went outside there was snow falling - there had been more snow that month than in the entire previous decade. Kearney asked Murphy where Jane was off to but Murphy had no idea. He then told Kearney about her elderly academic 'benefactor'.

'She lands on her feet all the time,' Kearney responded. 'Does she ever make a mistake or misjudge anything?'

Murphy let the observation pass while thinking the snow was a positive omen. Changing the subject, he mentioned Emily to Kearney who was not very encouraging about his prospects.

'How did she end up with that creepo Uriah?' Kearney quipped. 'Bit of a black mark there I'd say, what?'

'Who knows,' Murphy relied. 'We'll see how the plot thickens.'

'What plot? You may not see her for years. What are you going to do - sign on for a course of Middle English?' Kearney said in his usual sardonic tone.

'You underestimate the Renaissance nymph,' Murphy reminded him.

'True, true. And what about Grace? No hope of saving her at this late stage. Boy, she really picks them. She'd be better off on a bed of nails instead of being on a mattress with that oaf. Give me a break!'

'Changing the subject,' Murphy said. 'I suppose you didn't say anything to the nymph about Bibi?'

'Didn't get a chance and not sure if I'll mention it. There are some things gentlemen don't talk to ladies about.'

'Well if Bibi is one of the sisterhood then she is one waste of a curvaceous bod. Would I or what?' Murphy avowed.

They entered The Shack and Murphy thought he saw Emily for a brief moment and he was almost surprised to realise how much she had become present in his grand scheme of things. They were a bit taken aback to see the Frumpies in the distance as this was not one of their usual haunts. They immediately took evasive action and retreated into a kind of nook where there was a small bar and a gang of tall female Crusty types. There were the real thing - living on some bleak hill side in West Cork and up for the day doing their shopping or whatever Crusties do at Xmas. Their men folk were probably organising a Christmas supply of cannabis and other goodies. Murphy knew from experience that these were not really suitable candidates for a skirmish - not at least in the present context. There was nothing worse than an irate male Crusty coming in to find his mate talking to a non-Crusty. These Crusties in any case seemed to be the type who thought it fashionable not to have an ablution more than once a month. And anyway, women in big, shapeless woolly pullovers never appealed to Murphy.

They got a round of drinks and moved on further into the deep recesses of the bar, keeping an eye on the location of the Frumpies. Murphy felt a slight shiver as he saw the Bront looking around, as if searching for them. The last thing he wanted was to make pleasantries with that cantankerous malcontent. Rory Gallagher was blasting out a song, and though the music was loud, it was not intrusive. Kearney wandered off on walkabout while Murphy leaned against the counter, happily lost in the general atmosphere of carousing. He started thinking about Jane. She was definitely a gem, a rose in the desert and all that. Even her handwriting was so refined, so artistic. He wondered if there had been something between her and Bibi. He wouldn't ask her - despite her apparent openness there was an 'exclusion zone' that remained clearly off limits. Kearney eventually returned and they had another round of drinks while debating where to go next.

***

Meanwhile in Molloy's house in Mid Wales the arch rake and tom cat was awaiting the arrival of the bank manager's wife. She had only an hour to spare, on the pretext of doing some last minute shopping. She was wearing an expensive long black coat and a simple black mini skirt with the usual matching black lingerie underneath. She knew Molloy's taste so she obliged - it was Christmas after all! She wore the standard long slinky black stockings and suspenders that drove him bananas - she stood and then leaned against the table and slowly let the top part of her dress loosen until one of her very impressive orbs was visible and waiting to be pampered. Just as Molloy touched her cheek her mobile rang.

'Ignore that thing, don't even think of answering it,' Molloy gasped in a nervy voice.

'But I have to,' she volunteered. 'It must be him. It's not like him to ring when I have already made definite arrangements. It must be serious.'

Molloy suppressed an oath and went into the untidy kitchen and had a glass of water. He didn't even bother listening to the conversation going on in the next room. He wasn't very optimistic about congress at this stage and time was passing fast. After what seemed ages she stopped talking and was quite panicky.

'I think he suspects something. He was a bit strange and unusual. Don't know how he could possibly suspect anything. I'm supposed to meet him in The Lion and Lamb at eight - I mean he must believe me when I say I am shopping. I even bought stuff earlier to cover myself! Look at the time - we haven't a chance now. I can't arrive looking as if I have just been ravished.'

She was sitting on the sofa at this stage and Molloy was standing in front of her - so with new founded aplomb she unzipped him and 'did her duty' as he would have put it. Then in a flutter she left to dash off to The Lion and Lamb, with the prospect of no more sex for a few days at least, unlike Molloy, who had a large reserve of women lined up at his beck and call. He was planning to stay in Middle Earth until the

25th and then head over to his house in Ireland. The only problem was having to spend the festive season in Schull avoiding a psycho like McMicheal. He sent a text to his fellow rakes in Cork wishing them the season's best and then phoned one of his emergency supply of insecure women who always seemed ready to oblige. Within an hour there was a ring at the door and an fb was standing on the doormat with an open coat revealing a low-cut top showing impressive frontage, complemented by a short, tarty mini skirt and fishnet stockings.

***

Back at The Shack Murphy and Kearney were not having any luck as there was plenty of quantity but little quality. Both shared a deep dislike of Christmas and all the attendant hassle that went with it: the frenzy in the shops, the religious charade, the awful presents, family tensions, not to mind the desolation of Christmas Day. Earl finally came in but without the Ms Opera set. It seemed that she had to go and attend to familial duties, her friends having decided to disperse as well.

'How could anyone have familial duties at this time of night?' Murphy asked.

'Maybe she has a rendezvous with some vampire,' Kearney replied and then added, 'Molloy is venturing back to Schull on the 26th. He wants us to go down as well. We can stay with him as his body guards against the viper McMicheal for a bit of excitement. Course we all know who will want to stay at Sadie's.'

'Come on,' Murphy said defensively. 'It's hard enough having designs on Emily C without complicating things with a woman who is completely out of bounds.'

'Marriage never stopped you before. And you thought Emily was out of bounds as well,' Kearney reminded him.

'Well you must admit she's got the most attractive orbs you've ever seen. Pure Jane Russell pedigree. Would I or what?' Murphy said with an air of futility.

Earl wanted to know if he was also invited to the next Schull escapade. The two rakes were well aware of his ability to say the wrong thing at the wrong time and to act the loose cannon more often than not, so he was deemed the perfect candidate for Schull. There was always room for more drama. On this note all three decided to go to The High C for the last round of drinks and they made their way through the big crowd, aghast that there were so few romantic possibilities at this time of year.

The High C was full though there was an end of party feel about the place. The usual losers lined the counter in various stages of inebriation. There were empty glasses all over the place and a more than usual touch of squalor. Kearney was beginning to think that his encounter with Emma, the lady who worked in CERN, had been an aberration. It was nearly an axiom at this stage that they kept meeting interesting and attractive women in this pub only to never see them again.

They got their drinks and were lucky to find seats in a corner as a gang of Crusties just happened to leave at the right time. Murphy looked with satisfaction at his glass of Canadian Club on the rocks. Earl and Kearney were talking about the Ms Opera circle while Murphy looked over the clientele. He noticed a regular called Makeham who was one big reason for not believing in God. He was divorced from a beautiful woman who he had regularly beaten. He had an overbearing sense of self-importance and this was in inverse proportion to his intelligence. He sometimes acted as if he actually owned the bar and this led to various brawls with some incoming trogs or drunken zygotes, depending on circumstances. He was very drunk on this particular night and was leaning on the shoulder of some equally ugly, and even fatter being, who was 'technically female'. He had one stupid, glazed look on his bloated face. Murphy looked at him with total disgust.

Earl was telling Kearney that Ms Opera wasn't as bad as she seemed while Kearney disagreed – he rarely made mistakes in judging people.

'You just want her body Earl my boy, and you'll be waiting for an awfully long time,' Kearney advised.

'We'll see about that,' Earl mustered. 'It is Christmas after all. Maybe she'll melt after a brandy or two when I see her again?'

'Not the type anyway,' Kearney insisted. 'She's a goody goody. She wants to get married. She wants an engineer, or a doctor, to bring home to Mummy.'

Murphy finished his Canadian Club and decided to call it a night, telling Earl and Kearney that he would see them on the following afternoon for their traditional Christmas Eve pub crawl, not that there was anything to look forward to. He could see little to keep him in such a city for any long period of time. There was something too medieval about a lot of its bars and the basic nature of the inhabitants, not to mind the coarseness of the overall atmosphere and the underlying threat of violence.

He got a taxi before the trogs were back on the streets to get their fodder in the chippers - before going home to vomit and rut, though not necessarily in that order. It was snowing as the taxi reached his house. This was a real bonus and so rare that Murphy felt it as a kind of *déjà vu*, echoing forgotten experiences from his days in New England. He wasn't tired when he went inside so he treated himself to a mild Irish coffee while deciding what music to finish the day with. He decided on Bruckner's Fourth, an exceptional recording with Rattle conducting the Berlin Philharmonic. He always associated this particular music with majestic Alpine scenery and now for once there was even snow to enhance its glorious sounds. He loved the opening *Allegro* with its shimmering strings, a solo horn followed by the exhilarating build-up of more and more instruments until the whole orchestra blasted out the first subject. It was physically exciting and it made his heart thump. As he reached the glittering and invigorating scherzo, he was distracted by an unexpected text from Jane which simply read 'EC, Schull, 27th'. He smiled, as the music continued, impressed at her generosity of spirit in thinking of him at this late stage in the night. He returned to the symphony and listened to the finale - a final blast with the orchestra playing with absolute perfection. He then went to bed without a sign of the Black Dog's presence.

Part Four

CHRISTMAS EVE

Christmas was close at hand, in all his bluff and hearty honesty; it was the season of hospitality, merriment and open-heartedness; the old year was preparing, like an ancient philosopher, to call his friends around him, and amidst the sound of feasting and revelry to pass gently and calmly away...

The Pickwick Papers (Charles Dickens)

The sun shone, having no alternative, on the nothing new...

Murphy (Samuel Beckett)

Christmas Eve morning began with brilliant sunshine and a bitterly cold east wind. The snow had stopped, leaving the rarest of Christmas sights - a Breughel like snowscape which Murphy looked out at from a huge bay window. His house, which overlooked the entire city, had sweeping views. He always liked the earlier part of Christmas Eve - it was the night and the following day that he absolutely abhorred. The Dog always seemed to give him a break in the mornings. He had just ground some coffee beans and the aroma of rich coffee lingered in the light filled living room. He occasionally went to some trouble with the ritual of breakfast and this was one of those days. He was going to indulge in strong coffee and fresh croissants, and listen to music before facing the usual pageant of Christmas Eve. He had chosen the festive *Gloria* from Bach's *B minor Mass*. The music echoed with a brilliant resonance off the old timber floor and seemed to float out over the city as he listened and looked out at a brilliant blue sky and the snow covered city in the distance.

Christmas Eve was usually a day of endless casual encounters. He mused on the different people who would be in the next round of the ongoing saga. There would soon be the return of the irrepressible Molloy whose capacity to spin a tangled web had not diminished. Then there was the growing presence of Jane, who was becoming a key part of the rakes' circle. Kearney was expecting to have a festive skirmish with Karen despite occasional reservations. Earl seemed to be at an impasse with Ms Opera while Murphy himself was at a complete loss when he considered Emily Cardew. There was also the prospect of meeting the delectable, if unavailable, Sadie. She had a magnetism which made her so attractive that he made a conscious effort to keep her off his list of desirable liaisons, though this was easier said than done. In any case, Christmas Eve always threw up surprises even if the presence of the Motleys, Frumpies and Frosties had to be endured.

The remote, majestic grandeur of the *B minor Mass* was a perfect complement to the outside scene and he ended up listening to the whole work as the midwinter sun beamed down on his face. Afterwards, as he did not have any last minute shopping to do, he had the luxury of spending the earlier part of the day meeting people in cafés before the more serious socialising in the afternoon.

As time for the walkabout approached he got his long dark overcoat and headed down into the city. He had two CDs in his pockets - one was a gift for an ex, the Ravel *Piano Concerto in G* played by Michelangeli, and the other was the Benny Goodman 1938 Carnegie Hall concert. This was for Jane, the Renaissance nymph, as he still sometimes called her. Despite the extensive nature of her circle he sometimes got the impression that she didn't really have that many close friends. The Benny Goodman was a real blast and he knew that she would like it. He would even ask the barmaid in The High C to play it for the company later, depending on circumstances.

The usual pattern on Christmas Eve was to meet the other rakes in the afternoon and then, as the day wore on, they would wander from haunt to haunt in search of diversion and celestial beings. However Murphy's first social engagement was to meet a highly strung cousin for midday coffee in one of his favourite daytime bars - a big, light filled place with friendly staff and elegant décor. It was also the perfect place for private colloquies. By night he rarely visited it as it was frequented by primitive, grunting rap 'music' lovers backed by a simian DJ who seemed to be occasionally released from some local funny farm.

As Murphy sat down he saw his cousin arrive - she was about fifty and doomed to be a spinster. She had no siblings and both her parents were dead. She was very impulsive and capricious, constantly changing her life style out of a sense of enduring insecurity. She would take up the oboe one week and the next week her fixation might be skiing in the Alps. Fundamentally she was a kind woman made fragile and endlessly restless by inexorable loneliness. She usually went abroad at Christmas and if not, she would visit some hundred-year-old relation in an obscure part of Cavan where no one spoke English coherently. This Christmas she was staying at home alone. Murphy did for a moment yield to his better nature by asking her to join his fellow revellers in the afternoon but she declined.

'So what are you going to do tomorrow? Stay at home with the Black Dog?' he half-sighed.

'I'd prefer to stay at home alone than face the prospect of meeting all those odious relations of mine,' she replied. 'Call down in the evening if you are at a loose end - but no doubt you'll be wrapped round one of your floozies?'

'We'll see,' Murphy told her truthfully. 'I'll phone in any case. There is no chance of my ending up in a tryst by tomorrow.'

He really wished she could find someone. Ironically, given his usual stance, he thought that she was one of those women who would have been much better off married. There were plenty of men he knew who would have suited her, but there was so little opportunity for her to meet these - and she wasn't a bar person at all. Alas, he thought, there are so many women like her with so much to offer and yet doomed to lead a life with the Dog. She seemed in good spirits as she left him but he could sense the underlying loneliness as concretely as if it had been Chanel 5 perfume.

After she'd left, he stayed on to read *The Guardian* and take in the atmosphere before the next encounter. In a far corner he noticed the stunning but aloof Susan the coquette. There she was, as usual, in the most alluring and elegant of clothes with another equally attractive woman. Why she didn't ever seem to have a man with her was hard for the rakes to figure out, though Kearney insisted that she was just a gold digger and no more, biding her time for the proper catch. Murphy wasn't so sure. Whenever he talked to her he got the impression that she wasn't a complete bimbo though Kearney always disagreed.

She gave him a knowing smile and a half wave which he acknowledged, but he didn't get the impression that she wanted to be approached. Whatever about the gold digging he thought, he certainly wouldn't have minded her for an afternoon of sexual congress. As he was about to leave and head off for lunch in another haunt he got a text from Grace of all people, asking if he was in the neighbourhood. So he stayed and waited for her - always something to look forward to despite her impending marital doom. She was very edgy on arrival and as soon as she had ordered coffee she blurted out to Murphy that she was pregnant.

'Oh no, you cannot be serious?' he reacted. He was almost going to ask who the father was but decided it would have been 'slightly' tactless.

'When did you find this out?'

'Just yesterday. What am I going to do now?' she implored, as if he had the answer.

'Well you have a number of choices as you can imagine. Does your man know yet?' Murphy asked her directly.

'No he doesn't. You can't possibly be serious in suggesting the abortion option?'

'Why not? Think of your limited future with a sprog hanging off you for the next twenty years. What about your career? I mean what do you really want? Do you want to spend the rest of your days in some menial half horse town?'

'Well I suppose I'll have to get on with it and hope for the best. What a disaster. Kearney won't be pleased will he?' she added.

'Kearney!' Murphy asked. 'What about Daddy? What will he say?'

'Oh he'll be delighted,' she said plaintively.

'But answer me this one question,' he continued. 'Do you really want to marry him or not?'

'It's all arranged,' she evaded. 'Yes I'll marry him.'

So there it was. There was no point in pushing her any further when she wasn't going to answer the simplest of questions he thought. She was acting almost as if the news had not yet sunk home. Her edginess had given way to a kind of dreamy resignation. Murphy was exasperated but tried not to show it. It was the perennial struggle between a potentially brilliant career abroad (with the possibility of a later return to Ireland) and brute biology - and as usual nature was going to win. He knew so many women who had married in haste and procreated, and then spent the rest of their dreary lives regretting their rashness. They were enslaved financially, emotionally and geographically for the best years of their lives and lived in a kind of numbed discontent.

They ordered a light lunch and Grace talked about the coming Christmas activities expected of her by the family. She was like one of those passengers on the Titanic left on the doomed ship with all the life boats gone, knowing that she could have saved herself with a little foresight. She was forlorn and despairing. It was one thing to marry, but to marry a guy she really didn't want to marry was bordering on the absurd. Murphy was bewildered by her lack of coherence. Maybe a baby would make her happy. Maybe she didn't want a real career and would wallow in domesticity. However his instinct told him otherwise and he reckoned that she would be a single mother within a number of years. 'What a start to the afternoon,' he mused. 'Frosties in the corner and two forlorn women already, and it isn't even post lunch time yet.'

The omens were bad. There was not much he could do or say to Grace. She had got herself into an utter mess and there was no way out unless she had a dramatic reversal of attitude. She put on her things and left Murphy abruptly to meet her beau and tell him the wonderful tidings. Murphy felt sorry for her as she cut such a sorry figure leaving.

Time passed. He finished his dessert and saw that curvaceous music student, Kate, come in with her simian boyfriend trundling along behind. She reminded him of that drop dead gorgeous French pianist Hélène Grimaud. Whenever he saw the couple together he just winced. He would have to do some serious research on the reasons for the Second Law. And the way the ape ate with his mouth open - what did she see in him? Did she even notice these things? He looked over *The Guardian* again, gliding through the crossword, while casting occasional glances at Kate's geometry, and at the equally alluring aloof and sexy Susan (who still cast flirtatious half glances in his direction). He wondered how adventurous Susan was behind closed doors, not that he gave himself much chance of finding out. He briefly had this erotic image of her in black lace half-lying on a sofa, her nipples protruding though a see-through top, waiting to be ravished... he half-imagined that he caught her glance at that very moment and that she actually knew what he was thinking. If only.

As he was paying the bill and giving his favourite barmaid a Christmas tip (as in money) he noticed a woman called Donna Silver sitting at a table with her mother. He was really shocked to see how she had disimproved. She had been a stunner but since her marriage she had become haggard (as sometimes happened) and had really let herself go. He thought that there should be an escape clause built into the marriage contract – annulment in the event of spouses losing their looks.

He left and walked down a crowded street on his way to meet his fellow rakes. He passed a music shop but decided against going in - apart from the crowds there were a mere half shelf in the classical section, all that was on offer in the entire city. He headed towards The Wild Geese where he found Emma Larchfield sitting at the bar counter. He was glad to catch her by herself - he had a chance to give her the Ravel CD without any fuss from the others. She was another embodiment of the Second Law. She had a complete dipstick of a boyfriend, a grade one loser, an uncouth, irredeemable type who was loathed by almost everyone.

As Muphy spoke with Emma about Ravel and the composer's encounters with jazz musicians in the Cotton Club he noticed that Kate and her School of Music crew had landed in as well and were not far away from him. These were followed soon after by Jane who exchanged greetings with Emma before the latter wandered off to talk to some people further down the bar. Murphy gave Jane the Benny Goodman CD and it was received with enthusiastic gratitude. Not to be outdone, she took out a wrapped tome for Murphy - it was about the music of the spheres. Murphy was impressed. There were few who really knew what to get him, but here was one. They talked for a while about the ancient idea of the crystal spheres of the universe which made up that harmonious music, unheard by mortal ears. Jane had inscribed the book with a quote:

> *'How sweet the moonlight sleeps upon the bank!*
> *Here we will sit, and let the sounds of music*
> *Creep to our ears; soft stillness and the night*
> *Become the touches of sweet harmony.*
> *...look how the floor of heaven*
> *Is thick inlaid with patines of bright gold:*
> *There's not the smallest orb which thou beholdest*
> *But in his motion like an angel sings.*
> *Such harmony is in immortal souls,*
> *But whilst this muddy vesture of decay*
> *Doth grossly close it in, we cannot hear it.'*

'All very impressive,' thought Murphy. 'What would Kearney say now? And did she include him on her Christmas gift list?' Meanwhile the bar was following the usual ebb and flow of Christmas Eve and they sat in a comfortable silence for a while. Murphy told her about the curvy Susan but Jane didn't seem to think very much of her.

'You have too many encounters that are clinical and merely physical,' she lectured him. 'You need a real woman in your life.'

He was bemused by such advice from someone twenty years younger than himself.

'I know I have had occasional sexual encounters that were no more than physical,' she volunteered, 'but you lot really overdo it. Most women aren't into what you nefarious libertines want.'

'You mean most women in this part of the world,' Murphy

responded.

'No, most women everywhere!' she insisted. 'Women are more emotional about congress than men. And so the longer you go on having meaningless encounters the longer you will be without the woman you are looking for.'

'But it is all very entertaining,' Murphy added.

'Yes up to a point maybe,' Jane intoned.

'So what's wrong with having skirmishes until Ms Perfect comes along?' Murphy rallied.

'You become too spoilt sexually and don't give women a chance. You dismiss too many, too easily.'

'Not true. I only dismiss the ones I'm not really interested in. No point in not being the gentleman and leading them on. That would be a terrible thing to do.'

'Don't you take any women seriously?'

He was almost going to say yes about herself but veered over to Emily Cardew.

'Well you'd better treat her seriously,' she said emphatically. 'She is not to be trifled with. She is really a class act as far as I can see.'

'At the rate things are going,' Murphy replied, 'I'll never get close to her. What do you know about her Schull plans?'

'You promise that she is not on your skirmish list?'

'Claro.'

'Well I'm not sure myself but I will probably keep you informed. And may I add that I am not even sure if she suits you in the first place.'

'Give me a break! Wait and see for once.'

'Maybe you are mixing with the wrong women?' Jane said to annoy him.

'You should be in The Short Hill some nights - it's like a festival of virgins at times!'

'Come, come. You exaggerate. Really, you'll be lynched someday if you go on like that.'

'Don't care. I am right and you are wrong. Try being a single man for a while and you'll see.'

'Fine,' Jane said with an air of finality, 'I've nothing better to do these days.'

As it happened Susan and a few of her friends came in at this stage and gathered around the end of the counter. It was a bar where lots of people came traditionally on Christmas Eve so it was not really a coincidence for Murphy to see a lot of familiar faces. Emma returned and sat down beside them, agreeing with Jane about the rakes and their nefarious attitude towards the fair sex. Murphy felt an argument coming on as Emma was a bit on the serious side when it came to this topic but Jane digressed as she wasn't in the humour for a weighty colloquy. Murphy let the two women talk away for a while, being happy to sit back and watch the world go by. Jane was answering Emma's questions about her studies as Murphy was looking at the delectable Susan and her friends. He was again thinking of the pleasures of having congress with her. He was intrigued by her at times, despite Kearney repeatedly insisting that he overestimated her completely, and that the simple truth was that she was a grade one gold digger. Still, she was so physically attractive he thought that she could have been a Playboy pinup at the least. He caught her giving him the most fleeting of glances now and again. She reminded him of Pope's Belinda in *The Rape of the Lock*: they both had the same type of female glamour and charm, superficial and all though they were. Lines from the poem half-echoed in his memory:

> *'the daring spark,*
> *The glance by day, the whisper in the dark…*
> *Bright as the sun, her eyes the gazers strike,*
> *And, like the sun, they shine on all alike.'*

Of course he knew Susan was a complete flirt but that was part of the attraction. A bright and light liaison for the festive season would be just what the doctor ordered - but alas all that sex appeal and glamour would probably go to waste as she contemplated dreams of material wealth, courtesy of some moneyed zygote.

Kearney came in surprising the company with a new woman who he introduced as Lorraine. Seemingly she was recently divorced and was finding the single life more than liberating after the drudgery of marriage to a dullard teacher with a diminished sex drive. She was only staying for a while and she talked away to the other women while Murphy gave Kearney an update on the overall 'situation'. Kearney couldn't believe that his fellow rake was still even considering Susan the eternal coquette.

'But you wouldn't say no yourself, would you?' Murphy plied.

'Yes I would, Kearney asserted. 'She's not really even good looking beneath all that make-up and finery.'

'Well I don't care,' Murphy persisted, reminding Kearney that he had a date at six with his newly acquired librarian. Kearney himself had mixed feelings about this. On the one hand, he felt a bit constrained by having a definite rendezvous especially when the day was so potentially promising. On the other hand, the prospect of a night with the shapely Karen was not to be dismissed, though he had no intention of elevating her to his 'serious' list. Murphy went to the bar to order some drinks and was more than surprised to find the coquette next to him. He wasn't sure if it was a coincidence or not but she was vaguely friendly and even verged on being warm.

'So what is the plan for the day?' he asked her nonchalantly.

'Oh, no plan,' she replied wearily, 'just the usual round of places to visit and then the family stuff later.'

'Does she always look at all men with the same expression?' he asked himself. 'Maybe she doesn't even know she is doing it,' he mused. It was hardly a time to ask her about boyfriends and whatever. He could not deny the strong sexual attraction she exuded. Would he or what!

'See you later,' she suddenly said and that was that.

Murphy sat down next to Jane and waited for the inevitable.

'So how's Marlyn Monroe?' she quizzed. 'Did you get a date or what?'

'She's actually a really nice, bright and charming lady,' Murphy replied with a sardonic tone reminiscent of Kearney. 'Don't you ever just fancy someone out of sheer physical attraction?'

'Absolutely,' she replied with a wry smile 'but I don't spend years talking about it!'

'Get lost,' Murphy said while rumpling her hair a bit.

The newly divorced Lorraine enjoyed all the banter and its occasional sexual undertones. With the new found freedom of divorce she was beginning to enjoy her liberation, much to the amazement and disdain of some of her friends. She was intent on making up for lost time and was quite happy to have 'no strings attached' adventures for the time being.

'If only Molloy was here,' Murphy half-whispered to Kearney.

'He's coming soon. Lock up your daughters!' Kearney announced. 'Maybe we should plan a meeting between them for his Xmas present. I can't go off with her for logistical reasons and you're spoken for.'

'As it happens I wouldn't mind putting her on my list, but I don't think she's interested,' Murphy replied plaintively.

'How do you know? She is a bit obtuse at times. Wait and see,' Kearney advised Murphy. 'She'll be going soon but may turn up later - and with a coven from her work. The plot thickens. Meanwhile the most ideal woman you've ever come across is sitting across from you and you're doing nothing about it.'

'Give me a break!' Murphy retorted with exasperation. 'She isn't for me and that is that. I have spoken.'

'Maybe you're in denial?' Kearney persisted, much to Murphy's annoyance.

Jane seemed to know intuitively that they were talking about her and she made them change the topic very quickly. Murphy was sometimes surprised to remind himself that she was such a recent member of their set and, that despite the age difference, she seemed to be totally at ease with them all. He often mused that she was like one of those comets that traversed the night sky for a period before disappearing once more into the darkness of deep space. Intuitively he had thus resigned himself to accepting that she was a temporary member of the circle and would sooner rather than later be moving in more august circles in places like Oxford and beyond.

At the counter the gorgeous Kate was still drinking with her simian mate and other semi-arty types. Orangutan was definitely getting very drunk and was feeling her back, much to the disapproval of Murphy. A bit further down the counter was an fb well known by sight to the rakes. She was fairly glamorously done up and on the wrong side of forty five. She was formerly in the 'beautiful people/bimbo' category but now spent most of her social hours in a futile effort to capture a last minute knight before decrepitude ruined her completely. Beyond her there was a circle of drunken trogs complete with tattoos and attitude. The music being played in the background was Cole Porter, and as Ella Fitz did *Night and Day*, Murphy could see the sad expression of the fb. If she had been more amenable to a wider variety of people maybe she would have had more luck but she was a small town snob and so suffered the consequences.

The newly divorced Lorraine had heard Murphy mention the Second Law and when he told her what it meant she was keen to know all the other laws as well.

'Well, the First Law is that when A loves B, B usually loves C and so on. Then you know the Second Law - there are endless examples all around you. The Third Law is that no sooner than you find someone, you get interested in someone else as well.'

'And what about the Fourth Law?' she added, enthused by both alcohol and genuine interest.

'Women never forget,' Murphy informed her. 'As for the others - we'll tell you when we meet again.'

'That might be sooner than you think,' she replied mysteriously. 'It all depends on the plot,' and she slipped away to meet up with her work mates.

Kearney smiled a Heathcliff special as Murphy looked across the bar and caught another glance of Susan who seemed to be getting ready to leave. He felt himself mellowing in the glow of the festive atmosphere. Life was temporarily uncomplicated. The womb, the tomb and the toilet were three great places to be away from the 'cruel' zone - as was being in a cosy pub on Christmas Eve. Outside it was bitterly cold with a raw easterly wind stabbing the city, but here the Dog was at bay while Tommy Dorsey played *Opus One* - a real blast from the very distant past. There was a kind of lull while people decided where to go next. Murphy knew the music intimately - it was the Dorsey Brothers Orchestra recorded in Café Rouge in the Statler Hotel in New York in the mid-fifties. He had a nostalgic impression of that time with those gorgeous, curvy, elegant cars (and women), those great black and white movies and a certain kind of innocence long lost. 'Then again,' he mused, 'every age thinks the previous age more innocent.' *In a Little Spanish Town* was now wafting across the bar and he was probably the only one paying any attention to the music at this stage of the proceedings. The lull was becoming quite extended - everyone was intent on moving on but no one was yet moving.

As the Dorsey Brothers played *When the Saints go Marchin' in* the company finally began to stir. Jane remained with them while Emma had to go and meet her grade A 'off the wall' beau. Earl had sent a text saying he'd be in The Shack and surprise surprise, Sadie had sent Murphy a text asking him to phone her the following day. Murphy didn't delete the message - any message from the gorgeous Sadie was worth keeping, as he reminded Kearney as they moved towards The Shack.

'You'll have her yet,' Kearney predicted.

'Yeah, and you'll get the nymph,' Murphy countered.

'Let's get real. I predict that Lorraine and her posse - I said posse - will be here within the hour,' Kearney said as they walked into The Shack and found a recess that had just been abandoned by a gang of utterly ossified lawyers.

Murphy was beginning to wonder if the Dog had followed him. It was the exact same scene as last year and what had really changed since then? There was the same weekend routine - the usual encounters with boring and soulless people, the escape into revelry and drink to seek respite from the void, the meaningless banter with floozies and half-drunk fbs, the endless throng of Neolithic types who populated the city centre, the litter strewn dreary streets, the memory of a few more people who had killed themselves…

'Cheer up and pull yourself together,' Jane admonished him, 'It is Christmas you know. Is the Black Wuff Wuff biting you or what?'

'Yeah sure, just musing on the expanding universe,' he replied not very convincingly.

'So when is your date arriving?' Jane quizzed, turning to Kearney.

Kearney was annoyed at this and was about to tell her (uncharacteristically) to mind her own business when Murphy intervened.

'He has two dates at least so you'd better specify which one you mean.'

This pacified Kearney and he went back to his usual easy going, nonchalant and sardonic self again. Jane sensed that she had annoyed him and so veered the conversation to matters of more intellectual import.

'Did you see that they have discovered the most distant galaxy in the entire universe?' she asked.

'Yes. And where does that leave your God - inside or outside looking in?' Kearney quipped.

'Don't tell me ye are going to start another of those colloquies?' Murphy asked.

It was too late. They started talking about parallel universes, dark matter and the origins of the cosmos.

'The trouble with you is that you are too willfully absolute,' Jane accused Kearney in a good humoured way. 'Take the analogy of a trog trying to listen to a late Beethoven quartet - not that I'm saying you are a trog of course. For a trog the music is just a collection of incomprehensible sounds. He will never enter that musical world and see anything in the music. Likewise, you can't even begin to imagine or experience the numinous or the mystical. It is not even a possibility for you. I know it's not a perfect analogy but you get the point. Unlike the trog though you have the potential to see things differently.'

Kearney was about to respond when he saw Earl approaching from the distance. Suddenly he changed his tone of voice and whispered urgently to Jane, 'Whatever you do, don't mention anything about suicide in front of Earl. His brother killed himself on Christmas Day a few years ago. I'll tell you more another time.'

During the pause that ensued Murphy went to the bar and ordered an extra creamy pint of vitamin M for himself, a whiskey for the nymph and a bottle of American weed killer for Kearney. He sometimes thought his social life bordered on a kind of phantasmagoria with endless, meaningless encounters with people he half-knew. As he was waiting for the drinks he noticed Kate, Orangutan and the rest of her set arrive in, giving a well-timed validity to his musings. She gave him a half glance and wandered off towards the back of the bar to a nook that had a turf fire burning in it. Everyone was on the same traditional Christmas Eve pub crawl it seemed. He hoped that Orangutan would leave to eat his bananas so that he would get a chance to talk to the ethereal Kate. She probably hadn't forgiven him for the remarks he had once made about her simian companion. Still it was Christmas…

'So where is the Covent Garden set?' Kearney asked Earl as they all regrouped.

'They may be around later. Meanwhile I'm going to murder this vitamin G,' Earl enthused, sounding as if he had already been drinking for hours. 'And season's greetings to ye all.'

He was the least uncompromising of the Irish rakes. He was indeed less particular in some ways and less self-contained than the other two. His brother's suicide had made him more fragile and more dependent on other people emotionally. He was also easier to please and he often imagined getting on quite well with some uncomplicated woman who would live and let live, bake and keep house and beget an odd sprog or two.

Murphy noticed that the music was suddenly way out of sync for such a bar as The Shack. Instead of the usual rock and blues they had put on carols from King's College, Oxford, and these did indeed enhance the atmosphere, with the snow and cold outside and the scent of a turf fire inside. He noticed at the very end of the counter that Karen the librarian was talking to a barman and surprise, surprise to Kate. Murphy ambled down to see what they were up to. It seemed that Karen had just met Kate accidentally as she was asking the barman to put on the carol music. Karen, it seemed, like the traditional things of the season, and with Kate backing her up, the barman could not but acquiesce to the entreaties of the two good looking women to play the music.

'We're over there when you want to join us,' Murphy told Karen.

'I'm actually with other people down along. I'll be over presently,' she replied, leaving him alone with the stunning, willowy Kate.

'Well, I'd better be getting back to my set with these drinks. See you round,' Murphy managed.

'Sure,' she said and smiled as she walked her regal walk back to her own group.

'By the way, there's a concert coming up soon in the City Hall,' she turned and added. 'I'm playing the Mozart *Clarinet Concerto*, just in case you don't know.'

'Fine,' he answered. 'What a surprising thing for her to say. She's hardly about to dump Orang,' he mused. As he was walking back through the crowd he thought of all the new people he was recently meeting. They were all still strangers more or less but at least they were a better bet than having to put up with the Frumpy/Frosty/Motley brigades.

As he sat down Kearney and Jane were talking about the next trip to West Cork. Murphy hadn't yet got round to asking her about Emily Cardew but there was plenty of time. Jane mentioned some New Year's Eve party that was planned in Schull and the rakes were of course immediately interested. As they were talking a small bearded guy stopped at their table and said sarcastically to the two rakes, 'My friends from The High C!'

The two rakes were a bit taken aback and thought he was drunk. Murphy didn't recognize him at all but Kearney remembered him as someone who appeared now and again in their haunts.

'So ye don't remember last Saturday night in The High C?' he ranted. 'The two girls I was with had to leave because you two kept on staring at them. Ye obviously don't have any manners. We were sitting down near the window and ye made them so uncomfortable.'

The rakes knew that there was such a big crowd there the night in question it would have been impossible to notice anyone for more than a few seconds.

'Well they were lucky women to get my attention anyway,' Murphy declared with false gravity. 'What about you Kearney?'

'Can't say I recall what you are talking about,' Kearney drawled in his best Clint Eastwood accent.

All this maddened the interloper. He stood up to his full height and for a second they thought he was actually going to get violent. He was almost frothing at the mouth with indignation.

'Give the girls my regards,' Murphy taunted.

Fred Astaire, for that was the name the rakes gave him after this, stormed off and left them amused and slightly perplexed.

'What the hell was all that about?' Murphy asked as a bemused Jane looked on.

'Forget about it,' Kearney said. 'He's one of those people with a large sense of self-importance who's always looking for attention. Some of the women he hangs round with are dishy, though the cows who complained about us must be real tulips if you know what I mean.'

There was indeed a sub-set of people like Fred Astaire who thought they were 'intellectuals', who hung round the 'right people' at events like the film festival and who tried to look 'arty'. There were women all over the place taken in by such pseudos. Meanwhile Karen had joined the company. Murphy didn't have much of an impression of her as he had only spoken to her sporadically during the Schull visit. She looked dishy enough and there she was, finally seated at their table next to Jane, much to his amusement. Earl started talking to Karen about Schull and told her that they were all due to go down there shortly (much to the annoyance of Kearney).

'Seems to be a great place with lots of wild women and dangerous men,' Earl went on guilelessly.

The music being played was back to the more normal sort with John Lee Hooker blasting out a few numbers. As they were beginning to settle again Murphy looked towards the door and gasped, 'Oh no, not Satan, not now, not tonight!'

It was indeed the Evil One who had come in and was wandering round looking for people to talk to. Fatima was obviously elsewhere.

'So who's Satan?' Karen asked innocently.

'You don't want to know. Just don't call him by that name if he joins us,' Kearney told her.

Satan did as he always did and brazenly joined the company, not even considering for a moment whether or not he was welcome. He showed an immediate interest in Karen. Some chance he had. Still, he had a brass neck, and would even proposition a woman on her way to her wedding ceremony. He didn't even notice that the others were beginning to drift away to different parts of the bar - they knew Karen could take care of herself, even if it was the Evil One she was communing with. It wasn't long before he was showing her his vulgar and brazen self as he went on and on with lewd descriptions of the female anatomy and other such niceties. This technique of trying to shock or discomfit some women sometimes worked. However it didn't take the librarian long to see what kind of a pitiful and hollow creature he really was, not to mind so boring and without a glimmer of intellect.

As Karen endured the company of Satan, Murphy bumped into Louise Daunton, a woman he vaguely knew from his university days, and who was once in the same swimming club as himself. She was a type that seemed to him more fictional than real. She was the ultimate rich girl with a life seemingly unruffled by any great problems. Her family lived in a large, beautiful house on the Blackrock Road, with a sweeping view of the river estuary. Her papa was one of the city's merchant princes and one of the old school rugby types. She herself had sailed through college and became an established solicitor within a few years. There seemed to be no obstacles to her career or life in general. She had married a guy who could not be faulted - like herself he was bright, amenable, good at sport, handsome and financially well off. No family tragedies, no financial problems, a perfect family life, marital calm. Murphy mused that it had to happen sometime. She would have a huge Christmas tree in their house and do all the right Christmassy things. She was universally liked, though she did have an aloof quality which inhibited people from becoming overfriendly with her. Yet she always seemed to have a smile for others, and gave the impression that she had never suffered, though this was not really the case.

A few years earlier, near Christmas as it happened, she had been walking alone along the Marina by the side of the river not far from her family home. She was at a place where the river was wide with large ships passing by at regular intervals. It was almost twilight, when without warning, she saw a car career out of control and plunge into the cold, dark waters. Without hesitation she dived into the choppy river and swam to the car which was about to go under. The driver's window was open and there was a young woman inside. Louise managed to get to the window and gripped the woman's outstretched hand. She was just about to pull her through the window of the fast sinking car when a ship passed by, and its wake surged over them both, making the car plunge down into the icy darkness without a trace. Louise frantically did all she could but it was all in vain. An hour later she was brought home by the police, traumatised and haunted by the woman's expression just before she disappeared. As if this was not bad enough, when she was five she had nearly drowned in a lake while on summer holidays only to be rescued by an older brother. These incidents seemed to trigger off a mindset which would not allow her to sleep peacefully, leaving her with an ongoing series of recurrent nightmares. The two experiences seemed to merge and caused her no end of mental torture despite the best help available from medical experts. To the world at large she was a carefree and privileged woman with a charmed life, but to the few who really knew her she was a resilient woman who battled daily against her own terrible demons.

Murphy had a few words with her - he really only saw her every few years and there was no possibility of their becoming friendly alas, given that she was happily married. She was one of the pageant that passed before him at this time of year. 'It's all a bit ghostly,' he thought. They were forever to move in different circles like so many other attractive people he vaguely knew in the city. He regretted not knowing her better as he could sense instinctively that she was a cut above most people he knew. She moved off with a smile and that was probably that for another Christmas at least.

He wandered back to the table where Karen was still enduring the inanities of Satan's conversation. He gave a sigh of relief as Fatima came in the far door, making for her demonic beloved who could do no wrong. Jane and Kearney were heading back to the table as well and they were all relieved to see the happy couple move on to another set of people further off.

'Where the hell did ye dig him up? What an absolute jackal!' Karen exclaimed as soon as Satan was out of hearing.

'Well you passed the test,' Kearney told her glibly. 'Some women find him enchanting,'

'He's sinister beyond measure. He gives me the creeps not to mind the heebie-jeebies!' she responded with a shiver.

The bar was quite full at this stage and there was a higher than usual number of women coming in, with bags of last minute shopping, to have a drink before heading for home or suburban pubs. An attractive, blonde woman in her mid-forties came in, laden down with shopping bags from the most exclusive botiques. She was separated from the

Makeham brute who frequented the High C. The previous Christmas Eve she had involved Kearney in an untidy scene in that very bar. He had been sitting at the counter in the early afternoon, reading a book while waiting for some of his set to turn up. She was with her then husband and while she was getting a drink at the counter she became intrigued by Kearney, sitting there in splendid isolation and oblivious to the world at large. They struck up a conversation and it developed so naturally that she sat on an adjoining stool and stayed talking to the rake for quite a while. At first her overweight, brutish, dim husband didn't seem to take any notice as he was talking to some equally undesirable friends. She meanwhile was becoming increasingly more impressed by Kearney and was quizzing him in a charming and flirtatious kind of way.

'What are you reading? Why are you reading a book here on Christmas Eve? Where are your friends? Do you have a girlfriend? Are you married?' she demanded in rapid succession.

They began a diverting repartee, Kearney having no idea that her trog spouse was in the background. Sometime later he certainly found out as the uncouth lowlife charged over and ranted at the rake in a drunken voice, 'What the hell are you trying to do with my wife?'

Kearney remained cool and this drove the irate hubbie into a greater temper. He was pathologically possessive of his wife and couldn't bear to see her getting on so well with another male.

'Why don't you just get out of here now before something nasty happens to you?' the trog continued his diatribe. Kearney merely glared at him.

'Let's go,' Makeham then grunted, catching his long suffering wife by the wrist and dragging her away with brutish force. Kearney didn't like this at all and was about to stand up and send the oaf into the middle of the following week when some of the brute's group came over and pulled Makeham away. The unfortunate woman gathered up her shopping and left close to tears, half-whispering to Kearney on the way out that she was sorry. 'The number of apes with such wives is a depressing fact of life,' Kearney mused. He was later glad to find out that she had the good sense to leave her sottish partner and start a life of her own.

A year later there she was again but now she seemed far better looking and gave Kearney a half smile as she moved down the bar in search of friends. Kearney often thought that if her trog husband and his crew had been transported back to the Middle Ages they would have found themselves quite at home. What essential difference was there anyway between them and lowly brutal villeins from some twelfth century medieval manor? The medieval quality of Irish life was indeed a recurring theme of the rakes' conversations. For the brutes would always remain so and the civilizing effects of a thousand years of culture would never affect their basic lives. No wonder Kearney had a low opinion of the human race.

After all the milling about, the quartet of the two rakes, the student and the librarian, was again joined by Earl and once again they all sat down around a table. Murphy was taking time out and was just observing the comings and goings while the others deliberated on Satan and his popularity with so many women. As Murphy looked about he saw one of his exs come in and, as she passed, she half-glared at him. She was very attractive but he had ditched her because she was mean, moody and not very bright. She had not forgiven him, not that he gave a damn. He did occasionally miss her between midnight and morning but overall he was not unhappy that she was gone. Despite her curves and sumptuous orbs she was a hindrance socially and a no-no long term.

There was now an increasing amount of empty and dirty glasses all over the place and the floor was strewn with litter, giving an increasingly squalid feel to the atmosphere though most of the regulars remained oblivious to such details. The toilets stank at the best of times but no one ever seemed to notice or complain. It was passed off as part of the charm and atmosphere of the 'Irish pub'.

***

While the rakes and company were on their way to The High C, Molloy was having his usual busy pre-Christmas round on the sexual conveyor belt which was his life. It was actually getting a bit iffy for him as there was the ever increasing chance of two of his women meeting. He had already had a steamy romp with the bank manager's wife that morning. In the late afternoon he was expecting a twenty-six-year-old who was married to a complete bore and had two children. She was completely smitten by Molloy and he would probably have taken her more seriously if it hadn't been for the offspring complication. She visited him about four times a week and, as her visiting time was limited, there was little small talk and lots of advanced sexual congress. Her name was Annabelle and she was tall and attractive in a demure kind of way. Molloy was due to meet his own grown up children later that evening but this did not deter him from having a romp with a girl who was even younger. Annabelle arrived exactly on time, bringing the rake of rakes a case of expensive wine, which the two of them would indulge in over the following few months. On this occasion she was wearing a long overcoat and a simple loose full length red dress. Underneath she revealed the usual slinky lingerie of red and black complete with suspenders. Within a minute of her arrival Molloy had entered her, fogging up the windows in the bedroom in no time. She was very natural and good at congress and effortlessly glided from one position to another. As Molloy was about to ravish her once more his phone registered a text and he leaned over and read it. It was from the Cork rakes wishing him happy hunting over the festive season. He was amused and half-shouted to the moaning Annabelle, 'This one's for the Irish rakes,' and plunged deep inside her.

***

Back across the Irish Sea the rakes and company arrived at The High C as it was a tradition to have at least one round of drinks there on Christmas Eve. The streets they had passed through were littered with the usual rubbish and there was the standard amount of trogs lurching about from pub to pub. The women, who would normally have felt unnerved walking around the city centre by themselves, felt safe in the company of the rakes. It seemed so ridiculous that the city earned the title of European Capital of Culture when it wasn't even safe to walk the streets at night Kearney complained. They were lucky to arrive at The High C at a time when there was one of those intermittent lulls. They got a few seats in the best corner of the bar, near the fire with a view of the outside street. Kearney went off to buy a round, bemoaning the days long gone by when regular customers were treated to free Christmas drinks. Jane started talking to Karen about Schull and about Sadie and William. Karen, it seemed, did not know them that well but she was going to be about over the Christmas period.

'So how long have you known Kearney?' the librarian asked Jane innocently.

'Oh, we go back a long way,' the nymph lied with equal innocence.

As the conversation went on Jane realised that the older woman had had a rough enough past. Her husband had died in London - he was unlucky enough to have been in the wrong place at the wrong time when a no warning bomb planted by some IRA scumbags blew him and a six year girl to pieces. It had been a nightmarish experience but she had shown a lot of resilience in putting her life back on track again. Jane couldn't really find out what kind of relationship she was having, or hoping to have, with Kearney and she only prayed that she could cope with casual liaisons.

In former times this night would have been a fairly riotous affair until closing time and beyond. More recently though, the city taverns started to empty out about nine, leaving the rakes and company to carry on in a kind of eerie calm. As Jane continued her talk with Karen it emerged that the librarian was a Catholic. On overhearing this, Murphy was beginning to wonder if there was some kind of underground resistance movement which kept Mother Church going, in spite of the mounting forces pitted against her. Jane herself had little time for the institutional church. She deplored the moral cowardice of its clergy, despised craven 'political' bishops and despaired of the chasm between the spirit of the New Testament and the tawdry hypocrisy of the institution. In contrast Karen liked and needed the ritual and the rhythm of the church year calendar. Catholicism also helped her to recover from the death of her husband and find some kind of meaning in arbitrary events. Kearney listened to the two for a while, but when they both started on enthusiastically about epiphanies and numinous experiences his patience waned and he declared, 'You're sadly mistaken. It's a matter of psychology. Okay you walk in a forest on a windy day and hear the leaves rustling in the trees. You get carried away and the next thing you know you are having an epiphany. Give me a break.'

Jane explained to the bewildered Karen that this outburst was part of an ongoing dispute between herself and the nihilistic Kearney.

'Did you have an unhappy childhood?' Karen asked Kearney.

'Give me another break! This is real *Reader's Digest* stuff. Really!'

Kearney retorted with sarcastic vehemence.

'Why don't you even allow for the possibility of experiences beyond your own?' Karen replied with a sincerity that even impressed Kearney. 'Don't you remember Cromwell's words - *I beseech you think that even in the bowels of Christ you may be wrong.*'

'It's not a matter of allowing for experiences beyond my own,' Kearney countered. 'That is a red herring. The whole idea of God is illogical to begin with. And as for your God - there is no way you can seriously tell me that you believe in a story that was written down as hearsay so long after the main events!'

'You'll never win him over. He's too far gone,' Jane cautioned Karen, and then joked playfully to Kearney, 'What are you going to say when we meet in the afterlife? You'll be so embarrassed. Maybe we should have a bet.'

At this point Murphy intervened, saying, 'According to Kearney we're already in the afterlife! Look around you - we're in Purgatory at the very least.'

'Well we won't be continuing this colloquy for long more,' Kearney declared as he noticed the newly divorced Lorraine and two of her friends walk in. Her friends were not particularly alluring but they were good sports and there was worse company to be had at this hour of the evening. As there weren't enough seats for all, they took turns standing or just milling about.

One thing became quickly clear to the rakes - Lorraine was up for sexual congress and she didn't seem to mind which of them was going to be the lucky man. She was quite 'dishy' in Murphy's words and was wearing a slightly suggestive top with just a hint of impressive orbage. Murphy noticed that she was quite leggy - one of his favourite features in a woman. Much to Kearney's delight she was wearing fishnet stockings but he knew that he was out of the equation, as Karen was not going to allow him to disappear at this stage, and, in any case, she had decided against going back to Schull in the snow. Murphy was available but then he pondered what Jane might say to Emily Cardew. And of course there was the possibility of Earl, who was always available for a skirmish when it came to the fair sex. Indeed one of his more recent conquests told him that he needed a prescription of anti-Viagra tablets.

As it happened one of Earl's exs had come in and so he went to the counter to talk to her and give her the season's compliments. Kearney gave Murphy a knowing glance as if to say 'The field is clear - go get her boy.' Murphy smiled and looked out the window, trying to control his amusement. He liked these scenes. They raised the tempo. He loved being reckless and here was a perfect opportunity. He knew too there was the necessity of being occasionally tactical - some women were to be avoided as they were too local and there was the danger of too much fall out. However sometimes he just didn't care and once he set his mind on having a steamy romp he tried his best to succeed.

Earl as it turned out was not having a good time. His ex looped the loop now and again and was occasionally shipped off to some funny farm. She seemed to be on the verge of another round of instability. She was bordering on the incoherent and Earl knew her well enough to realise it was not just alcohol. Every time he tried to say anything she just kept saying 'fizzy, fizzy, fizzy!' She glanced over at the company in the corner and said, 'Aren't you going to introduce me to your fizzy, fizzy friends?'

Before he could answer the half crazed dweeb had gone over and introduced herself to the whole group.

'All we need,' Earl complained. 'A loopy dame to round off the festivities. It'll be Satan next.'

'Well look out the window Earl ol' chap because it seems your wish may be granted,' Kearney observed sardonically.

Satan was indeed approaching with Fatima in tow. Murphy decided to take emergency action and moved next to Lorraine while the others stood around. Lorraine's friend had the other chairs so he was safe from Satan for the moment. As the cloven footed one approached he eyed up the company in the corner with jealousy. Lorraine, not aware of what was going on, began to engage Murphy in conversation about Schull, giving the impression that she wanted an invite. All he needed when chasing the gorgeous Emily! He caught Jane's amused expression and reciprocated. Lorraine meanwhile seemed to be moving closer and closer to him until her knees were touching his.

Despite Fatima's presence Satan managed to get talking to the women who were with Lorraine and he was obviously intent on getting as much info as possible about her. Meantime, at the counter Doyle the wife beater was getting increasingly aggressive towards the girl behind the bar. At first no one paid much attention but as his ranting grew louder people began to take note. It seemed that the unfortunate barmaid had told him that he was not being served any more drink. This caused the brute to rear up. He started by fisting the counter with his paws and then swept a pile of glasses onto the floor. This was a step too far and a few other customers took hold of him, trying to restrain him. Murphy phoned the police and told them that there was a riot in The High C. The drunken wife beater was still out of control when two policemen finally arrived in as he was about to break a bottle against the counter and use it as a weapon. Murphy could only imagine what his wife would have to endure when he staggered in home later.

This interlude cast a shadow over the rest of the evening. The crowd thinned out even more as soon as the police had left. Satan and Fatima were also leaving for some party. Jane told the rakes that she would probably see them all down west while Karen was keen on exiting quickly with Kearney. After a few minutes Murphy was left alone with Lorraine while Earl was in the background talking to her two friends who were by now completely blotto. He was good at taking advantage of drunk women - for a lot of them it was their only way of facing congress. His problem was how to offload one of them so that he could have his way with the other. Lorraine told Murphy that one of her friends could take a taxi with them and they could drop her off *en route* to his place. This was all music to Murphy's ears - a liaison on Christmas Eve was always a special treat. So Lorraine helped her friend, a civil service secretarial type, out of the bar while Murphy went in search of a taxi. Earl stayed behind with the other woman who was slightly more coherent then her friend.

Lorraine and Murphy sat in the back of the taxi while her wasted friend was consigned to the front seat. Lorraine was certainly in a very sexual mood. She took Murphy's hand and placed it under her skirt and moved it slowly in an upward direction while Murphy tried to keep it stationary. He wasn't very comfortable with this as the taxi driver was talking to him about soccer. The drunken woman in the front seat kept interrupting, talking incoherently about Manchester United while the taxi driver tried to ignore her slurred comments.

As they approached Murphy's place, having dropped off Lorraine's friend, the snow began to fall once more. Murphy was looking forward to a brandy and cigar before ravishing the hot Lorraine. Overall it had not been the worst of Christmas Eves and the Dog was still out of sight. They went in and before Murphy had time to turn on the kitchen light Lorraine was kissing him hungrily. She wrapped her legs around his and had him against the wall for a long time before he managed to restore a temporary order. She calmed down a bit. Murphy didn't like rushing things.

He liked the full menu to be savoured. He took her onto the sofa and poured her a small cognac. She put a finger into her drink and wet her nipples with the cognac enticing the rake to try a different way of savouring his five star night cap. There was a kind of abandon in her, as if she hadn't had sex for ages and ages. The rake had to slow her down and so he steered her to the master bedroom while he had a quick shower after a day in the trog filled taverns. When he came back he found her calmer but looking a bit depressed. 'Oh hell, don't tell me she's going to start crying and tell me about her divorce,' he mused. He took her in his arms and gave her a deep kiss that made her fairly breathless. She was off again... she wanted to be on top so he obliged. There was plenty of time for all the other positions. She had very firm breasts and erect, pointed nipples.

Then it happened. She kind of froze and turned on her side and started to cry. And after such a promising start! All he needed. That was obviously going to be that. He knew from experience that he was not going to have a night of steamy congress and after a few minutes waiting, this view became a certainty. The chances of a taxi at that time of night were not great - and would she go in any case? She started whimpering about her ex-husband and murmured something about his violence. Charming. All Murphy needed on Christmas Eve night. She then rather pathetically put her arms round him like some kind of lost child. He resigned himself to a night of 'nursing' and after what seemed like an eternity he fell asleep. When he woke up about nine in the morning she had gone. She didn't, he supposed, what to face the embarrassment of an encounter in the clear light of day.

***

Christmas Day was the least favourite day of the year for all the rakes but especially for Murphy. The morning was okay - he got up late and tried to put the Lorraine visit down to experience. The weather was still very cold and the snow was due to stay for a few more days.

Christmas in the snow was such a rarity that he took a few black and white shots of his garden with the city backdrop below in the distance. Through the bare trees at the front of his large garden he could see the outline of St Fin Barre's cathedral in the far distance. The snow glistened off the roofs of numberless houses and was an invigorating sight. He fell into the usual Christmas Day routine almost fatalistically. Like the previous day the morning was his favourite time, the time when the Dog never seemed to be on the prowl. He went into the music room with its panoramic view of the city and the harbour beyond. The scent of strong coffee he was preparing wafted about the house as he went through his music collection, musing on what to play. He wanted something energetic and uplifting, something with intellectual rigour and emotional panache. He finally picked out a vinyl version of the Brahms *Double Concerto for Violin and Cello*. It was such a riot, a real fusion of the classical and the romantic, pure reason allied to passion. A bit like Jane's personality in a way - he wondered what she'd say if he told her she was like this concerto? He certainly knew how most women would react.

Later in the afternoon he lit a fire and indulged in a big fat Cuban cigar while going through his wine collection. He settled for a ten-year-old Rioja reserve and then, trying his best to keep the Dog at bay, he put on a Louis Armstrong *Hot Fives* recording from the late twenties. He read a history of the Victorians for an hour before flicking through the TV channels only to find the usual reruns and predictable Christmas fare that seemed to be churned out each year. Time passed. At about nine the Dog arrived with a vengeance. He was overcome by a black sense of desolation, a kind of dark night of the soul without the Christian comfort of a dawn. This desolate feeling extended to a kind of physical pain and a bleak sensation of futility, an apprehension of death which overwhelmed and stifled him.

Part Five

HUNTERS IN THE SNOW

Now in Vienna there are ten pretty women.
There's a shoulder where death comes to cry.
There's a lobby with nine hundred windows.
There's a tree where the doves go to die.
There's a piece that is torn from the morning,
And it hangs in the gallery of Frost...

Take this Waltz (Leonard Cohen)

Murphy, Jane and Kearney headed for Schull on St Stephen's Day - Boxing Day according to the sardonic Kearney - and were there before noon. Molloy was to arrive later while Earl half-threatened to turn up at some stage. The accommodation arrangements amused Kearney no end. He was to stay with Molloy until he met Karen on the following day. Murphy had decided to stay with Sadie rather than with his fellow rakes. The Renaissance nymph was also a guest of Sadie's, a fact which gave Kearney plenty of ammunition with which to assail Murphy. They were not expecting a repeat of their last visit, that being like a sexual conjunction of the planets, a rare event not likely to be repeated for a long time.

They had a light lunch in one of the Schull pubs, and as Sadie was busy for the afternoon, they decided to go on a mini tour while the going was good. William was nowhere to be seen but that didn't surprise anyone. Murphy's old Saab purred along with Jane seated beside him while Kearney sat in the back offering occasional wry comments, but generally just as happy to take in the wild, rugged scenery.

'Sadie is very alluring Murphy don't you think?' Kearney asked rather abruptly of his fellow rake after some time.

'Indeed,' Murphy agreed with a hint of sarcasm.

'Don't tell me you have her on your list as well?' Jane gasped, looking at the driver with bewilderment.

'Me and Sadie? Course not. She's a married woman,' Murphy joked.

'But if you had a chance you'd take it wouldn't you?' Jane half-sighed. 'What a philanderer. I give up!'

'I wonder if Bibi will be around this time,' Kearney then asked, with just a hint of amusement on his face.

'Yes, she will be as a matter of fact,' Jane retorted with a straight face. 'I'll introduce the two of ye to her. She is really not as bad as ye make out. I told her she has been renamed Queen of the Frosties.'

'You what?' Kearney complained. 'We'll never get anywhere with her now.'

'Bloody hell. You always said that you wouldn't go near her with a forty foot pole,' Murphy reminded him.

They both liked Jane too much to make life uneasy for her so they left the Bibi topic and moved on to discuss other matters: the quality of the pint in The Short Hill, Susan the coquette's sex life, the Good Fairy in Myles na gCopaleen's *At Swim Two Birds*, stone circles of West Cork, Mozart's 1788 summer in Vienna... The journey through Bantry and beyond Glengarriff was over in no time and they stopped now and again to dwell on the stunning views over Bantry Bay. In Murphy's mind no part of Ireland had scenery to surpass this region. The Beara Peninsula indeed was as near as one could get to the soul of Ireland he had often declared.

They then made towards Castletownbeare at a leisurely speed and, on arrival, went for a walkabout before heading to McCarthy's bar, which was a haunt of theirs well before it had acquired its more recent literary fame. This was one of the last of the old style bars, functioning as a shop as well as a drinking haunt. Murphy liked visiting it as there always seemed to be at least one diverting customer to be entertained by. As it was St Stephen's Day there was a fairly serious drinking session going on. There was a very mixed crowd of locals and foreigners. The latter were mainly Dutch and Germans with the odd Spaniard to be seen. Jane of course was rattling away in German to some semi-Crusty after a few minutes while Kearney started a colloquy with some musicians in the corner. Murphy nursed his pint of vitamin M at the counter and had a talk with one of the girls who was serving. He was more than content to just lose himself for a while in the general atmosphere of merriment and conviviality. Next to him there was a battered looking sailor who turned out to be a Basque fisherman. Murphy talked to him in Spanish, extolling the green, mountainous scenery of the Basque Country and the distinctive character of the Basque nation. The fisherman was from a village called Bermeo which Murphy knew well from his travels. The mariner had rugged looks and his sea battered face gave him a kind of ageless aura. They went on about the delights of San Sebastian and its restaurants, the beauty of Basque women, the excellence of Basque food, the coast road from Bilbao west towards Galicia, the Roman village of Santillana del Mar, the August fiestas, and the new cleaned up Bilbao with its upcoming Guggenheim museum.

Before the trio knew it daylight was fading and they had to get back to base. Murphy had only had one drink because he was the driver but the others had a good three or four. He was always impressed at the nymph's ability to take her liquor. They didn't stop on the way back and so on reaching Schull Murphy dropped Kearney off at Molloy's house - the Welsh rake had arrived early after all it seemed as there was a light on inside.

'Hope he's not in the middle of something,' Kearney muttered as he rang the bell, just in case, before entering. Murphy and Jane then went off to Sadie's where there was the usual hospitality and feeling of being at home.

As night fell an image of the ancient Anglo-Saxon hall came to Murphy's mind once more as he looked out into the cold darkness from the light and warmth of the big timbery house. There was even a Grendel out there somewhere, a monster who would (and did) smash a woman's head to pieces without compunction. There was something almost too perfect about being inside this house for Murphy. His comfort and feeling of being at home was counterpointed by a sense that it was all very temporary, that some dark force would not let it go on for long. There was also something in the Sadie-William relationship that he felt wasn't quite right.

After dinner Jane and Sadie sat down near the fire while Murphy looked through some of the latter's vast library of books and music. Jane quizzed Sadie about the murderer of the German woman and the ongoing rumour that the perpetrator was supposedly still in the locality. Sadie didn't like talking about this at all but did reveal that there had been one or two incidents of late which resulted in the police issuing a new warning to local women about walking about by themselves at night. All three then moved on to discuss other topics and Jane gave an account of the progress of her thesis and of the old Oxford scholar who was sharing such academic treasure with her. By all accounts, he was one of the last of the old school, a professorial type whose wife was dead and who seemed to find satisfaction in helping along an Irish student of prodigious ability. Murphy guessed (rightly) that the old boy was probably most impressed by her naturalness and unassuming personality.

Meanwhile back in Molloy's house there was actually a fire going as well, though not as big as Sadie's log fire blaze. A local woman who did the cleaning and kept an eye on the place for Molloy had come in earlier and made the place cosy for the Welsh rake. His affair with Rose was over it seemed as he didn't appreciate the idea of being hunted down and shot at close quarters by a pathologically possessive McMicheal. Much and all as he liked her she wasn't worth becoming extinct for. And anyway, from what he could see the place seemed to be a veritable gold mine of women of all kinds. If his fellow rakes could succeed here then he would surely have a ball. He was after all their mentor.

'So who have ye lined up for me?' he asked of Kearney.

'You can forget about Sadie and Karen. The rest are all yours,' Kearney advised, giving him a list of possibilities and non-starters.

'Who are the rest? I didn't have much time to notice the last time with that sub-normal psycho McMicheal out gunning for me,' the tomcat pressed.

'Well there's Jane who is certainly not your type,' Kearney advised. 'Murphy would go ape if you were to try anything.'

'Since when is he interested in her?' Molloy asked.

'He swears that he has no interest though of course he may be in denial,' Kearney explained patiently. 'He's a bit taken up with this Cardew woman who frankly seems to be more of a ghost than anything else.'

'And who else is there for me?' Molloy persevered.

'There's the gorgeous, sexy but cold Bibi, who may or may not be in the sisterhood.'

'Keep going. I want a good choice,' the incorrigible Welsh rake demanded.

'Talk about a ravenous wolf, Kearney retorted. 'We'll see who Karen brings along. And speaking of Karen - don't you even think about it!'

'Never! And what about, what's her name, the potter?'

'How could you have forgotten her name after your antics on the last visit? Haven't heard much about her of late. She may turn up - she does live round here so it seems likely. Is that enough to keep your one tracked mind sated for a while?'

'Hmm. What time are we due at The Bull?'

'About nine. Now what about you getting victuals ready while I phone the librarian.'

Molloy was not exactly an *haute cuisine* chef but he did manage to rustle up some kind of half presentable pasta dish based on cold turkey brought by his adoring cleaning lady. His house was simply furnished and spacious, having a great view of the harbour. By night he was always delighted to watch the glimmering lights of an occasional boat coming or going. He was gradually filling up his library with a collection of books - whatever about being a complete tomcat, he did have an interesting mind and was very well versed in history and literature. Sometimes he went on a roll and would recite poems by Dylan Thomas or tell stories about The Valleys. His own poems revealed quite a refined sensibility but his obsession with sexual matters was so great that it put the rest of his persona in the shade.

While they were eating the pasta he told Kearney about the background to one of his own more recent poems, a work called *The Private and the General*. This was based on a true story from the trenches of World War I. A Welsh eighteen-year-old soldier, Owen Thomas, was shot at dawn for cowardice one raw winter's morning in 1916 near Arras. However Molloy's extensive research had revealed a darker tale. It seemed that Thomas' commanding officer had received the wrong orders but was intent on forcing his group of men over the top in any case, to impress a visiting general. Thomas and others knew the lie of the land much better than any superior officer, having been there for a much longer period of time. The Welsh youngster confronted the pompous English general, informing him of the true state of the nearby German trenches, telling him in no uncertain terms that they would all be mown down in about a minute if the orders were to be obeyed. This resulted in him being arrested for insubordination and subsequently shot after a brief, summary trial. All Thomas' comrades did indeed die very quickly as he had predicted. To make matters even more depressing, Molloy discovered that the commanding officer in question had an ongoing reputation for being a totally craven louse and had enthusiastically sent a number of other young soldiers to a dawn firing squad over the course of a few months.

'This will really impress some women,' Kearney suggested.

'Yes,' Molloy replied with a lupine look on his face. 'I can see the nymph swooning over me as I translate my latest masterpiece for her.'

'Not a chance. She is not your average, impressionable, vulnerable, under-educated woman who falls for your inane charms,' Kearney said.

'Ah ha. Do I detect some kind of undercurrent of repressed passion?' Molloy challenged.

'Beam me up! How do you do it? Maybe it's your aftershave?' Kearney said with evasive bewilderment.

'Dream on my boy. Jealousy is an ignoble emotion,' Molloy said smugly. 'It's my astral body! But don't forget you have the librarian and I have no one so far.'

***

By nine the entire company had arrived in The Black Bull for a night of carousing. Sadie as usual had managed to get a table with a view of the harbour, and the night started with her proposing a toast to the Renaissance nymph for the amazing way her thesis was progressing. This was enthusiastically seconded by Molloy, much to the annoyance of the other rakes. They were soon joined by the English woman George who they had met on their previous visit, and this time her husband was with her as well. He was a brusque but diverting character straight out of a Victorian colonial world. He read the right wing Telegraph, followed cricket, was a high Anglican, hated the Labour Party and unions and was the quintessential Tory of the old school. Despite all this he was not at all offensive and was generally liked.

After a while the company broke up into different groups as they discussed the state of the cosmos and the meaning of life. Sadie began talking to Murphy about Beethoven's *Diabelli Variations* and became flushed with animation when discussing the last piano sonatas, impressing Murphy with her insights and almost reverential attitude.

'The amazing thing about *Opus. 111* is the serenity of the last pages,' she pronounced. 'If you look at the actual score it is black with notes and yet there is this amazing sense of stillness and transcendence.'

However she asserted that it was in the *Hammerklavier* sonata where Beethoven had ventured furthest into the world of the spirit. Murphy disagreed, saying for him it was in the *Arietta* of the last sonata, *Opus. 111.*

'So where does this leave Benny Goodman?' the nymph inquired.

She told Sadie about Murphy's present and true to form Sadie was well up on the big band era, loving the music of the forties and fifties especially. Molloy was being low key - the relief of not being hunted by McMicheal was comfort enough for the moment. He eventually got into a colloquy with Henry, George's sidekick from the days of the Raj, and they soon became engrossed in talking about rugby, one of Molloy's interests outside womanising. They debated the effects of professionalism on the modern game, and the other rakes were surprised to see Molloy spend more than half an hour without scanning for women. It must have been a near record.

Kearney was half-listening to the two sets of conversation but George eventually got talking to him once more about the afterlife and its connection to the material world. Kearney tried to be patient. He treated her views as being on a par with someone who was trying to make him believe in astrology.

'There's only one thing for it - I'll go to one of your séances and then we'll see about all these spirits of yours,' he said to her half flippantly. She agreed and suggested making a date right there and then. He looked on her as if she was demented, someone who needed a room with a good strong straight jacket. Her husband, in contrast, was full of bluff common sense and stiff upper lip. How they got on he could only imagine.

The bar was now quite full and there was a convivial atmosphere. Murphy always liked this night after the tedium and darkness of Christmas Day. He was taking one of his time outs surveying the clientele when all of a sudden he noticed the door opening and a woman in a long black overcoat came in with two men. There she was. Emily Cardew. Back in the homeland. He looked at Jane while Kearney gave him a wry smile.

'The penny drops. The cookie crumbles,' Kearney intoned. 'Wheels have been set in motion. The die is cast. Time for action ol' chap. What's the plan?'

'There's no plan sleazebag. Don't get on my gimp,' Murphy responded with a slight degree of irritation.

Jane sat next to Murphy and told him that she would go talk to the trio and he could come over when she gave the signal. She then went off to talk with Emily and her companions.

'What a nymph to know,' Kearney said without any sarcasm (for once). 'She should become your personal trainer. Murphy, it is becoming quite ironic that the woman who suits you most is trying to fix you up with a friend of hers. When are you going to see the light? I do not jest.'

'Get lost,' Murphy countered. 'As you well know there is a slight disparity between how a woman suits someone on paper and what happens in the real world.'

'I think we'll put a bet on the whole thing.' Kearney said smoothly. 'I'll give you four to one that you will be involved with the nymph before next Christmas! Come on, there are odds you can't refuse! If you're not going with her by this time next year I'll give you four hundred and if you are, you'll give me a hundred!'

'You're on,' Murphy said as he got up and walked in the direction of Jane and Emily. 'Now go away and die. I'm a man on a mission.'

The rest of the company pretended to ignore what was happening, but at the same time there was a general interest and excitement in what might ensue.

'Can't you look into your crystal ball and save us all the suspense?' Kearney jested with George.

'It's more exciting this way,' the medium explained unconvincingly. 'I hope your friend is successful. He looks like a man who needs a good woman.'

Murphy was introduced to the companions of Emily - two cousins as it happened. She seemed a bit worn looking up close but was still very fetching. She was drinking a brandy and port - always a good sign in a woman. Murphy didn't mention her dead sister as they were really still strangers. He was even uneasy at being there at all. She assured him he wasn't in the way and that she was glad to meet new people.

'So how long do you know our Jane?' she asked.

'Oh I'm not quite sure, he explained. 'She seems to have a knack of meeting new people all the time. She's more or less part of our circle these days. I heard about her thesis and how highly rated she is in academia.'

'Not only in academia,' Emily added enthusiastically.

The conversation stayed on fairly safe grounds and it was impossible for him to judge if she had any interest in him or not. Molloy then appeared next to them at the counter, seemingly innocently, as it was his round. Emily started talking to him about Welsh literature but Murphy didn't mind. He could stand back and take things in and he knew for certain that she was not interested in the most lascivious tom cat in Middle Earth. To add a touch of spice to the whole scene Bibi and her circle sauntered in. Murphy caught Kearney's amused look and half-smiled to himself. There was a growing circle of people at the counter at this stage and before long Bibi was talking to Jane and Emily, while Molloy took the drinks back to the table.

'Stay!' Kearney told Molloy.

'I'm not a dog!' Molloy replied laughing.

'You're a tom cat,' Kearney advised. 'Let the plot thicken first. Then you can go and get Bibi or one of her friends.'

As Jane introduced Bibi to Murphy he could not but talk to the Frosty. She seemed aloof enough, as if she was only allowing him an audience because of Jane. Jane told him that they were all going to go hill walking on the following day - a trek up and around Mount Gabriel. This was meant for Emily as well. There was something about Bibi that Murphy did not like - no matter how much he tried to commune with her she was cold and exuded a slightly superior aura. In any case, he could see Emily getting ready to leave. It was all becoming an anti-climax.

'So we're all to go hill walking tomorrow,' he said to her as she was heading for the door with the cousins.

'Yes. I'll see you all bright and early. Good night.'

Murphy went back to the table and the others wanted a report.

'Well, have the wheels been finally set in motion or what?' Kearney asked him.

'I'm not sure,' Murphy sighed. 'She's VHF for definite - Very Hard to Follow not to mind Very High Frequency. We'll have to wait and see.'

'But what about your lupine instinct?' Molloy joked.

'She is being coy but we'll have a liaison tomorrow night,' Murphy told him sardonically.

Jane had returned as well. Bibi and her friends had taken a table at the other end of the bar.

'There is something about Bibi which leaves me cold. I just do not take to that woman,' Murphy told the nymph.

'I can't understand that. She is really friendly and warm,' she countered. 'You have to give her more of a chance. She is not used to wolves.'

'There are just some people we never like. There is no reason for this - it just happens. And she is a prime example,' Murphy explained unconvincingly. 'So where is the Welsh bard gone to?'

There was no sign of Molloy for a while but then there he was, having taken the scenic route back from the toilets, sitting at Bibi's table as if he was her long lost friend.

'If there is an afterlife, one of the first questions I'm going to ask the Big G is what women see in that tom cat,' Murphy declared. 'Looks like we could be stuck with Bibi and co later.'

'Well one of her friends seems about a 7.25 if the worst comes to the worst,' Kearney drawled.

'What's a 7.25?' George asked innocently.

'Oh we're talking about tyre sizes,' Murphy smiled turning towards her husband.

'All's well?' Henry said benevolently as if he had the backing of the former British Empire behind him. 'Having a spot of women trouble?'

'I thought people like him only existed in films,' Kearney whispered to Sadie.

'Oh he's okay really. Just a bit out of sync with the time-space continuum,' she said.

Meanwhile Jane sidled up to Murphy with a wry smile on her face.

'Everyone seems to be taking great interest in your latest romantic escapade.'

'What escapade? I don't think she is very interested,' Murphy replied.

'Well what did you expect her to do?' Jane exclaimed. 'Jump on top of you? Whisk you out the door and ravish you on the wall?'

'Okay, okay,' Murphy allowed. 'But usually a fellow gets some kind of vibe.'

'Wait for tomorrow and you'll get lots of chances to speak to her all by yourself,' Jane advised. 'Anyway she's just after leaving her husband and burying her favourite sister.'

'Aren't you going off to join Bibi and her set?' Murphy asked.

'No. Molloy has cornered the market. I'll let them be.'

The conversation went on as the snow began to fall outside. It would be years again before they would see such snow in this part of the country. Jane started talking to Murphy about the attractions of Old English poetry and he began to give her his interpretation of *Beowulf*, while at the other side of the table Kearney was having a talk with Sadie about some artists they both admired. Molloy showed no sign of coming back to join them but that was not a big deal. George and Henry left as they were not really carousers like the others. It was all getting very calm and undramatic. Murphy looked down at Bibi's table and whenever he caught her glance she just looked through him like a sharp east wind. He would have loved to know if there had been something between her and the nymph. Meanwhile there was the blazing fire, a few creamy vitamin Ms and the prospect of a day on the hills with Emily.

Molloy eventually came back and was not at all in a good mood. They jested with him, wondering why he hadn't kidnapped Bibi or one of her friends. As it happened, he was more than unhappy for other reasons. It seemed that Bibi's set was well up on the ins and outs of Schull life and had imparted to him the bad news that Rose could not appear anywhere in public for a few days, as her callous husband had given her a bad beating. They rakes were all very put out at this news and were more than angry.

'Nothing can be done because she is afraid to go to the police,' Molloy explained. 'If they don't get a complaint then they can't act.'

'Well then we'll have to teach the scumbag a lesson,' Kearney suggested.

'Yeah and then Rose gets the worst of it afterwards,' Molloy retorted.

'There must be something that can be done,' Jane asked. 'Can't she leave him and go somewhere else? She must have friends or relations.'

'She is terrified of the brute,' Molloy told the company. 'She wouldn't and couldn't leave him.'

All this put a damper on the night and not long after this they decided to leave - in any case it was near closing time. Kearney and Molloy went off, the latter firstly going in the direction of the Bibi set and asking them back for coffee - an offer they surprisingly accepted. As Sadie and Jane moved towards the door, Kearney gave Murphy a knowing look as if to say, 'There is Jane, what are you waiting for?'

Back at Sadie's the trio all had Irish coffee by the fire. Sadie explained that William was in the UK for a few days and shortly after she went off to bed. 'If Kearney could see me now,' Murphy mused as he sat near the fire with the nymph. They finished their drinks as the snow pluffed against the big bay window. Murphy went over and stood looking out at the harbour and the falling snow. He was going to tell her in jest what Kearney was always suggesting but decided against it. She joined him at the window and he joked about the old hall in *Beowulf* and the monsters lurking outside.

'We're a long way from *Beowulf* now but there are still monsters out there,' she mused.

'Indeed. But don't worry - we protect nymphs and sylphs all the time,' he laughed.

'How chivalrous. Well goodnight Sir Galahad,' she joked, kissing him lightly on the cheek before disappearing to her room.

Meanwhile at Molloy's things were not so calm. It seemed to Kearney that Bibi's two friends were in the same Frosty mould as herself. What annoyed him was that even though Bibi was fairly sociable while they sat around and had some whiskeys, she had spent a very long time ignoring him in the city despite knowing him by sight for years. After they had finished talking about the Rose situation he turned to her and said, 'So what's the problem with saying hello to people you know to see for ages and ages?'

'What do you mean?' she replied, taken aback at the forcefulness of his question.

'You know very well what I mean,' he snapped. 'It's not a difficult question to answer.'

'I usually only say hello to people I've been introduced to,' she replied with a certain steeliness.

'Give me a break. Jane Austen is dead, as you may have gathered,' he retorted. 'What do you expect? A silver tray with a calling card on it?'

'Maybe we were brought up differently?' she said in a catty tone.

Kearney came from a working class background and while this was never a big deal for him, he smarted at the implication.

'What do you mean by that?'

'Nothing much. I didn't mean it like that... only maybe you shouldn't be so quick to judge,' Bibi uttered defensively.

This put Kearney slightly off the path he had intended to take. He relented somewhat, seeing that in any case she was on the verge of tears. All he needed!

'Okay, okay. Relax. It's just I don't really understand what's the big deal about acknowledging someone's existence,' he countered in a more placatory tone.

This Kearney-Bibi duel was causing a tense atmosphere, not that Molloy cared - he always said a bit of drama before bedtime was good for the heart. However, he finally intervened, taking the edge off the tension, asking, 'Anyone for another round of whisky? I brought it especially for Christmas - you can't beat that peaty Scotch scent!'

Kearney however had decided that Bibi had some more explaining to do. When he was in one of his Heathcliffian moods he was hard to stop.

'So what about the way you were brought up?' he persisted crossly.

'Don't keep on. Give the girl a break!' Molloy intervened. 'You can ask her all day tomorrow on the hills.'

'It's okay. We'll continue the conversation some other time maybe. Now I'm going home,' Bibi announced with such finality that that was that.

'Well you really did a great job getting us sexual congress tonight,'

Molloy ranted at his fellow rake with exasperation after the women had left. 'What am I going to do? A whole day without a woman?'

'They're not the type,' Kearney said with a certitude which didn't seem to convince the tom cat at all.

'Meanwhile back at Sadie's,' Molloy intoned.

'Murphy's having all the luck indeed,' Kearney went on. 'He's in a house with the gorgeous Sadie who has the most bodacious curves I've even seen, not to mind his getting on exceptionally well with the nymph! And then he has the beautiful Emily on the moors tomorrow.'

***

The following morning saw an unusual assortment of people assembled outside the bank in Schull. There were the Emily and Bibi sets as well as the rakes, Sadie and the Renaissance nymph. They headed off in three cars towards the base of Mount Gabriel.

'Today or never,' Jane reminded Murphy as they walked towards the Saab.

'Really,' he replied sarcastically.

The snow made the scenery extra special and once they got to the base of the hill they walked up along a path with the sea glittering in the winter sunshine below them. They went at a brisk pace at the start, with Molloy of course setting the pace with one of Bibi's set. One of Emily's cousins was talking to Kearney about planning corruption in Ireland and Sadie was bringing up the rear with Murphy. Bibi was talking to Jane. Places were being swapped around as time passed. After an hour they were all strung out about a quarter of a mile apart. Murphy still hadn't got Emily by herself but his chance was coming soon as Jane moved away to let him try his luck. Emily seemed a bit rapt, looking at the rugged scenery. The snow made it all rather surreal.

'So what piece of music would you choose to match this scene?' she asked him with a smile. He liked a woman who could ask such questions.

'Well that's a hard one,' he answered. 'It could be Brahms' Second Symphony or Beethoven's *Emperor* Concerto or possibly Sibelius' Fifth. I suppose the sweep and majestic power of the Beethoven would do perfectly.'

They walked along and for the first time since their original meeting Murphy felt somewhat at ease. She was indeed interesting company - a kind of older version of the nymph he thought. She had the most beautiful hands. They appeared to have been sculpted by some great artist they were so fine and elegant. He often noticed women's hands, much to the puzzlement of Molloy who noticed hands a good deal later than other things. As they skirted round the top of Mount Gabriel Murphy began to probe with more personal questions.

'So how are you after your separation?' he asked naturally enough.

'Oh fine,' she said nonchalantly. 'I should have done that years ago but I never listen to my friends. I'm too obdurate.'

'You must still be in shock after your sister's death?'

'Yes. But there is nothing to say about all that is there?'

'Do you believe in an afterlife?'

'Not really. I'm an agnostic I suppose. I have very occasional moments when I indulge in the possibility of a God but they are really very rare.'

They moved on to other topics. She commented that Molloy was an interesting kind of character judging by what Jane had told her.

'So you have all our files?' Murphy said ironically.

'I wouldn't go that far but I know quite a lot about you all thanks to Jane. I don't mix or become friendly with students in general but Jane is different.'

It was all very low key after that but what was a rake to do up a hill with a woman who had to endure the loss of a sister not to mind marital woe. The rest of the walk was a mixture of everyone talking to everyone. Even Bibi and Kearney passed some civil words and she even managed the ghost of a smile at one stage.

'What a scream it would be if you ended up with her,' Murphy joked with Kearney as they stopped to have some food.

'Could do worse,' Kearney responded sarcastically.

Meanwhile Molloy was getting acquainted with one of Bibi's set, a secondary teacher who was reasonably good looking but who had been dismissed earlier by Murphy and Kearney as being in the goody goody mode. She had a job in a convent in north Cork but lived in the city. Her name was Helena something or other.

'The quintessential nice girl - and with that wolf,' Murphy noted. 'Should be interesting. If he has his wicked way with her then I'll buy him free drink all night.'

'Better tell him then,' Kearney suggested. 'He may need an extra incentive when there's a goody goody in the picture.'

They all faced the view of the wide ocean with Emily standing somewhat apart from the main group, cutting a slightly forlorn figure.

'Why don't you go talk to the French Lieutenant's Woman?' Kearney asked Murphy in his usual sardonic tone.

'Why don't you go and give Bibi one from us all?' Murphy replied.

'I'll just go do that,' his fellow rake joked and moved away.

Murphy went over towards Emily. She seemed to look indeed both forlorn and fragile - vulnerable Kearney would have said. And that was the best time to take advantage he had often advised.

'So are you going to be round Schull for long more or what?' Murphy asked her tenuously.

'Another week but I have to do some work while I'm here,' she explained. 'I'm in the family house but there is no one else with me at the moment. Some cousins may be along in a day or two. Come and visit some evening if you want. I like talking about music but most music academics are so boring. I'm not a great cook but you can have something simple. Bring some of your gang if you want.'

'Charming,' Murphy thought. 'Not a good sign to have others come along as well,' he mused.

'I'd love to,' he told her enthusiastically. 'I'm not sure what plans the others have for the next few days. I'll let you know.'

'Well, why not make it tomorrow evening, say around seven. We can ask the others later.'

'Fine but maybe it would be better to let that Bibi out of the equation as some of us don't click with her.'

'That's surprising. She seems really nice.'

'So everyone thinks - that is everyone except us.'

Kearney came in their direction at this stage and so that was the last chance Murphy had to speak alone to the beautiful Emily for the rest of the hike. She walked off ahead of the others with her long, wavy hair blowing in the wind.

'Touch of the French Lieutenant's Woman indeed,' Murphy muttered to Kearney.

The rest of the hike passed quickly. It was getting colder and the wind was picking up. They straggled down the side of Mount Gabriel and headed back to The Black Bull where the plan was to have one drink before regrouping later that evening. Murphy was disappointed to find that Emily was not one of the company there. It was about five o' clock and as usual there was a big blazing log fire to greet them. 'If only such taverns were more common,' Kearney wished as they sat down with their usual drinks. Molloy saw McMicheal passing in the distance and was not at all pleased to be reminded of that orc's existence. Jane and Sadie were milling around 'meeting the people' while Bibi and her friends were at the counter talking to some locals. The rakes began a discussion about the Rose problem.

'The thing to do is get rid of him completely,' Murphy suggested earnestly. 'Hire a hit man in Dublin and all problems solved for a few grand.'

'And how do you go about finding a hit man?' Molloy demanded.

'Are ye all looping the loop or what?' Kearney reminded them. 'The trail would lead back to Molloy and then we'd all be bunched.'

'And who would pay for the whole thing in any case? Molloy asked.

'Well, what about giving him a warning and see what happens?' Murphy suggested.

'That's a possibility but he is very dangerous and has some fairly shifty allies round the place. Anyway, I thought Sadie's William was the answer to McMicheal?' Molloy asked.

'Well one way or another if something isn't done he'll end up doing permanent injury to Rose,' Murphy added.

The conversation gradually veered away from the nefarious McMicheal and some minutes later the Bibi set came and joined them.

'Thought you didn't believe in miracles?' Murphy asked Kearney.

'Give me a break,' Kearney half-growled in reply.

Jane, seated beside Murphy, asked some predictable questions about his progress with the elusive Emily.

'All very tenuous and iffy,' he reported. 'A matter of patience perhaps.'

'That really suits you then,' the nymph said with a hint of sarcasm.

Contrary to the usual routine the company did not stay on for an extended drinking session but broke up after an hour as they all had different agendas and things to do. Later Murphy expected a repeat of the night before but it seemed there was going to be a lessening of numbers: Molloy had some writing deadline to meet for a literary journal, Kearney was going off to Karen's place for high tea on a low table, Sadie had to go and finish some sculpture for a New Year's Eve exhibition and Bibi and her set were due to go to some upmarket dinner party. That left Jane, though Molloy threatened to come out later. After dinner and before the inevitable trip to the pub Murphy had a chance to get Sadie's reading of the Rose dilemma. It was the usual story of everyone knowing what was going on but no one prepared to do anything about it. Even the local police couldn't do anything without Rose or someone else making a complaint and that was unlikely to happen in such a small place. And after the brutal death of the German woman people were even less inclined to get involved in anything remotely controversial.

'William will be back in a day or so and we'll tell him about the latest violence to Rose,' Sadie suggested. 'He has his own network around here.'

'As if William is some kind of Superman who will deal out justice to the wicked,' Murphy thought to himself. 'And where the hell was he in any case?' Sadie gave Murphy a house key and went off to her workshop saying she would go down to the pub for a late drink if she had her work done. She was looking exceptionally sexy that night he thought as he tried to keep his eyes away from her delectable, curvaceous body. Would he or what!

Kearney sent him a text saying, 'You and nymph alone in pub for the evening. Only a matter of time.'

The nymph was actually out somewhere with some of her mysterious contacts, having a tenuous plan to be in the pub later. At the rate things were going Murphy thought he would be spending the evening drinking alone despite all the hype of the night before. Sadie told him to indulge in some music before going out so he sat on the floor and went through some of her vinyl collection. He came across a Colin Davis recording of Mozart's Thirty Ninth Symphony and so put it on a state of the art Swiss turntable. Davis conducted the work with a white heat intensity, capturing the visionary splendor of the work, leaving Murphy feeling quite exhilarated.

When the time came to go out he didn't want to interrupt Sadie at her work. As he put on his coat he could hear Leonard Cohen's decadent *Take this Waltz* coming from her studio down below. 'Great taste that woman has,' he thought as he headed off towards the town below. He walked along in the cold and the dark under a starry sky wondering how scared local people really were about the possibility of a murderer in their midst. The whirlwind finale of the Mozart symphony echoed in his head as he walked along, casting occasional glances at the sky. He was in one of his rare optimistic moods by the time he got to the town centre.

In The Black Bull there was no one he knew so he took up a strategic seat on a stool at the end of the counter. He savoured the taste of the creamy vitamin M and looked around to see who was out and about. It was a pub that was easy to be on one's own and he was quite content to sit there for a while and let the world go by. 'There is a kind of art in being alone and content in a pub,' he mused. A fellow had to take in the surroundings gradually during the first drink and then slowly ingratiate oneself into the company of the people serving. Usually a conversation with the barman led to a customer joining in and then one was off.

As he finished his first pint he got a text from the nymph saying she would be along presently and hoped that he was coping. He really had no idea what her angle on him was. 'Probably all very innocent,' he thought. The owner was behind the counter with his wife coming and going. They were all very friendly without being over inquisitive. He talked intermittently to them about the tourist business and the weather, about the book shop and the planetarium in the school, about everything local it seemed except the murdered German woman. He thought it would be in bad taste to discuss the topic he most wanted to talk about, and in any case, he was fairly certain that the locals did not want to talk to every stranger about the whole saga. In the background Miles Davis could be heard playing some melancholy number - in some sleazy smoky jazz bar or so Murphy imagined.

When the nymph finally arrived she had a big surprise for Murphy, for as the door opened, she came in accompanied by the 'French Lieutenant's Woman' herself. Murphy was taken aback to find Emily there - and indeed wearing a kind of cloak that had more than a touch of the FLW about it.

'So you spend all your time drinking Guinness in pubs?' she asked him in an amused voice.

'No, he replied 'I spend all my time drinking Murphys in pubs.'

He persuaded her to have a glass of the said vitamin M and she was quite surprised to find how different it was to the tangy taste of vitamin G. The nymph was drinking Carlsberg for a change. They were all sitting on high stools with Emily in the middle and Murphy feeling almost elated. What he liked about the two of them was that unlike most stuffy academics they had a real love of knowledge and were very well up in all sorts of fields besides their own. So the three of them had a diverting colloquy that began with the news of the furthest, most recently discovered galaxy in the known cosmos and then modulated to music and Mozart's summer of 1788, Rose's predicament and Molloy's exploits, different types of Scotch whisky and hangover cures, the trog situation in the city and possible solutions (Murphy refrained from mentioning concentration camps), the West Cork music festival and Banville's overuse of seedy old codgers in his novels.

Murphy was informing Emily about the merits of the Bantry House summer music festival when Molloy arrived in, looking like one thirsty hound and obviously in top hunting form. Murphy was quite happy to see his fellow rake as it would give him more of an opportunity to speak to Emily. He knew that Jane had no interest in the Welsh Casanova and so he was quite at ease seeing Molloy making an ongoing fool of himself with the nymph.

Time passed. Molloy did indeed get involved in a lively conversation with the nymph while Murphy and Emily had a one to one about life in the city and the increasing domination of the trogs. All this bemused Emily and she refused to believe the city was as grim a place as the rake was painting it.

'Well come and see for yourself some time,' Murphy suggested. 'I'll take you on a tour. You can even bring some nuts and bananas for the trogs and the other Neolithics as you walk around.'

He then went on his usual rant about the city's medieval roughness and its orc population, the young trogettes who wandered round in a drunken state, the high rates of depression, the Frumpies, the Frosties and the Motleys, the paucity of symphony concerts, the unprovoked violence, the coarse nature of nocturnal life and the high suicide rate.

As soon as he mentioned the suicide word he regretted it.

'I'm sorry for bringing that up,' he said ruefully.

'Don't worry. I don't live in a cocoon,' Emily responded. 'Actually I am half aware of the high suicide rate. If all of what you say is true then maybe I'll get a better idea of the reasons why people do it. I've been out of Cork for so long except for the odd seminar and Christmas visit.'

He then told her about all the worthy, young people he had known who saw fit to do away with themselves in the city over the last decade. He didn't want to stay on such a morbid topic but she seemed really interested and it didn't seem to upset her in any outward way. He gave his well-worn theory about the reasons for the alienation and isolation felt by so many.

'You should read an essay in *The Cork Anthology* called *Internal Exile in the Second City* by Paddy Woodworth,' he sermonized. 'It's a good starting point in understanding the complexities of the suicide problem in the city, though the essay isn't explicitly about suicide at all – it's more about alienation.'

Molloy and the nymph then rejoined them and, as it was nearly closing time, Murphy treated them all to Irish coffees. There was no sign of the Bibi set and Murphy wondered if the nymph was going to see the Queen of the Frosties later. Meanwhile Emily was going to walk home by herself, having refused Murphy's repeated offers of an escort. He didn't want to be too pushy and she was firm in her wish to go alone. Her house in any case was quite near she told him. As she put on her 'FLW' cloak she bade them all goodnight and then, just as she opened the door, she turned and gave Murphy one of those glances -

the kind she had given him on their first meeting, a real *Tristan and Isolde* special he felt, hearing a surge of the Prelude to Act 1 in his head, feeling slightly flushed.

'Romeo, Romeo, wherefore art thou?' Molloy intoned, much to the amusement of Jane.

'True love! I am impressed,' the nymph declared with a delicate sense of irony.

Outside under the stars Molloy invited them back to his place for coffee but Murphy declined, not being in the humour for more banter after such a thrilling end to the night. Jane however accepted and so Murphy headed off to Sadie's by himself. He was a bit annoyed by the nymph's decision to go with Molloy but what the hell.

When he got back to Sadie's she was in the kitchen having a night cap. She was dressed in a satin dressing gown that showed all her curves especially her stunning cleavage. He wondered if she was aware of the effect she had on men and considered the possibility that she was either a complete *femme fatale* or else so unselfconscious as to be almost saintly. What he would give to part her dressing gown and sample her film star body. Such infidelity so soon after his encounter with Emily! But he was so weak when it came to gorgeous women!

No, he decided, Sadie was not the saintly type, unaware of her charms and beauty. If she wasn't married... if he hadn't met Emily... if, if, if... He knew that she knew what he was thinking and there was a heightened sexual tension while they chatted about the night and the plan for the next day.

'You really like Emily don't you?' she asked coyly.

'Yes, she's special,' the rake managed, trying to keep his gaze away from her Kim Novak bust.

If she didn't leave the kitchen soon he would just go and kiss her to pieces she was so damn attractive.

'I think you and she are equally beautiful,' he almost said aloud. 'Horror of horrors,' he thought and wondered what she would have said if she had heard this.

And almost as if she had, she leaned over and gave him a light kiss on the cheek and was gone before he could say 'orbs'. So he eventually went to bed after another whiskey and read himself to sleep. He had a dream which was a complete muddle of images that combined Sadie, the French Lieutenant's Woman, a high mountain summit and a fleeting hint of Emily. The next morning he was woken by the nymph shaking him. He almost never overslept but this was one of those times.

'You must have had a wild night?' she asked more than once.

'You can hardly talk. What time did you get back from Molloy's?'

'I didn't,' she said boldly but with a glint in her eyes.

Murphy's expression showed a clear disapproval.

'Yes, we had wild sex all night long and he walked me home just now,' she laughed. 'Sadie's finished breakfast ages ago so you have to get up and talk to me over your bacon and eggs.'

He looked out the window at the sea and the hills and thought how lucky he was to be in such a spectacular place in the company of two classy women with the prospect of a rendezvous with a third later that day. When he got to the large, bright kitchen Corelli's *Concerti Grossi* were playing in the background and there was an aromatic waft of freshly ground coffee to savour. He brought up Emily's invite for that evening.

'Well why can't you go alone? We don't want to be in the way do we?' Jane asked.

'I can't,' he explained. 'It would be too obvious. You're going to go, aren't you?'

'How do you know I'm free?' she teased.

'You cannot let me down, of all people.' Why did he come out with such things he wondered?

'Well I suppose I could do you yet another favour. Molloy will go of course but Kearney will be wrapped around the librarian I suppose. Ask Sadie, your number two.'

'Give me a break. You are too smart at times. The things you do come out with.'

'Well you spend ages admiring and lusting after her so called celestial orbs among other things.'

'I most certainly do not,' he retorted wanly. 'I don't fancy every woman I know believe it or not - even if she looks like Sophia Loren in her prime. Of course Molloy will go anywhere if there is even the slightest chance of meeting a woman. I swear to God if I were married and he was in the house on a visit, I'd tie him to a table if I had to leave him and my wife alone for a minute.'

'Whatever about Molloy, I know and you know that if Sadie was single - and Emily not around - you would go for her in a big, big way.'

'Why don't you get a job as an oracle somewhere? You spend so much time in the medieval world when you rejoin the modern one your judgement remains a bit shaky.'

And so the banter went on as they had breakfast while looking out at the sea and the blue sky and the hills beyond. It was a kind of moment that lingered in the memory long after, a kind of step outside time that he would later often reminisce about. Kearney arrived out of the blue towards noon and he was not a happy camper. He didn't say anything to Jane but when he got a chance to talk to Murphy in the yard he told his fellow rake that Karen wanted a relationship!

'You can't be serious. What? A relationship?' Murphy joked. 'How demanding and unreasonable. Women - they are just so pushy,'

'Well she wants a husband and soon, as far as I can see,' Kearney muttered, giving his standard opt out speech. 'I mean she's good company and all that but I'm not even going to start sliding down that road. I just have no long term interest in her. She's too nice for me anyway.'

As there was a gale forecast for later the two rakes decided to round up a few people and head off to the Sheep's Head for a drive and a walk. Molloy turned up with Helena.

'God, he should get a doctorate for womanising,' the nymph could only say as she saw them.

There was no sign of Bibi who seemed to have gone to ground completely. Murphy drove the Saab along the winding coast road towards Dunmanus Bay as the nymph sat next to him with the other three in the back - the innocent Helena wedged between the two cynical rakes. Kearney surmised from her body language that the Welsh wolf had not tried anything yet with her. They got near the end of the peninsula with its spectacular views of Bantry Bay on one side and

Dunmanus Bay on the other. They had to leave the car and walk the last mile or so to the very extremity of Sheep's Head. Murphy glared at Molloy as the latter was doing all he could to ingratiate himself into Helena's favour. 'Surely even Molloy can't have his wicked way with such a droll goody goody,' he mused as they sat around on big boulders having coffee. 'She probably wears bloomers for God's sake.'

The walk out to the lighthouse at the tip of the peninsula took some time but it was worth it for the sweeping view of the stormy Atlantic and the panoramic prospect of the Beara Peninsula. All was going along smoothly even if the wind was beginning to pick up. Molloy had by this stage taken to holding the hand of the secondary teacher, with Murphy betting Kearney that the Welsh cad would have her ravished by the next day. As they made their way back Molloy got a text from Rose saying that her oaf of a husband would not be at home before nine and would Molly risk visiting her. All he needed! He didn't reply - he would do so later when he had thought about it more. A visit to Rose's, with the possibility of an encounter with that psycho husband, was not an enticing prospect, even if she was sure that the coast was clear.

'So where's the librarian?' Jane asked Kearney as the others walked some way in front.

'She's consigned to the history book of rakish conquests,' he informed her.

They stopped off at a pub on the way back - one of those pubs where everyone looks when a stranger walks in the door, giving the newcomer the impression that he or she is intruding on a private conversation. There were some seriously obese American women in one corner by a fire, true heavy weights! Murphy could never comprehend what some men saw in the 'beached whale' type but seemingly they were indeed all married. As well as being grossly overweight they were loud and their voices grated on Murphy's ears more than any other.

'No international scenes?' Jane half-pleaded.

'No indeed,' Murphy agreed and went off to a table as far away from the beached whales as was possible.

'Americans, with some exceptions, are beyond doubt the least educated and most intolerable nation in the whole wide world,' he declared to the company as they settled into afternoon coffees.

'Oh no, he's off,' Molloy volunteered.

Helena, the secondary teacher, was irritated at Murphy's blanket statement. She started on about American hospitality and how the place was a haven for so many unemployed paddies over the years and about the wealth and opportunity offered by Uncle Sam.

'We are not going to have this conversation,' Jane pleaded.

The beached whales seemed to have picked up on the gist of what was being said. The others were in no mood for another of Murphy's tirades against Uncle Sam and American foreign policy. Meanwhile one of the whales trundled in their direction and there was a pause while she lurched past them on the way to the toilets. Murphy wondered if she could actually even manage to squeeze through the toilet entrance, so obese was she.

He started going on and on about Americans in general knowing so little about their own government's foreign policy, their near absolute ignorance about the world at large, their facile amiability, their lack of irony, their incredible arrogance, their lack of compassion for the downtrodden and the huge numbers of poor in their own country...

'Boom, boom,' he then intoned as the beached whale made her way back slowly from the 'powder room'.

'You are really so bad,' Jane half-giggled.

Helena was looking far from pleased. She had a big sister (as in older) across the pond and she had a certain unspoken, and indeed unquestioning allegiance to Uncle Sam. Jane used all her charm to get the topic of conversation changed. She started asking the earnest teacher about her travels while the rakes discussed the Rose situation. She got Helena to talk about her school and told her that she too had spent some time teaching in the north of the county. (She had decided to do a teaching diploma in case her academic career did not work out - an example of a certain insecurity and lack of self-confidence). She did not get on very well with the other teachers though she survived a year dealing with a student body largely made up of indifferent, mediocre students and downright hooligans - though it was not pc to state such things. The parents, more often than not, were as bad, a sordid case of abject ignorance breeding more ignorance. The small minority of ambitious students had their educational lives ruined by the constant misbehaviour of the yob element which was all too prevalent. Jane's fate was sealed one dreary wet Wednesday near the end of term. On the previous day the vice-principal - a Ms Gillhoughly (not related to the Sinn Fein druid) had overheard her mentioning Beethoven's Seventh.

'You don't listen to that kind of rubbish?' she asked Jane casually.

The next day at the morning coffee break Jane half-threw a copy of the score of Beethoven's Seventh onto the table in front of the VP and asked the all-knowing one with acidic coolness, 'So can you show me exactly where the rubbish is?'

There followed an embarrassed silence followed by the VP turning her back on Jane, acting as if she had suddenly become invisible. However the point was made, and Jane began to realise that teaching for her was not a career to be pursued in Irish schools where all the rights were on the side on the yobs and where many ignorant types held managerial posts. The VP never spoke to her again, unless it was in an official capacity.

Meanwhile the rakes were agreeing that it was not a good idea for Molloy to go and see Rose that evening.

'There's a storm brewing,' Murphy joked. 'The scene is set for a showdown - Molloy of Middle Earth duels with the Schull Psycho.'

Outside a strong easterly wind was picking up with the prospect of a blizzard to come, an event almost unheard of in those parts.

'And by the way where the hell is Earl? He's supposed to be here by now?' Kearney asked.

'He's probably been kidnapped by Ms Opera and as we speak they are probably having a table job,' Molloy, the said expert suggested.

'Be careful or you will have to explain to Julie Andrews what a table job is,' Murphy quipped.

The afternoon lingered. The odd shaft of sunlight came through the bar window. The American whales trundled off to another port of call. Despite earlier pronouncements Molloy and Helena were due to go to Emily's as well as Kearney. Murphy was at first not at all pleased but then he realised that with a few people there he would have more of a chance of speaking to Emily than if he had gone with Jane only.

It was dark by four thirty so they headed back to Schull, the Saab purring along nicely. Helena went back to Bibi's where she was based and Molloy and Kearney went to the Welsh rake's place for a respite and ablutions. A visit to the famous Emily was an event according to Molloy and he was sure that it would be the setting where he could do some more work on the shapely if virginal Helena. Meanwhile Sadie told Murphy and Jane that she would not be going with them, while pouring them some light white wine to put them in the mood. Outside there were snow flurries, with the wind picking up, as they indulged in the cosy atmosphere created by the log fire, the wine and the view of the town and harbour lights in the distance.

'Real *Wuthering Heights* stuff,' Murphy suggested to Jane who was reading some book on Chagall.

'And not a Heathcliff in sight,' she sighed.

Murphy looked through a copy of Ted Hughes' *Birthday Letters* while she seemed to have become totally lost in the world of Chagall. Sadie was doing some work in the studio. After a while Murphy put on an Arvo Pärt CD and fell into a kind of reverie as the fire crackled and the snow pluffed against the windows. Pärt's hypnotic *Kanon Pokajanen* began with its strange mixture of the modern and the traditional. It was indeed very calming and in harmony with the atmosphere of the room.

It was not long before the time came for them to head off. They said goodbye to Sadie and walked down to Molloy's where Helena had already arrived and then they all walked along towards Emily's house. It was about half a mile up a narrow lane on the west side of the town.

'Not a great place for a woman to be walking alone,' Murphy said to the others as they sauntered along. He was not at all pleased at the idea of Emily walking up such a dark lane by herself with all the goings on that had taken place. They saw the lights in her house while they were still only half way there. As they approached they could see footprints in the snow in front of the house - footprints of at least two people. Murphy rang the bell. There was no answer. He tried a few times but still he got no response. He could see the table set inside and a fire lit beyond.

'See if the door is open,' Jane suggested.

He did so and turned the handle, slowly walking inside and calling out Emily's name. The others followed him hesitantly into the hall and still there was no sign of the hostess. Jane walked into the dining room where everything was laid out for dinner. She went into the kitchen and noticed that there was something in the oven which was more or less baked. She told the others to go into the dining room and suggested that Emily could have been out the back somewhere. Murphy felt distinctly uneasy at this stage - it was not a place for a woman to be by herself. It was too isolated and in view of past events it seemed to be almost tempting fate. He followed Jane out the back door. It was quite dark as they couldn't find the light switch for the yard. There was a kind of barn at one end of the yard and there was a dim light coming from there. They both called out Emily's name but there was nothing but an eerie silence as the snow swept round in eddies. By the time they reached the door of the barn they were both in a kind of nervous sweat. Murphy called out Emily's name one more time before opening the barn door and peering in. In the dim light he saw her hanging lifelessly from a rope that had been slung over one of the beams supporting the roof, her beautifully crafted hands tied behind her back.

***

By the time the police arrived the company were huddled in the front room all in a state of deep shock. Kearney had the presence of mind to put some stones around the footprints they had seen outside - and indeed he had measured them with a measuring tape he had found in the kitchen. It was he who also had cut Emily down and placed her body on the ground, making them all stay inside until the police came. They tried not to disturb anything in the house while waiting for the police. Jane was holding Murphy's hand as both looked completely desolate. Helena was sobbing incessantly and Molloy was glaring out the window angrily. As the police questioned all of them separately Molloy mentioned to a detective that McMicheal had been out of his house until nine. When the same detective phoned Rose's number she asserted that her husband hadn't left the house all evening. There was nothing more for all of them to do and so after a long wait the police drove them back to Sadie's house warning them to say nothing to anyone for the time being.

Murphy and Jane were too stunned to say anything coherent. Molloy and Kearney looked as if the whole evil event hadn't yet sunk in. Sadie was putting on a brave show to keep the others consoled in some way. She had sedated Helena as the teacher had become completely hysterical.

'It must have been that psycho,' Molloy gasped, speaking of McMicheal, as he revealed to Sadie what Rose's text had said earlier.

Sadie disappeared for a while on hearing this piece of news and they seemed to hear her on a phone in another part of the house. It seemed to Murphy from the tone of her voice that it was William she was talking to. She returned with a tray on which there were bottles of cognac and Scotch. They all had a stiff measure of drinks. There were long silent lulls and the only sound to be heard was the wind rattling the windows. A little later a detective arrived at the house and joined them in the living room where there was a big fire going. He reiterated that they were to remain silent and stay in the neighbourhood. He brought Molloy aside into the kitchen and left some time later taking the Welsh rake's mobile phone with him. The detective seemed to spend a long time talking to Sadie as she walked him to the police car outside.

'All we need,' Sadie half-whispered as she returned to the room with the fire. Murphy found this a very strange thing to say but the others didn't react. Time passed. Molloy and Kearney went back to the Welsh rake's house while Sadie put the secondary teacher into one of the guest rooms.

Much later Murphy went off to his room after having a third cognac. Jane retired later after an extended talk with Sadie. Murphy couldn't sleep despite the cognac. He was numbed by the whole experience which had a surreal and ghostly feel to it. He kept seeing Emily hanging there limp and lifeless and cold, swinging slowly with the wind rattling the timber walls of the barn. After about an hour his door opened and the nymph appeared wearing a long white T shirt. She slid into his bed and put her arms around him and there was not a word spoken - she stayed like that for hours and left the bedroom just before dawn.

Part Six

REQUIEM

Her voice was ever soft,
Gentle, and low - an excellent thing in woman.

King Lear

Get thee to a nunnery; why wouldn't thou be a breeder
of sinners? I am myself indifferent honest...

Hamlet

The days that followed passed in a kind of numbed blur for those who had found Emily. The funeral took place a week after her death, in the same church as her sister's had been. Murphy and Jane were treated very well by the family even though they were all complete strangers to each other, not to mind the fact that Murphy was almost a stranger to the dead woman. At the funeral Mass - Kearney couldn't believe that Emily also was a Catholic- the family insisted on sharing the front seats of the church with Murphy and his circle. The music had been already chosen by Emily, and her brother who was the executor of her will, carried out her instructions to the letter.

Murphy was relieved to see that the priest officiating was not the 'bacon and cabbage' Fr GFH - though the odious Sinn Fein druid was in attendance. The music was played from various works in Emily's library. There was the *Kyrie* from Bach's *B minor Mass* and a chorus from Purcell's *Funeral Music for Queen Mary* - both played before the actual Mass began. Then there was a pause in the middle of the ceremony as the *Larghetto* from Mozart's last piano concerto was played and then, as the coffin was taken from the church, there was the closing chorus from the Bach *B minor Mass*.

At the grave side Jane clung on to Murphy while the rest of their set stood slightly further back. Unlike most funerals the mourners waited until the earth covered in the coffin completely, giving the whole ritual an added sense of finality. Murphy caught a glance of Kearney wincing as the priest invoked the words '*I am the resurrection and the life.*' On the way out of the cemetery Fr GFH passed Murphy and put out his hand to sympathize. Murphy refused to accept his sympathy - his opposition to the IRA was implacable and he was not going to accept a facile handshake from one of its most enthusiastic supporters.

'Go to hell,' was all the 'bacon and cabbage' priest got from the rake.

Murphy and Jane were almost the last to leave the graveside. After a long silence they made their way back to Emily's house at the insistence of her brother. It was a very painful visit but they went for the sake of the family. Murphy experienced endless flashbacks to the moment when he saw the hanged woman, her eyes staring down at them. After a respectful amount of time had passed they went to The Black Bull to meet the others. Molloy had to go back to Middle Earth on the following day. He hadn't been out with Helena since the murder, she being mainly with Bibi and her set. His efforts to get Rose to change her story about her husband's movements had failed. She was obviously living in terror of the brute and there was no way she was going to tell the truth and risk getting killed herself. The police had concluded that McMicheal was indeed the only suspect but there was no way of getting at him. The footprints in the snow were not his size – but the brute could have been clever enough to wear a larger shoe size and then throw the shoes away after. That two women had been brutally murdered in such a small town in a relatively short space of time was bordering on the incredible. That no one had been arrested defied belief.

They all headed back to the city some time later. Sadie was not around for some reason - she hadn't been in Schull for a few days and like William no one seemed to know of her whereabouts. Jane was to go off to Oxford for a few months and so Murphy and Kearney were left to face another year in the city of trogs with little to look forward to.

Part Seven

TROGVILLE

I arrived at Cork, the dullest and dirtiest town that can be imagined. The people met with are yawning, and one is stopped with every minute by funerals, or hideous troops of beggars, or pigs which run the streets in hundreds...

There is no town where there is so much needful to do to make the place agreeable to a great number of the poor inhabitants. The spirit of commerce and self-interest has laid hold of all branches of the administration...

Chevalier De Latocnaye
A Frenchman's Walk Through Ireland 1796-97

'There's no such thing. Forget about it. You just cannot be serious. It just doesn't exist. I am talking *ex-cathedra*,' Kearney advised Murphy as they sat at the counter near a window in The High C early on a Wednesday night. 'The only way there is any possibility of a near platonic relationship between a man and a female friend is when they've had sexual congress at some stage in the past. As in exs.'

Murphy had mentioned that the Renaissance nymph was due back from the lofty towers of Oxford and the conversation had turned to platonic relationships between men and women.

'But you are wrong,' Murphy countered. 'I have no designs on her and yet she is a friend of mine - more or less.'

'But there must be an underlying sexual tension of some kind?' Kearney demanded. 'Maybe you haven't tapped into it or more likely you're in denial.'

'And anyway, she doesn't have big orbs - and you know I am an orb man myself,' Murphy joked.

'Well that really changes everything,' Kearney agreed. 'Are you telling me you have never considered a skirmish with her?'

'What's the point in having this colloquy when you won't believe me,' Murphy insisted.

'There is always something between men and women who are just friends as you put it,' Kearney maintained.

As they talked away a leggy eastern European girl of about twenty five came in with cards promoting a lap dancing club. She was a stunner, but out of bounds, as they knew from past experience.

'Going to a lap dancing club is like trying to play the piano with your gloves on,' Murphy told her while having extremely lustful thoughts. 'All those beauties and you can't even touch them. Give me a break,' he added gruffly.

They took the cards to please the temptress but had no intention of going near the place.

'How about a platonic table job with her?' Murphy wished aloud. 'Would I or what!'

'What this city needs is a good bordello,' Kearney intoned.

'Some chance of that happening,' Murphy replied mournfully.

In the corner there was a gang of Frusties - these were typically in their early forties, frustrated sexually but lacking the confidence to do anything about it. They were friendlier than the Frosties and potentially more sexual than the Frumpies, but they remained in a kind of Limbo both socially and sexually. Kearney heard one of them complaining about the smoking ban. She was an fb but still had a kind of sex appeal. She was a teacher though she looked more like a nurse - hence the touch of sex appeal! She wanted a husband as well as sex though and that was the thing that got on the gimp of the rakes.

It was coming up to Easter and one of the better parts of the year's cycle was upon them - the annual International Choral Festival, which occasionally threw a few foreign babes their way. Patrick's Day had earlier passed in its usual way - the garish parade for the intellectually challenged followed by even greater amounts of litter than usual strewing the city centre, the customary violence, the vomit and trog urine on the streets, the 'in your face' brutality. At least the Choral Festival brought some civilized dimension to the place as it did not impinge upon the reptilian consciousness of the trogs.

In The High C the usual line of assorted drinkers lined the counter as things got busier. Murphy had been drinking a little too much since the events of Schull, and even though drink was no consolation, he still liked losing himself for hours in bars, indulging in long conversations with whoever he encountered. He hadn't listened to any music since the murder - there was a kind of spiritual black hole at the very centre of his life. He was more than surprised that Jane had become so distant and her e-mails were becoming almost a rarity. No doubt she was suffering in her own way.

The two rakes discussed the Choral Festival and later planned to go off to the hotel where its festival club late night festivities were to take place. A guy came in wearing a V-necked pullover and was accompanied by a fairly dashing looking brunette with long frizzled hair. He was a teachery type and looked boringly avuncular, sensible and rich. They were married it seemed and Murphy just raised his eyes to heaven muttering his usual disapproval of the Second Law. Meanwhile one of the losers who lurched against the counter was bemoaning the death of some guy he knew. It seemed that his buddy had done away with himself by jumping off a ferry in the middle of the

Irish Sea.

'At least they saved the expense of a funeral,' Kearney could only add.

A sauropod (a kind of bront but even bigger) made her way to the counter to order a round of drinks for her equally weighty companions. She half-pushed against Murphy and a shiver of cold repulsion ran down his back. His female friends gave him endless grief for being so 'superficial' in dismissing women who were not exactly 'lookers' but who could be 'really nice'. But he didn't care, he liked beauty whether it was in the shape of a woman or a piece of music or a tree.

'Why do you always go for looks?' Debbie Wright had often taunted him.

'So what do you want me to do - go for dogs?' was his standard reply, sometimes said with a certain amount of exasperated earnestness. There was usually a lot of wincing and annoyance after this proclamation, but he even cared even less than before as his sense of reckless abandon grew.

Some workmates of Kearney wandered in. Kearney exchanged pleasantries with these arrivals as Murphy had one of his many memories of those terrible days in Schull. His life was a nightmare of flashbacks and he only survived by having a doughty resilience which kept the temptations of suicide at bay. At that moment he was remembering his harrowing yet serene talk with Emily's father while he and his set were paying their respects at the family home after the funeral. This man was a retired sea captain, imposing, tall and cultured looking. He had an eerie and deceptive aura of serenity about him. He was gone beyond grief after the deaths of his two daughters in such a short space of time. Murphy was at a complete loss as to why the old man wanted to see him so soon and so privately after the death of Emily. It was a brief encounter. The old man was obviously very bright and was tuned into the life of his murdered daughter. In the end the meeting was not very consequential. It seemed that Emily had mentioned the existence of Murphy to her father and joked about the possibility of having a first date for years. It was the first time he heard her laughing since the death of her sister and it was also the last time he ever heard her joke about anything. Murphy it seemed would always hold a central place in the drama of his daughter's death.

As it was too early to head off to the Metropole Hotel where the Choral Festival crowd would be the rakes stayed on in The High C to see who or what would turn up next. As it happened the door opened and in came Ms Opera with a female friend. There was no sign of Earl and they had no idea of Earl/Ms Opera relations. They both still had a low opinion of Ms Opera - she was the ultimate small town snob, superficial and impressionable, with notions of her social status that had no bearing on reality. They could not comprehend what Earl saw in her and they knew very well that she certainly had no interest in him, as she knew that he wasn't very rich. She wanted to marry a pilot or an engineer, putting money above all else. She lived in a Mickey Mouse size apartment in one of the city's more prestigious areas. She could have bought a big house in another part of the city but then that area's name did not have the same social resonance about it. She and her friend stayed at the back of the bar, seated in a corner. The rakes were glad not to have to engage in exchanging social niceties with these shallow types. A few minutes later, the Motleys came in one by one, but as the bar was getting fuller the rakes also avoided the tedium of having to commune with them. So too with the Frumpies, who followed in *en masse* (in every sense of the word) after the Motleys.

'All we need now is the Frosties and we'll have the complete works - Motleys, Frumpies, Frusties and Frosties. Every man's social heaven,' Murphy chanted.

Some of the Motleys were actually making conversation with the Frumpies (and no annihilation resulted despite Murphy's prediction) while the Frusties stayed in their seats looking forlorn and slightly desolate in their faded beauty.

'Brightness falls from the air Queens have died young and fair,' Murphy quoted for no particular reason and launched into another pint of vitamin M.

***

The table was set in a cosy and informal way and there were even two bottles of Rioja reserve opened on the table. The homely smell of baked lasagne wafted all over the house and there were some CDs on top of the music system as if already chosen for the evening ahead - Corelli's *Concerti Grossi*, Bach's *Brandenburg Concerti*, Vivaldi's *Guitar Concerti*, King Oliver, Ella Fitzgerald doing Cole Porter. There was a log fire and the whole room gave the impression of an almost Dickensian cosiness made complete with the snow outside. Murphy often imagined arriving into such a scene with the beautiful and intelligent Emily there to greet him. Whenever he did have such a fantasy it was inevitably followed by the memory of what he encountered after opening the barn door... the noise of the wind, the eerie swinging of the rope, the stare in the dead woman's eyes, the smell of dung, the brutal terror...

***

Earl eventually sauntered in and joined his fellow rakes without noticing Ms Opera and her companion.

'So why aren't you shooting the breeze with Ms Opera?' Kearney asked.

'Ideological differences,' Earl mustered not at all unhappily. He was half-considering another round of internet dating, one last spin of the wheel - things could only get better. He scanned the bar and spotted a good looking Frosty and mentally took note, putting her (unrealistically) on his skirmish list. Only Molloy ever had a skirmish with a Frosty as such experiences were by nature alien to his fellow libertines. The Welsh rake usually only succeeded by telling a pack of ungentlemanly lies and the fallout was all grief and angst.

Meanwhile Murphy and Kearney discussed the disappearance of Sadie from their lives as Earl tried to make conversation with some Frosties he half-knew. They had not heard from her since Christmas and thought she must have been travelling. Murphy mentioned the esoteric George and suggested that they have a séance in the near future. Kearney only glared at this idea and Murphy let the topic drop. Time passed. The Motleys were still in the background, one looking at the floor while another looked at the ceiling and the third looking all over the place with not a word from any of them. 'Beam me up,' Murphy thought. 'Do the wrong people die or what?' Out of the blue his phone registered a text - it was the nymph asking to meet him the next day for lunch. He was quite happy to do so as there had been a kind of bond between them since the Christmas murder. He still didn't have any romantic thoughts about her (or anyone else for that matter) and didn't expect to have any in the near future, despite Kearney's insidious suggestions.

For Murphy death whittled things down to the essence. There was the trog universe - factual, brutal, deterministic, human nature at its despicable worst, people fundamentally selfish and greedy without any poetry in their souls. On the other hand, there was the universe of Emily and the nymph, the ethereal and the poetic, the mystical and the musical, the remote and majestic grandeur of the *B minor Mass*, the transcendental late Beethoven quartets, the universe in which people sacrificed themselves for a principle or a loved one, the realm of faith. His instinct leaned him towards the latter type of cosmos but his logical side and experience of human nature pulled him away and forced him to reject such a meaningful world. It was to be mankind as the 'quintessence of dust' rather than as the 'paragon of animals'. In the end the leap of faith into the darkness was too much for him.

The murder had put him into a kind of Limbo while his breach with the world of music was beginning to be severe. He looked haggard and dishevelled, there was darkness under his eyes and he was increasingly reckless in his drinking and thoughts. And the person he most needed to commune with was the absent and almost incommunicado nymph.

The bar was now fairly full though Ms Opera and the Frosties had left. The Sauropod belched and trundled off to the toilet, Doyle the wife beater slurped back another pint of lager, one of the Motleys uttered a few monosyllables, some types in the corner discussed soccer and an undersized Crusty of the hobbit class rolled a joint. The music was a surprise - Rachmaninov's *Third Piano Concerto* could be just about heard above the noise level - the throbbing strings of the opening followed by the romantic entry of the piano. For some reason this music always reminded Murphy of Boston in the thirties or forties - the winter snow, those big black curvy cars...

Earl was back saying that he had been impressed with the best looking of the Frosties and was considering making a date with her despite the drawbacks. As Murphy often noted in the past, of all the rakes Earl was the one who most needed the security of a long term relationship - he was not really a rake deep down but had just kept a certain rakishness going for want of anything better to do.

'One more here and then off to the festival club,' Kearney announced.

'Maybe we'll get lucky like last year?' Earl said hopefully.

'You mean you got lucky. I ended up with the virgin of virgins,' Kearney replied.

They were almost finished their drinks when Lorraine entered with a few of her girlfriends. All they needed - frigid women. To their relief, the frozen ones stayed well away from them, though Murphy caught a glimpse of Lorraine in the big bar mirror looking a bit flushed and embarrassed, as well she should have been after their Christmas liaison.

'We should definitely open a finishing school for young ladies with an emphasis on advanced sexual congress,' he suggested.

'And I suppose we'd have to do all the tutorials?' Kearney added.

They headed off to the festival club, avoiding occasional drunken trogs and gangs of trogettes shivering in their cheap, skimpy pink skirts and plastic white boots. Patrick's Bridge, as usual, was like the storm scene in *King Lear,* with incoherent denizens of poverty and alcoholism muttering and shouting at passers-by.

'*Poor Tom's a cold… the foul fiend bites my back… what art thou that dost grumble there in the straw?*' Murphy intoned as they crossed the river.

There was a good party atmosphere in the Metropole with a band playing jazz and big band numbers, with occasional songs from various foreign choristers in between. The rakes milled around separately and did their usual scan. Kearney was pleased to see a higher than usual percentage of dishy women to choose from and he wandered around aimlessly seeing who was there to seduce. He saw one leggy eastern European stunner, Russian probably, but she was in the company of some ugly Boris type and not likely to be free for a sapient colloquy on Peter the Great and Tchaikovsky and *Lady Macbeth of Mtsensk.* He then moved on and stood by the bar counter for a while. There was a bevy of Polish women at a table nearby, some of whom looked quite fetching but they seemed to have a lot of male company. As one of the women went to the bar to get a drink he engaged her in a conversation about the festival. She had good English but was a bit reserved in a coy kind of way. 'No congressional prospects,' he thought. She smiled at him and wandered back to the table. He had always liked the Poles and thought of how standards of music were so high in all those eastern European ex-communist countries. 'At least that was one good thing the commies did,' he mused. He remembered being at a concert in Warsaw one summer's evening. It was the most memorable

Beethoven's Ninth he had ever experienced - either live or on record. The conductor had such an amazing grasp of the work's architecture and the orchestra played as if on fire. There was a complete communion between audience and orchestra and such transparency of playing, such incandescence. After that, as he and a friend walked along a street towards the centre, they came across another concert going on in a Baroque church - so in they went and heard part of a dazzling performance of the Mozart *Requiem*. What a place for music compared to the dreary and philistine city they were now living in.

He then wandered on through the various bars of the festival club, getting into conversation with some local women he knew - and who frequented the same haunts as himself. There was a shapely woman in their company who he had not seen before. Her name was Nuala, she was quite tall and had a certain glint in her eye. He ended up joining them and started to engage her in conversation as the others talked about holidays, clothes, Coronation Street, car insurance, babies, *Sex and the City*, …

Murphy meanwhile found himself at the entrance to a kind of large alcove where people from lots of different choirs were milling around in between songs from various individuals. When someone sang the rest maintained a respectful silence and drank away happily. A tall sallow faced Russian lady, a fine woman as all the rakes would have described her, got up and sang the Gretchinanov *Credo* with some backing from a few of her friends. It was really impressive. Murphy could never get an angle on the Russians. They were so unfriendly when he visited St Petersburg, so endlessly gruff and dour. And yet, there was Tolstoy, Dostoevsky, Gogol, Tchaikovsky, Rachmaninov, Shostakovich… Maybe long decades of totalitarian rule did things to a nation's psyche. After the Russian singing, a few Italians, made happy by numerous pints of vitamin G, sang the drinking song from *La Traviata*. Murphy at this stage had managed to get a seat near the back and was more than happy to lose himself in the ongoing revelry. Such international gatherings were rare in the city. He sat there for ages drinking pints of vitamin M, the quality of which was not really satisfactory. He wondered what stories the nymph had for him and what her state of mind was like after recent events.

Earl was in a different part of the ballroom, spending a lot of the time ignoring Ms Opera and her friend who had turned up out of the blue. He was in the mood for a long night of congress with some nympho. His ears picked up when he heard an American accent and there on his left were a group of American women with not a man in sight. What was the catch? Surely they were not in a lesbian choir though knowing his luck... He started talking to the nearest of them - an ordinary enough looking Yank from some obscure town in Kansas where no one had ever heard of anywhere outside its state line. She introduced him to the others and he was immediately taken by an older woman (not quite an fb) whose name was Barbara Witch. He tried to keep a straight face when she was introduced and just about managed to succeed. She was certainly very friendly and he got her away from the group after a while, suggesting they go and listen to the band nearer the front. She seemed to be an American version of the Frosties - but he knew well that when Frosties were away from base they could be very naughty indeed. He bought her a whiskey and soda and she was well on the way to becoming merry. He was still not very sanguine about the prospects of having congress as he knew a lot of such women who used guys for company and free drink only to say goodbye at the end of the night with a chaste kiss on the cheek. However he gradually got to find out that she was resident in the hotel and, oh happy night, had a room all to herself.

It turned out that she was one of those who was more than aware of the limitations of her fellow Americans and was really interested in a world outside the shores of her own land. She was prepared to try and find out why her nationality was one of the most hated worldwide. She embodied much of what was best in Americans - an easy going friendliness which was not merely facile, an intelligent sense of humour which actually encompassed irony, a healthy and good looking physique, an appreciation of the material things in life without being obsessed by them, an openness and above all an optimism which people like Kearney would have found incomprehensible. As closing time approached Earl was getting more unsure of which way the cookie would crumble. Then it all turned out fine as she suggested he come with her to room 502. Just like that. 'Come with me to room 502.' When was the last time he heard a woman speak with such directness?

She was typically American in her sexual confidence even if she had been a bit out of practice. He got the '*a la carte* menu' rather than the 'menu of the day' so to speak. She wore (unsurprisingly) very tasteful lingerie and was very experienced in the art of slow seduction. She had a very attractive, tanned and athletic body. Her breasts were firm to buoyant and she was quite leggy and curvy in all the right places. She went through a lot of the usual sexual positions quite naturally and then, for what he thought was going to be a grand finale, engaged in a very long sixty nine, much to the enjoyment of Earl. He was amazed at her ability to keep going. She engaged him in lustful congress for most of the night and sleep didn't seem to be on the agenda. Alas for him she was to go to Kerry and places further afield on the following day and he would not be seeing her again, unless he planned a transatlantic tryst.

Meanwhile Kearney was getting on with his new contact Nuala and she seemed to be quite a sport compared to the rest of her set. When the time came to leave, she casually took hold of Kearney's hand and they went off to his place quite nonchalantly. Success for two rakes in one evening was not a common occurrence and Murphy would be impressed by the 'trend' Kearney thought. While he was not as badly afflicted as his fellow rake after the events in Schull he was still fairly shaken up. Like Murphy he kept as busy as possible and looked to all kinds of diversions to keep away from brooding over the death of Emily. The whole affair only intensified his nihilism and his attitude to the human race became even more pessimistic and cynical.

Murphy eventually went off home alone and had his inevitable, ongoing encounter with the Dog. He tried going to sleep after a long bout of reading a history of the Spanish Civil War but sleep eluded him. He looked out the window at the city lights shimmering down below and half-muttered *'Seest thou yon dreary plain forlorn and wild/The seat of desolation.'* Desolate was the word alright. A stage beyond depression, a feeling of being alone in an inimical universe with no prospect of any refuge, even of a temporary nature. The prospect of an unending dark night of the soul made death quite an attractive proposition.

***

Next morning Earl was in his usual café listening to his romantic adviser Natasha giving him her stock sermon on the meaninglessness of his amorous adventures.

'I really don't know which one of ye is the worst,' she lectured. 'You cannot go on being a tomcat. All these futile flings. I mean what do you really want? Are you going to be screwing women when you are sixty? Okay, are women going to be screwing you at that age? Surely you didn't give internet dating a chance?'

'Give me a break,' Earl countered. 'Internet dating is a last resort - apart from looking for the right woman in a convent.'

'Women aren't just sexual objects there for your gratification. Why don't you try and go to West Cork some weekend and meet real women. Not Schull after all that's happened - but what about places like Clonakilty?'

'So what am I to do? Book into a B&B in Clon and go down to the local pubs and announce myself?'

'Well why not? Better than your usual routine here. Same places, same people.'

'Wasn't the same people last night,' he boasted with the smugness of a tomcat.

'Well, you will be a long time waiting for another American nympho to come your way. Don't you remember your Confucius - desire is the cause of all human suffering.'

'She wasn't a nympho. She was just a regular American woman. Not like the irregular women we have to put up with here. And sod Confucius. Bet he never had an American babe.'

It was like Ground Hog Day most of the time - the same variations on a theme with the same people. His eyes wandered round the café as he talked to his unhappily married friend. There was a very fetching blonde at a table quite nearby with another female. He tried to stop looking at her but it was difficult. Where did such women go for a social life he wondered?

'You need to go to a clinic like Michael Douglas,' Natasha advised.

'Well you book me in,' Earl suggested.

'And I'll have to get you all some bromide tea as a matter of urgency. Imagine the chaos if all males were like you wolves. There'd be pandemonium to say the least.'

'Imagine if all women were as interested in congressional matters as us. Now there's a thought.'

Earl was lucky as his papa owned one of the city's biggest auctioneering businesses and he worked in the main office with plenty of flexibility for coffee and lunch breaks. He actually was successful in selling houses. He tended to overprice things if he didn't like the buyer and did the opposite if he liked her (it was usually a 'she' when it came to a lower price). His inconsistencies were overlooked by his long suffering papa. And in any case he didn't really come across that many dishy women who were buying houses. He had propositioned the pretty secretaries in all the offices of the company and had some success with a few of them until his exasperated papa gave him a stern hands off warning.

Kearney wandered in. Because he was a research scientist in the local university he had a certain amount of flexibility in his day as well. He sat down and told them the story of his latest encounter - casual congress with no certain future meeting in prospect. Not that he cared. It was a diverting skirmish and that was all. As the two rakes talked about the previous night Natasha thought that she did in one way envy the freedom they had and their ability to try different sexual partners on an ongoing basis. She missed the excitement of the chase and the romance of a liaison. Being stuck with one partner indefinitely was not a very satisfactory option in hindsight, and even worse was having a partner who had lost all interest in romance. However, she had been brought up in the arms of Mother Church and there was no way she could or would leave her overweight, boring, incommunicative, slightly simian, smug but rich husband.

Both rakes were a bit wrecked as it was quite unusual for two of them to have had conquests on the same night but the Choral Festival always was a bit of a sexual purple patch. Natasha did not of course articulate her thoughts about the joys of marriage and soon left them to do domestic chores and get hubbie's lunch.

'So who's the stunner over there?' Kearney asked Earl, nodding in the direction of the blonde.

'Don't know but she's a real beaut,' Earl exclaimed.

'Never saw her here before,' Kearney noted. 'Must come here at this time tomorrow. You never know.'

'Maybe Natasha is right,' Earl pondered. 'Maybe we need to go to a clinic for our lupine impulses?'

In any case he was in no humour for a serious conversation and had to go off home for a few hours in bed (thankfully alone). Kearney, being made of sterner stuff, stayed on reading *The Guardian,* and glancing occasionally at the shapely blonde who was now also alone. Time passed. She suddenly left and he looked at her disappearing curvy shape with a certain melancholy and weary desire.

Meanwhile Murphy woke late having fallen asleep about four in the morning. He had to meet Molloy and get an update on what had been happening over in Middle Earth. He thought the Welsh rake was planning a trip to Schull and this was not at all to his liking as he knew his fellow rake would want him to go along as well. All of West Cork, not to mind Schull, was out of bounds for him at this time. How could he look at the rugged scenery there and not be reminded of the horror? He got into the Saab and headed off to the local ferry port to pick up Molloy - the Welsh desperado was afraid of flying, something which really got on Murphy's goat. He had no patience with such a fear - what was the big deal?

As he drove along in the black Saab he unthinkingly put on the radio and was taken by surprise to hear the closing bars of Mozart's *Jupiter* Symphony. It was one hell of an exciting performance whoever the conductor was. He was more than moved as if it was a long lost friend suddenly found. The amazing finale was like summer, 'full of the warm south' and here it was out of the blue, such a surprise, such spiritual uplift despite all recent pessimism and grief. No less than five different melodies all interwoven into the most divine kaleidoscope of sound. Music from Mount Olympus - out of the clearest azure sky, a divine gift for mortals.

Later he let Molloy get his bearings while he went off to meet Jane at about four in the afternoon. Meeting her would bring the whole nightmare flooding back but at the same time she was the only one he really wanted to speak to about it all. He met her in a café which he didn't often frequent. He didn't want to meet other people he knew. She was already there when he arrived, dressed down as usual, though still quite fetching in an unconventional, demure kind of way. She never wore make-up but still looked better than a lot of dolled up Frosties he reckoned.

The reunion far less emotional than he had expected. They began by talking about her time in Oxford and she regaled him with a few stories about various academic types. Sleeping with lecturers to get good grades was still a custom that was alive and well. One particular don, one of Oxford's ugliest, seemed to have the highest bedding score, which reminded the nymph of the Second Law. She said that the rakes' laws of the universe were becoming common knowledge all over Oxford and that one of them should go and give a talk on the said laws, not to mind their associated axioms. She expected her studies to be finished by the autumn and then she was going to go on a world tour for at least a year, ignoring the advice of her career advisers.

'So how are all the wolves?' she asked.

'Oh the usual. Kearney seems to be getting even more nihilistic if that were possible,' Murphy informed her.

'And Schull? I take it that you haven't been back since?' she enquired gently.

'No, if that's a surprise. It has all been so strange. I mean I barely knew the woman and yet in other ways... And I haven't seen or heard from Sadie for ages. She may be out of the country.'

He thought they were going to talk more about Emily's brutal demise but she veered the talk away to other matters. After a while he mentioned that Molloy was going to Schull within a few days.

'In that case maybe we should go,' she suggested. 'At least go and see Sadie if she is on the planet. We can't avoid the place for ever can we?'

'We'll see,' he sighed unconvincingly.

It was such an awkward relationship in a way. They were both good at hiding their emotions and were also quite cerebral and rational when at times the opposite was what was essentially needed. Emily loomed above and about them but there was nothing more said about her.

'So what is the plan for later if there is a later?' she asked.

'Don't you have lots of people to meet? Parties? Boyfriends?' he probed.

'Not particularly,' she replied wistfully.

This always mystified him but he never said anything.

'Doesn't it ever bother you that we are all older than you?' he asked, changing the subject.

'Why should it. What a stupid thing to say. Ye are all quite diverting and underestimated.'

This was pleasing to hear at any time but coming from the Renaissance nymph it was a treat. He told her about the Choral Festival club and said he'd ring her later with a plan.

'Is Kearney going to be there tonight?' she asked a bit tentatively.

'We'll all be out - isn't there a full moon?' Murphy assured her.

Outside the day was still bright as spring was upon them. The streets were full of the tattoo/tracksuit brigade. The usual litter swirled around and the cracked pavements were full of puddles of various sizes. They passed a long row of ugly shop fronts complemented by an equally uncouth assembly of trogs. Above them there was a sky of towering cumulonimbus, growing higher and larger and more dramatic by the minute, fed by huge up currents. Murphy mused fleetingly that such a skyscape was the visual equivalent of the opening movement of Beethoven's Seventh, with its equally towering sense of architecture and energy, the build-up of enormous, creative, natural forces.

Sunlight glinted off the clouds as the nymph went off to her family home while Murphy headed for the Saab and the grocery shop. He had almost forgotten that there was a rake from Middle Earth to be fed. He still had no designs on the nymph despite all that Kearney predicted. On paper she was as close to the ideal as he was likely to meet (she could always get an orb job done). However the spark was not there and so that was that. He got back to the ranch to find Molloy engrossed in a history of the Allihies copper mines.

After both had a coffee Murphy went upstairs to look over his e mails. On his table there was a CD of Bach's *Well Tempered Clavier Book I*. He played it while checking his mails and then, having finished, he continued to listen to the ethereal music realizing that he was in no mood to face another evening on the town. However, with Molloy as guest and the nymph to meet, he had no choice other than put on a show and endure it all.

'So the story goes on. I'll have to go to Schull in the next day or so. Come along if you want,' Molloy said as Murphy entered the living room.

'I'll see. Not sure if I want to face all those people and places again at the moment,' Murphy explained.

'Like who? It would do you good in the long term,' the Welsh rake argued. You're hardly going to avoid West Cork for the rest of your life?'

Molloy did not fully realise the extent of Murphy's fragility and solitariness after the murder and was merely being well intentioned. He himself had had no contact with Rose for months. She persisted in telling the police that her unbearable husband was at home the night Emily was murdered, despite her text to Molloy indicating the contrary. Murphy spent a lot of time thinking how he would react if or when he came across McMicheal. He was not given to violence but, at the same time, it had its uses in dealing with the sub-human, scumbag side of human nature. After all, not all human life was sacred.

'Suppose we're doing the usual route tonight?' Molloy asked.

'Any better ideas? There will be a change later when we go off to the Choral Festival club. Earl and Kearney have already got lucky there. Course we've warned all females of your arrival and your sordid, lascivious, ruthless, conniving, amoral, caddish reputation. Welsh tomcat prowls around the festival club!' Murphy joked.

He was always open to new suggestions but the bottom line was that there was a terrible lack of choice in the city centre. There were the student bars which were okay once in the blue moon. Then there were the bars full of loud 'grunt and rap' music with gangs of trogs and lowlifes falling all over the place. And he certainly didn't like the characterless, factory type bars full of utter morons. In any case, he was getting vague notions of leaving the city again and going on another round of travels.

Some German choir was doing the Brahms *German Requiem* in the City Hall but he was not in the right frame of mind to go. There was also a choir, conducted by some woman he vaguely knew, doing some Renaissance motets in the School of Music but he'd just pretend he had attended if he was to meet her by chance in her usual haunt, The High C. A lot of people he knew in the classical music world however lived outside the world of bars and carousing and would have found the social round of the rakes to be completely meaningless, bizarre and futile. Their circles were self-contained oases of high culture scattered very thinly about the city. Ironically these were the very people that Murphy would have most liked to meet but their invisibility socially made them more than difficult to befriend. He could empathise with their attitude towards the pub scene but on the other hand...

'You forgot the Dog,' Molloy reminded Murphy as they walked down St Luke's towards the centre.

'He'll follow us later,' assured Murphy.

The sky had cleared and there was a spring like feel to the air. There was a full moon and the city spread out before them full of a promise and potential that were rarely realised. Molloy gave his fellow rake a rundown of his most recent adventures. The banker's wife had been removed from his congressional list as the liaison was getting too dangerous. However he had recently met an arty type in her early thirties who had lured him to her apartment on their first meeting and had seduced him. It seemed to Murphy that Molloy's exploits were like a run through the pages of the *News of the World*. Then again Welsh and English women were so forward and direct in comparison to some of the Vestal Virgins Murphy and Kearney had to deal with at times. It was the norm for Molloy to have sexual congress with at least two different women every week. He was not closed to the idea of a serious relationship but, as it happened, most of the women he got entangled with were married or divorced with children. He wasn't pushed about it all - if the right woman came along so be it. If not, the sexual merry-go-round would go on.

Murphy was in theory quite interested in having a serious relationship but not in compromising a whole lot. There were fairly okay women he knew who he could have married but he was going for the jackpot or nothing. In any case, one went through life alone and anything else was a bonus. There was also the consideration that most women wanted to procreate and he certainly didn't want to perpetuate himself - a fellow got one spin on the merry-go-round and he had no intention of being tied down by a brood of take, take, take sprogs. He knew so many people whose lives were a perpetual struggle to bring up a duo or trio of ungrateful, trying children who left no room in one's life for any space or spiritual freedom. As for the hassle in putting up with infants and all that stuff - it amazed him how so many people swore they didn't want offspring and then off they went and spawned a brood of noxious, ungrateful runts who became the bane of their lives.

Occasionally he would come across some really well mannered, bright and radiant child and think it would have been nice to have had 'one like that' but it was a rare wish and it didn't last longer than a few seconds. He could see from people he knew that offspring filled up a void in relationships as the romance faded away and there was less and less to talk about.

The rakes headed for The Shack. Murphy was in the mood for a real drinking session and Molloy was equally enthusiastic about the prospects of acquiring a new conquest. The others had not yet arrived and it was still a bit on the quiet side. Molloy was enjoying his vitamin M, and as there were no women worth looking at yet, they were shooting the breeze about alliteration in Old English poetry. The mention of *Beowulf* reminded Murphy of Schull and Sadie's retreat on the hill. This led on to a talk on the elemental nature of life in The Valleys with the preponderance of trogs and Neolithics, dilapidation and grime. Molloy had once had a slightly romantic vision of Wales but it was being seriously undermined by an influx of tattoo/tracksuit types who turned towns into frightening zoos, especially at night when they went on the rampage. Murphy, on occasional visits, was disgusted at the utter brutality and coarse nature of the denizens of the pubs in towns like Newtown. So many examples of human nature at its most odious and despicable. Then again the trogs were becoming a dominant force in Ireland as well and there was little to stop their forward march short of a revolution or a benign dictator who could eliminate them completely. As the two rakes went on about Celtic matters and the impossibility of Welsh independence, Kearney arrived in with his latest conquest, the flirty and confident Nuala. Earl was around somewhere while the Renaissance nymph was going to be late. Kearney was having an unusual spring fling in that Nuala was also only interested in a liaison. She used Kearney as much as he used her - it was mutual and there were no complications. He suspected that she was involved with someone in Dublin but he didn't really care. To outsiders it seemed that she was completely smitten by the rake as she routinely wrapped herself round him when they were in company.

Earl finally turned up and, after a few words with Nuala, he started talking to a trio of separated women who were fairly close to them. All three were in their early to late forties and were fairly well done up not to mind well sozzled. At first all went smoothly but as often happened he found that one of them was a rather embittered piece. She had a residual dislike, or even hatred, of men and this often resulted in vituperative scenes, especially when drink was involved. After a few minutes of small talk another of the trio commented to Earl, 'Oh your friend and his girlfriend seem to be really in love. They make a lovely couple.' Earl found this a bit of a laugh and he retorted typically, 'Oh they're only having a fling. Nothing serious. Spring impulses and all that.'

This really got on the gimp of the oldest of the trio and she exposed a real virago side to her nature by almost hissing at Earl, 'Why do you men always use women so badly. She should stay well away from him so!' The venomous nature of her tone made Earl turn his back and ignore the old bag. He got the message and that was the end of that.

'What a shower of battleaxes,' Earl said to the others instead. 'No wonder they're all separated.'

Murphy did point out that there was also another type of separated woman (who he encountered very occasionally). These were liberated from a frustrating marriage and were sexually confident and adventurous. Their children were grown up and they tended to be independent and liberal. He had a fling with such a woman a few months previously and she remained in his top five all time sexual encounters. Her name was Missy Atkin and he initially viewed her as a conservative goody goody. She was really a friend of a friend and having met her accidentally on the street one day he invited her to his house on the following Saturday. He had no notion of having sexual congress with her but after a late lunch they were in the warm drawing room with a view of the city lights shimmering as dusk was falling. She was wearing a fetching enough navy dress and once the conversation got round to romance she started quizzing him closely on past liaisons and girlfriends. Even at this stage he didn't really think his prospects very encouraging but he spun a few stories about past adventures and happened to mention the word 'seduce'.

'So how do you seduce someone?' she asked coyly.

He wasn't quite sure what to say in response. She was sitting on a large armchair facing the city view. He was a little further back so he got up and walked behind her.

He put his hands on her shoulders and said, 'Well it all depends.

Firstly you must know if the woman wants to be seduced. After that it's all very natural and easy.'

'So let's say I want to be seduced?' she purred.

He was taken aback a little. Some goody goody she was turning out to be, that is if she wasn't just playing a virgin's game.

He massaged her shoulders a little and she seemed to like this, reacting with a sensual shiver. Then he had to go across the 'line' and hope she wouldn't jump like a scalded cat. He slowly moved his hands down under her arms and gently placed them on her well sized (silicon) orbs. Her dress was very light and he could feel her erect nipples. She didn't seem to mind his exploring at all and he knew he was in for a torrid romp for the whole evening. She turned out to be one of his best ever sexual partners. She was passionate, wild and adored sex like a true nympho. Unluckily for him she shortly afterwards moved to the UK and so faded out of his life. Similar such women lived in the city but alas they were not at all easy to come across as in general they did not frequent bars and the haunts of the rakes.

The Renaissance nymph finally arrived and they were all struck at how pale and wan she looked. She was (uncharacteristically) wearing all black and this added to her pallid demeanour. She sat next to Murphy, and after the usual preliminaries, the conversation fractured into different themes - Earl talked to Kearney and Nuala about the pitfalls of internet dating while the nymph and Murphy talked about life at Oxford and the variety of things to do there. Molloy had disappeared, off on one of his extended walkabouts. Then the nymph got serious and told her fellow sufferer that there was talk about a memorial service for Emily to be held in Aberdeen and how she was expected to attend.

'So if I go will you come as well?' she half-asked and half-pleaded with Murphy.

He was not ready for all this and said he would have to see if he could get off work for a few days. He didn't like talking about the Emily tragedy in such surroundings so the subject was dropped and so they all finished their drinks and headed off to the festival club. The Bitter Lemon Trio gave Earl glares of disapproval but he just walked past them as if they didn't exist. Kearney reminded Murphy that their bet re the nymph was still on. Murphy smiled and started asking

Kearney's latest about her social life as they walked along through a crowd of leggy trogettes.

They got to the lobby of the hotel encouraged by the buzz about the place. Foreign types from all sorts of exotic corners came and went. Kearney ideally would have preferred to be without Nuala but wasn't too put out by her presence. It would just mean he would have to watch his fellow rakes do all the hunting. They went to the main ballroom for the second night in a row and this time there was a more frenetic atmosphere with a much bigger crowd. Murphy wandered around by himself for a while. He liked floating around aimlessly and bumping into tall babes from Uzbekistan. He was feeling more than usually reckless and had an even greater sense of abandon than usual. He took an automatic turn to the left when he saw the Frumpies in the near distance. He wasn't in the mood to humour the Bront and the Sauropod. He was annoyed that they were there - it was really not their scene. He bumped into a Frosty in his bid to escape from the dull Frumpies - more like he collided with her impressive celestial orbs. She was someone he vaguely knew to say hello to. She looked more nursey than teachery. He hadn't noticed before how impressive her orbs were so he stopped and asked her a few pc questions about the festival and her mummy and holidays. He then moved on, making a mental note to give her more attention in future. 'There are Frosties and Frosties,' he thought. He went back and mentioned the dreaded phrase 'Frumpy alert' to Kearney while Nuala was off somewhere.

'Give me a break!' Kearney reacted with vexation.

'Maybe they won't see us?' Murphy said wanly. Maybe they'll start doing their knitting in the lobby?'

Meanwhile Jane, looking demure, was sitting down listening to a small jazz ensemble. She shared Murphy's liking for occasionally losing oneself and letting things just float along. In any case, she was free from academic stress for a few days and needed to chill out. A girl could not live in the world of medieval knights and magic indefinitely. She was taken aback a little when she saw a Bibi lookalike but it was a false alarm. She was not at all happy in herself after her steamy liaison with the curvy Bibi - she couldn't understand how she had let it all happen so easily. She certainly didn't consider herself one of the sisterhood. It was just one of those things as the song said.

Earl came and plonked down a round of drinks at their table as

Jane rejoined them all. He had been smitten by a non-English speaking Croat while he was at the counter and was watching her commune with what appeared to be fellow nationals at a nearby table. She had the typical features shared by many eastern European women, with her fine bone structure and intelligent looking face. There were some people whose intelligence shone through so clearly just as there were the coarse and dim brutes who were on the Caliban level. Earl didn't see much point in trying to win her over because of the language barrier.

'So she's an accident?' he joked with Kearney.

'Absolutely,' the arch pessimist asserted. 'A mixture of atoms and nothingness. Soon to be all gone.'

'So what happens if you're wrong and we all meet in the afterlife?' Earl demanded.

Kearney picked up a beermat and let it drop to the floor.

'Extinction is as inevitable as that hitting the floor,' he pronounced.

'Well you are going to be one hell of an embarrassed angel if you're wrong,' Earl half-laughed.

Kearney was not amused. It was outside his comprehension to even consider the possibility that he was wrong. It was like trying to deny the existence of gravity or the other three fundamental forces that kept nature ticking over. Belief in an afterlife was a fairy tale, a saving illusion to keep the abyss at arm's length, the Big Lie perpetuated by tottering institutions like the Catholic Church to give the faithful some semblance of hope.

'Emily is NOT extinct you know,' Jane exclaimed all of a sudden.

They were all a bit taken aback at her tone, especially as she hadn't been in the conversation at all. Past conversations about such matters had been serious but were always sprinkled with a touch of humour. However this time her tone of voice had a new steeliness in it.

'Really? And how do you know?' Kearney demanded.

'There are times when I can sense her presence,' Jane averred. 'I just know! You can't tell me what I experience. There are ghosts in the machine.'

'Seems we'll have to have that séance after all,' Kearney said sardonically.

'That may not solve anything,' the nymph retorted with exasperation. 'You can't just expect the dead to turn up when you want them to!'

Kearney was surprised at her strength of conviction. Past conversations had always been of a general nature but now with the death of Emily there was a more personal side to the argument. It was an impossible impasse. There were two polarised opinions and absolutely no chance of a meeting place in between. What annoyed the nymph was Kearney's refusal to respect her side of the argument. It was as if she was some kind of loony astrologer such was his degree of contempt for any kind of belief in an existence after death. They let the subject drop as there was no point in going about it.

'Speaking of death, look over there,' Murphy announced. 'It's the bleeding Shroud of Turin.'

'The what?' the nymph asked.

'That woman over there with the mournful weeping Madonna expression, the one with the white top,' Murphy explained, pointing in the direction of a table a few yards away. He knew the woman from his days working in Heathrow. She had been a British Airways agent for a number of years and he had nicknamed her the Shroud as she was always so glum. She was one of those really passive, dull types who would never initiate a conversation and would just sit there expecting to be entertained. All stimulus-response. Ask her a question and she'd answer it and that was about all. A real pain at the best of times. She was one of those people with no poetry in their souls who lived in a world of pure fact. Why she didn't just jump off a cliff or stick her head in an oven was beyond him. If she had been a landscape she would have been an arid desert.

'You are so bad,' Jane smiled. 'You'll all come to a bad end.'

'Maybe we're in Purgatory already?' Kearney suggested with a touch of levity.

As if looking at the Shroud was not depressing enough there was a rustic oaf at the counter and before Murphy could avoid his glance he had been spotted. The brute was a friend of a cousin who lived in some remote place near the Cork/Kerry border. Murphy could only presume the creature was there for the drink and not the cosmopolitan company. He had met him a few times when visiting his cousin. He was one of those people who had the table manners of a polar bear. He ate with his big mouth open and spewed pieces of food all over the place. He was an earnest if blind supporter of Sinn Fein/IRA, a support based on an utterly ignorant, black and white view of Irish history. His ranted about Irish history as if he was some kind of history professor. He was the 'basic' model in all respects and had a self-important air about him which was so at variance with his coarse and ignorant nature. He strutted over to Murphy's table with his big gut hanging out of a dirty shirt. Murphy only hoped he wasn't going to join the company. He was in no humour for tolerating rural trogs. The brute, on the other hand, found a sense of moronic pride in being seen with Murphy's set. As it happened there were no free seats and so he stood talking to Murphy for a few minutes. There were no introductions. Murphy was praying for him to go away and jump into a big incinerator. When the oaf started eyeing the nymph he was really beginning to get on Murphy's nerves. All that was needed now was for someone to leave a seat and they would be stuck with the galoot for the night. He had absolutely no sense of being in the way or interfering. He was so egocentric that such thoughts didn't register. Fortunately for the company he went off to get another pint and got talking to some buck toothed, weight lifting sauropod for whose existence Murphy was eternally grateful. He had less and less tolerance for the brutes he came across in his daily life. And there were so many of them he thought wearily.

After a while the company broke up - Kearney wandered round with Nuala, Earl stayed put, content to listen to the music and cast occasional furtive glances at the curvy Croat, while Murphy and the nymph went off to an alcove where they had heard impressive singing on the previous night. They just about got into the alcove which was brimming with people and they stood against the back wall. Surprisingly, there was a pretty Czech violinist and a guy at the piano who had just launched into the opening bars of Beethoven's *Spring* sonata. The audience were very attentive, appreciative of such talent and spontaneous playing. However three heavy looking trogs barged in and stood near Murphy. To his consternation they talked as if they were at a football match or at the trough feeding. He was so enraged he literally gave the nearest a thump on the shoulder and hissed, 'Shut up or get out!'

The nymph was horrified and expected a huge brawl. A woman

next to Murphy held her breath. Others nearby approved of what he had said but were not so sure about the advantages of thumping a trog who had fellow Neolithics for back-up. However to everyone's surprise, not to mind Murphy's, they shut up and left after the first movement of the sonata had finished. Jane put her eyes up to heaven and smiled a wry smile. The woman near Murphy gave him an approving look. He enjoyed the rest of the sonata as it was played with panache and a lightness of touch. After that, various singers volunteered to sing all kinds of songs from light musicals to grand opera. The nymph was delighted to have been present at such musical revelry. When there was a pause in between singers someone she knew (one of her post-grad friends who happened to be on the other side of the room) shouted out to the pianist that there was 'a great Bach player' present, pointing at Jane who was aghast with embarrassment. Added to her woe was a very enthusiastic audience who gently pushed and cajoled her towards the piano. All this had Murphy bemused - while they had christened her the Renaissance nymph he didn't know that she had studied music as well. She sat down and there was an expectant hush as she tried to compose herself. She looked quite fetching in a cream linen jacket and jeans. He admired her coolness and versatility, her ability to glide through all sorts of scenes and happenings with such style. That was the word indeed. Style. Almost shades of the gorgeous Hélène Grimaud.

She played the opening aria from the *Goldberg Variations,* followed by the next five variations. Her playing was very impressive, crystal clear and not without a touch of the rhapsodic. There was a huge burst of appreciative applause when she finished and such was the crowd's delight that she had to repeat the fifth variation as an encore. Again there was wild applause as she excused herself from more playing by telling them all she was due a well-deserved drink. She got back to Murphy and they went out to the bar to get her a stiff whiskey.

'I am seriously impressed,' he enthused. 'How do you know the music so well?'

She explained that she had once mastered the first half of the *Goldberg Variations* for a big bet but that was a long time ago (at least for a nymph). Her late father was equally musical and she owed her whole musical education to his encouragement. Kearney would be impressed! There was no sign of the rest of the company so they stood by the bar and enjoyed their drinks. For the first time since Emily's death the two of them seemed more at ease in each other's company.

Meanwhile the trogs who Murphy had earlier put in their place happened to be milling around not far from him and the nymph. She noticed them first as they approached to exchange pleasantries.

'Look who's here. Our good friend the bouncer,' the ugliest of them said. He had glazed eyes and was clearly far back on the evolutionary ladder. Jane slipped away while Murphy faced the trio. He knew she would be getting help so he had to try and stall them before things got serious.

'So why don't you all just crawl on home to your caves or wherever you go when you need to vomit?' Murphy replied, much to their astonishment.

One of them had a bottle in his paws and was about to use it as a weapon against Murphy's head when several of the hotel bouncers appeared. One of them tried to take the bottle from the simian scumbag but the latter managed to land a blow across the cheek of the bouncer. This really enraged the other bouncers and all hell indeed broke loose as the three trogs were literally hurled out of the bar and into a paddy wagon outside on the street.

'Three reasons for not believing in God,' Murphy quipped to the nymph as they continued enjoying the free drinks given to them by the bar staff.

'And how many reasons for believing are there in the *Goldberg*?' she countered.

'Indeed,' Murphy said, not really wanting to get back into <u>that</u> conversation again.

The problem with the trogs who had been evicted was that they would be in the city centre another night and there might not be bouncers about to deal with them he thought. In any case it was nearing closing time. Earl was to be seen at the table of the Croats having some kind of sign language going with the woman he had earlier admired. As the nymph and Murphy were wandering through the hotel lobby they came across Molloy, who was after more than his usual quota of vitamin M.

'Where the hell were you?' Murphy asked the Welsh tomcat.

'It's a long story and you won't believe me in any case,' he replied wearily.

As was often the case Murphy would indeed believe him as the Welsh tom cat was always getting himself into the most incredible and bizarre situations. It seemed that he had earlier met some Ukrainian siren in the hotel who had lured him to her room. She was very sexy and alluring but unfortunately for him it was not going to be a purely romantic encounter. She was a hooker and demanded three hundred euros as soon as they were in her spacious room. He was indignant and annoyed at this turn of events as she had showed no sign of being a pro when they first met. She wouldn't let him leave and he didn't want to cooperate. She then rang someone and a few seconds later a heavy looking orc arrived. He was seriously ugly and demanded that Molloy pay the 'lady' or face the consequences. There was a long period of arguing. Molloy protested that he didn't have that much money with him so the orc suggested he visit a nearby cash link machine. Molloy had no choice but to go along. As they approached the cash point he decided to do a runner. He was nothing if not fit and he could leave a lot of people far younger than him far behind in a race when it came to the crunch. As they got to the machine he legged it down towards Patrick's bridge and then shot along the main street with amazing speed. He ended up in a police station where he told his story to a sympathetic policewoman. He was driven back to the hotel in a police car, much to his amusement. There was no trace of the orc or his alluring partner. He was about to get a taxi back to base when he spotted Murphy and the nymph.

'Aren't you coming with us for a nightcap?' Molloy asked Jane.

'No I'm not. And you should go and read a book and be a good boy,' she advised. 'You're in enough trouble now with the Russian mafia after you.'

She went off into the night leaving the two rakes to get a taxi back to base.

'I can't believe you tried to lure her back. You are a complete sleazebag,' Murphy admonished his guest. 'I wouldn't even trust you with my wife. You are utterly incorrigible and you have no bottom line.'

Molloy smiled at such praise and wasn't too unhappy to go home without a conquest considering how much worse things could have been. As the taxi passed through Patrick's Street there was a huge brawl taking place outside the old Savoy building. They crowd fighting seemed to be all in their early teens and there was a significant number of females involved. It seemed to be a serious enough affair with blood all over the place and broken bottles and knives being used.

'Trogs fighting trogs,' Murphy said to Molloy.

'No big deal. So long as they are only killing each other there's no harm done,' Molloy asserted.

The taxi had to slow down as there were so many people on the street, while a bottle landed on the bonnet and skimmed across onto the ground. Up close the rakes could see an assortment of individual fights. Two trogs were kicking a guy on the ground who seemed to be in a lifeless state. Another group were wrapped around each other with trogettes pulling at each other's hair and screaming all sorts of interesting profanities. A foursome of brutes were hell bent on cutting each other to pieces with a few nasty looking daggers. The police and ambulances arrived with wailing sirens but it would take quite some effort to restore calm.

'They need a few of those big hoses for crowd control,' the taxi driver commented as he drove past the melee.

As Murphy was walking in the driveway of his house he got a text from the Bach playing nymph reminding him to think about the memorial in Aberdeen. How could he refuse her? Molloy was too restless to shoot off to bed and so Murphy poured the two of them a large Hennessy as they sank into armchairs looking out at the city lights glimmering in the distance. He mentioned the yokel he had met from the Cork/Kerry border - where the men are men and the sheep are nervous. He rattled on a bit about the baseness of human nature. Molloy insisted that the brutish side was balanced out by the spiritual and the artistic. Murphy strongly disagreed.

They sipped the cognac while Molloy brought up the topic of McMicheal. It was a very difficult topic for Murphy - McMicheal was indeed the only suspect for Emily's murder but they could not be conclusively definite. In any case, there was now an even greater fear lurking around the Schull area with a possible double murderer lurking about.

'What about a hitman?' Molloy suggested with complete

seriousness.

'As in how? Too dangerous. We'd be traced,' Murphy said.

'Think of the double advantage,' Molloy enthused. 'McMicheal would be done for the murder, if not murders, and Rose could have her life back.'

'Well why the hell doesn't she just get up and go in any case?' Murphy replied with an air of exasperation.

There were so many women like Rose. Murphy knew a woman living in a north Cork town whose husband was a complete monster. He was pathologically possessive and even timed her visits to the local gym. She had a good job of her own but like Rose she did not have the will or the courage to just walk away. Men like her husband had a power over them and he supposed they feared such husbands more than they desired to be free.

'In any case let's go down there for a day or two. No point in me having a house there if it's not used,' Molloy suggested.

'We'll see,' Murphy said quietly.

Part Eight

SPRING IN THE CITY

The outsider, a figure who arouses interest in most cultures, whether he or she is interesting in themselves or not, is at an unusual disadvantage in Cork. The native community is so self-contained that it needs nothing beyond itself to add spice or difference to its comfortable and familiar flavours... It does not reject newcomers; it simply does not see them.

Paddy Woodworth
"Internal Exile in the Second City" (from The Cork Anthology)

181

They were all in a bar called The Woodbourne in the centre of town - though it seemed more like a café than a bar during daylight hours. It was a big and spacious place with shafts of light coming in big windows which faced out onto a busy street. It was mid-morning and the three rakes were there with the nymph and Emma Larchfield. Earl was due to turn up but was late as usual. Kearney's latest conquest was *en route*. They were all there at Murphy's suggestion of a hill walk later in the day. At the counter there was a real dipstick who Murphy and Kearney took a special dislike to. He was an ungainly and obnoxious pseudo-intellectual of the worst kind, who was always at the edge of various circles whether it was the film festival or some art exhibition opening. Murphy especially took exception to his endless smugness, not to mind the impression he gave of knowing everything about the arts and sciences, when in fact he was a complete bluffer who lived in a world of mere facts, a world where all things poetic were alien to him. He was a good friend of the runt Emma had been seeing but the rakes did not want him in their circle at any cost. Cork was such a small place - once someone like Pseudocream became too familiar he would haunt them indefinitely and the only remedy would be to find new places to socialise or else to eliminate him altogether. Emma's circle was suspect at the best of times and some of her friends were candidates for a mass grave. 'Too many egomaniacs and too little space,' Murphy had often commented.

The rakes and company were going on about the expanding, accelerating universe and morning grouches and sex without alcohol and BIBs (big ignorant breakfasts). Molloy was trying to cope with the difficulty of doing without daily congress. Murphy was telling them of some updated news - Bibi, he had been told, was going to live in Dublin. Grace, meanwhile, wasn't to be seen again until after her nuptials as Lance was afraid she'd do a runner if she kept meeting Kearney. And last but not least, there were rumours that Fatima was not in a good state after being roughed up by the one and only Satan.

The conversation veered round to the Choral Festival. Murphy had originally considered going to the closing concert but tickets for the balcony in the City Hall were all gone, mainly to corporate booking. This really annoyed him as there would either be lots of empty seats or else the 'see and be seen' set would be occupying them: business types and local 'dignitaries' who didn't know Mozart from a banana sandwich.

'Speaking of bananas, if that idiot even comes near this table I'll go spare. There are some people I take a complete and immediate dislike to and he is one of them. What a complete dipstick,' Murphy declared to Jane as he saw Pseudocream glancing over enviously.

A woman Murphy vaguely knew came in and sat at a table fairly close by. Murphy raised his eyes to heaven as she took her seat.

'And what's wrong with her?' the nymph asked.

'Give me a break. She's straight out of a J.B. Keane play. She meets this guy once a week in a suburban bar and they tuck into the same BIM (big ignorant meal) every week. Then they go back to her place and have congress and that has been going on for the last nine years. Seems he lives with his mammy and doesn't want to 'extend' the relationship.'

Murphy continued talking to the nymph. At least she wasn't a morning grouch. There were some people he knew who were completely out of bounds for at least an hour after they got up. They were always in such bad form and unable to function until enlivened by strong coffee. This was another group Murphy had little patience with - life was short enough without all this grumpiness so early in the day.

Meanwhile Molloy was fascinated at the antics of a fat, ugly woman at the next table. She was with a man who seemed to be her long suffering husband. He was thin and wiry and didn't look at all happy. While he was sipping a coffee intermittently, Dragon was launching into a full Irish breakfast and by God she was going to lick (not to mind eat) the plate as well. Her side of the table was a complete mess and she was spewing bits of rasher rind out of the side of her big fishy mouth. Molloy could only imagine the squalor she lived in judging by the condition she left the table in. There was sugar spilt as well as pieces of toast and a pool of tea around her plates. After the BIB she ordered a chocolate éclair and Molloy looked on in fascinated disgust as she squashed half the cake into her gob in one mouthful. There was cream on her nose and moustache - Molloy looked away in disgust as Jane smiled in sympathy.

'Imagine sharing a bed with that heap of blubber,' he said aloud to no one in particular.

Nuala breezed in about this time and there was more shooting the breeze about diverse matters. Kearney made a special effort to be 'nice' to Jane as he felt slightly guilty about his dismissiveness towards her on the previous evening. Emma was telling Murphy that the world at large was amazed that Jane had not been snapped up by either himself or Kearney.

'And what about the age difference?' Murphy asked Emma, not for the first time.

'It doesn't make a difference in this case, when there is an obvious meeting of minds,' Emma advised. 'Maybe you are afraid to get seriously involved?'

'That angle doesn't work so forget about it,' Murphy explained. 'As for the meeting of minds - yes I suppose there is that and all. But life is not a fairy tale just because people theoretically suit. No chemistry, no romance. Get it?'

'Maybe it could develop?' Emma persisted.

'Maybe it could. What do you want me to do in the meantime - rent some?' Murphy replied sarcastically.

Meanwhile Dragon, having finally finished her extended breakfast, trundled off with her sidekick while Pseudocream scuttled off a bit later. The company finally gathered their things and headed off for the planned hill walk. The nymph, out of habit, took the passenger seat in the Saab with Molloy and Emma in the back. Kearney drove with Nuala and Earl in a battered old VW Beetle that Kearney thought was a piece of class while everyone else thought it was an ongoing embarrassment. Murphy mulled over the constant flack he was getting about the nymph - people were so predictable in their perceptions. As if life was not complex and surprising. Surely there were all gradations of relationships? Why people had to simplify everything down into silly Hollywood notions of romance. They drove towards Macroom and then took 'a severe left' just before the town that 'never reared a fool' and headed for Inchigeela.

'Not so sure I agree about the bit about the only town that never reared a fool,' Murphy said as they veered away south west.

When they got to the scenic village of Inchigeela they took the South Lake road and headed for Shehy mountain, a good choice for the first venture of the new hill walking season. It was an easy walk more than a climb. The scenery was indeed spectacular - to the south west was the rugged Beara peninsula in the far distance. The Kerry mountains were seen to the north west and even Cork could be made out thirty odd miles to the east. They had some food on the summit and Murphy was especially relieved to be away from the trogs and the lowlifes of the city. He felt a pang of pain as he took in the wild scenery in the general direction of Schull. He would probably go there with Molloy the following day. He had to face the place sooner or later and sometimes sooner was better - otherwise he would have to avoid one of his favourite places indefinitely.

As they all trekked down the mountain he asked the nymph if she was going to go to Schull. She was unsure but when he mentioned his possible trip with Molloy she assented. He was still amazed and surprised at her piano playing of the night before. So what indeed were her faults or weaknesses? He was indeed hard pressed to come up with some. She could commune with paupers and princes. She was musical, witty and intellectual; she had a natural intelligence unlike the narrower sort possessed by most academics; she could play a good set of tennis and enjoy a day at the races; she had a very original mind and, as he had often said to the others, even her handwriting was classy. In the looks department she was tall and lithe and good looking in an understated kind of way. Her only weakness physically (apart from her small orbs) was a tendency to be pale and to border on the gaunt on occasion. Perhaps she was a bit too controlled but then again who was he to talk? Some people found her cold and inaccessible but these were generally a bit overawed by her.

They got back to the cars in the late afternoon and headed off in the general direction of the city. They made one stop at a roadside pub in a small village and had one round of drink. The village idiot was at the counter as they sat at a table near a turf fire and he kept staring at the women as if they were aliens who had just landed from some remote part of the galaxy. Jane winked at him eventually and he suddenly scuttled off back to his shack on some remote hillside.

Murphy liked old fashioned bars with real log fires. The walls were lined with old photos and there was an old valve radio (wireless) on a shelf next to photos of De Valera and an infamous Provo warlord, guilty of many cold blooded murders. Murphy winced when he saw the smiling face of this psychopath - he often thought of a line of Chaucer whenever he saw his loathsome photo: *'The smiler with the knife under the cloak.'*

'The lowlifes get away with so much murder,' he mused to himself, not wanting to start another colloquy on the dreary, sectarian North. Dusk was falling but light still shone through the dirty windows.

'That scent should be canned and sold in the USA,' Emma suggested as the aroma of burning turf wafted all over the bar.

'That's one country where you could sell it and become a millionaire,' Kearney informed the company. 'I've seen cans of Irish air on sale in Boston.'

'There is another side to the Yanks,' Jane spoke out.

'Oh no, not another run in with Kearney,' Murphy thought.

'And what side would that be?' Kearney joked. 'You mean they have more than one?'

'Very funny. They are not all morons,' Jane asserted. 'Remember the Vietnam war - they didn't all go with the flow. There are the ten percent who know what is going on and can even speak foreign languages! They did get to the moon you know? Some are really embarrassed to have idiot presidents. And they are not all beached whales.'

'Indeed,' Kearney admitted. 'But you must admit for all their wealth and power they could do so much better - in treating their own people not to mind the outside world.'

'Agreed,' she replied.

For some reason the debate fell flat and there wasn't the usual repartee or sparks. The last daylight had gone and it was time to hit the road and face the trogs and other sub-groups. Sometime later as it happened the nymph invited herself to Murphy's place - her mama was having a few of her awful relations for high tea and she didn't want to be anywhere near them. So Murphy found himself in the kitchen with her while Molloy vegetated in the front room and had a beer while looking out at the city lights.

'I suppose you have a few degrees in *haute cuisine* as well?' Murphy teased.

'Not exactly,' she said with some irony. 'But why don't you go and have a beer and discuss independence for Wales with Molloy and I'll rustle up something here. I am the woman after all, and you boys really think this is the place for us.'

Murphy went off only too happy to be free of cooking duties. He found Molloy wondering when he was going to get himself a wench.

'JFK wasn't the only one to suffer if he didn't have congress every day,' the Welsh tomcat complained.

'Well, don't panic,' Murphy advised. 'You can always bring a wad of notes and pick up a Ukrainian babe in the festival club.'

They started on about the lack of sexually brazen women and brothels and other matters relating to Molloy's main reason for living. Gradually they noticed unusual and slightly exotic odours coming from the kitchen. Murphy tried to go and see what the nymph was up to but she told him to go away until she called them.

'If you put her in a novel people would not believe you were all there,' Molloy quipped.

Jane eventually allowed them into the kitchen and they sat around the big pine table as she tossed a simple radish and fennel salad. The dressing was exceptional and the rakes were impressed yet again.

'For the main course, especially for hungry wolves, there is roast breast of chicken with roasted asparagus and some cherry tomatoes, black olives and basil,' she announced.

The roast chicken was simple but she had jazzed it up with various herbs and whatever and once again they were all appreciation and compliments. For dessert she had conjured up a simple but very tasty fruit crumble - all golden and hot on top with the most exquisite blend of fruits underneath.

'All I can say after all this feast if that if he doesn't marry you then I will,' Molloy declared.

'Off you go,' Murphy retorted. 'There's the best offer you've had all day,' he said, turning towards the nymph.

She just smiled one of her pale smiles and took a large glass of wine into the front room, telling the two rakes to do the wash up. After that there was a kind of lull as they had some time before going to meet the others. Molloy lost himself in a book on Seamus Heaney, casting occasional glances at the nymph, who in turn was practising some Beethoven *Bagatelles* on the piano, while Murphy was in his sanctum checking e mails and making himself generally scarce. There was also a sweeping view over the city from the second floor and he could see a full moon and a few stars as he finished off various mails. He couldn't help but feel the presence of the nymph as her playing echoed round the house. If all his circle had its way he would just go and propose to her. 'Give me a break,' he half-muttered to himself as he came back downstairs.

'Everyone got their anti-trog spray and bullet proof vests?' he asked his two guests as they readied for a night on the town.

He wasn't in the humour for yet another night in the centre. He was fed up of the same places and the endless hassle with trogs and other prehistoric types. He would have been quite happy to stay in and read himself to sleep, even with the Dog about.

They walked down St Luke's and went along McCurtain Street which had the usual few winos and Crusties heading for their drinking dens. They passed through Coburg Street which was a bit dimly lit and had a few real types hurrying off on their high heels to meet various primates. An occasional sad looking African passed them. They passed the brutally ugly Stalinesque wall of the Opera House and went along past the river towards the Coal Quay where there were still one or two old fashioned bars. As Molloy talked to the nymph Murphy was more than happy to walk a few paces behind them and muse. He did think she had a certain attraction but whatever the world said there was just not enough chemistry. When he thought about Emily or Sadie there was just no comparison in terms of sheer physical attraction. The very vaguest of hints that she could really be in the sisterhood flickered across the furthest part of his consciousness for a fleeting moment but he immediately dismissed such a notion. She was communing in an animated fashion with the tomcat about the fortunes of Welsh coal mining villages. If there was one thing she was good at was tuning in to people with a real naturalness. Murphy liked such people who could change stations, depending on who they were with. She could tune into everything from long wave to short wave so to speak, without the least effort or strain.

Patrick Street was the usual mixture of louts gathered outside fast food joints and small gangs of trogs going to meet their fellows. The air of threat was not tangible yet - that usually developed a bit later. As usual there wasn't a policeman to be seen. In the Market Lane Inn they got a table at the back and it was a relief to savour a round of drinks without hassle. This bar did not usually have many trogs about but there were a few types like Pseudocream scattered here and there as well as an assortment of Frosties and Crusties. There were also a few journalist and arty types who always seemed to wear the same clothes and sit on the same stools. Kearney joined the company just as he got a text from Nuala, ruling herself out of the night's proceedings.

'We can all see you are overwhelmed with disappointment,' Molloy said with some irony. 'No lopsy paw tonight for you.'

'Completely grief stricken,' Kearney returned.

Next to them was a group of American women who seemed to be in the city as part of the Choral Festival. They were all a bit on the plain side except one, who in Molloy's eyes was a definite nine plus. He got into conversation with her and it seemed that she actually had been living in the city for more than a year while the others were just visiting. She was doing some course in the university and he quizzed her about living in the city of trogs and dogs.

'Well it does, dare I say, seem to live up to its reputation for being on the cliquey side,' she said hesitantly.

'Don't you find it a friendly place?' the rake continued.

'Not at all,' she elaborated. 'Not at least compared to other places. People are friendly enough in the shops or if you ask for directions. But overall I can't say I am overwhelmed with the natives. They seem so self-contained socially.'

'And what about romance?' Molloy delved delicately.

'Well for sure the men here can't really take the direct approach,' she averred. 'It seems to me that they can only talk to a new woman after a lot of lager. Maybe being American doesn't help. I mean we seem to be hated everywhere. Only those obnoxious Israelis seem to be more hated than we are. And we're not all bad you know. Some of us are even educated for God's sake.'

Kearney and Murphy were beginning to listen in and were amused to meet one of the 'ten percent' who was okay and well up on things. She told them she had to go off with her friends and Molloy said they'd all be at the festival club later.

'So guess who the big bad wolf is after?' the nymph asked the

189

others after the Yanks had moved on. Molloy indeed had that lupine look on his face. Murphy assumed he would not be coming back to the ranch that night. He was such a sleazebag.

'So what about her remarks on how unfriendly we all are?' Murphy asked the others.

'She's right. I know people in this city who go for years without meeting new people,'

Kearney said.

'We don't have a clannish and cliquey reputation for nothing. I think all this crap about the friendly Irish is really off the wall, not to mind about this city,' Jane ventured to suggest.

'Charming talk in front of a visitor,' Molloy reminded them. 'Whatever about you horrible paddies, I am friendly as she will find out later.'

'What number will she be? You must be close to the three hundred mark?' the nymph asked him sarcastically.

'About that, child,' Molloy replied.

'Don't child me you randy tomcat!' she retorted.

Murphy was amused. He liked that spirit in a nymph. As she and Molloy went on one of their occasional tangents about medieval poetry, Murphy and Kearney continued the conversation brought up by the American.

'There is definitely a lot in what she says,' Kearney averred. 'Consider the people who own the bars we frequent. I have been going to The Wild Geese for years and even though the same people still own it not one of them knows my name. I spent a year in Antwerp and I could go to three bars where not only was I known by name but the proprietors often stood me a freebie.'

He went on this vein for a while until Murphy noticed a woman come in who was on his skirmish list and who was talking to Fred Astaire of all people.

'Better not stare at Pearl or we'll be in the doghouse with Fred again,' Kearney advised Murphy.

Murphy had christened her Pearl one night as she was at a table in candlelight and she reminded him of Vermeer's *Girl with a Pearl Earring.*

'That little bearded dollop really needs to be put back in his hobbit hole' Kearney ranted.

'He is so goddamn self-righteous and pseudo. What a total dipstick. The way he struts around the place like some Venetian *doge*. And she probably thinks he is some sort of high intellectual.'

Murphy caught Pearl's eye as she was talking to Fred. There was a flicker of a smile. Fred looked over. Murphy and Kearney started staring at Pearl and Fred turned away in nervous and flustered distress.

'Spare me. What about a skirmish?' Murphy asked.

'Forget it,' Kearney snapped. 'She'd want to get married first. Waste of space. And look who her friends are.'

Jane was looking at the two Irish rakes while Molloy went on and on about some Welsh metrical structure in one of his poems. She caught Murphy's glance and there was for a millisecond a rapport, a kind of spark, a mutual smile of complicity. It was so fleeting he wondered if it had been his imagination. Molloy eventually rejoined the conversation. Kearney asked him for his esteemed opinion of Pearl.

'Fred will really get attitude if one more starts looking at her,' Murphy advised.

'Bit on the rough side,' Molloy opined.

'I can't believe it. You of all people. Your standards go down to non-league levels and you call her rough. You cannot be serious,' Murphy said John McEnroeishly.

'Well I wouldn't say no,' Molloy replied.

'You wouldn't say no to anything that looked remotely female,' the nymph admonished him with a smile.

'I'd say no to you,' Molloy could only reply.

'No you wouldn't. You would be sooo lucky though.'

The banter went on and they eventually left, passing Pearl, who gave Murphy another amused half glance.

They arrived at The Short Hill to find it fairly full of the usual amount of nondescript types, and a few ossified Crusties at the round table at the very back of the bar. Murphy had often said to the nymph that she should set up tours for students of the Middle Ages to come to these kinds of places. They were so very medieval in their elementary roughness and appearance not to mind the noises the denizens uttered, all kinds of guttural grunts and raucous shouts. Molloy had a quick scan to see if his new American lady was about but there was no sign of her. Numbers from Ry Cooder's *Jazz* album wafted in the background, giving the place a surreal feel. A Romanian girl served behind the bar. Murphy got the impression that she was very unhappy and downtrodden. There was no sense of friendliness between her and the owners. If the American found the place unfriendly what chance did this poor girl have? She was tall and pretty with dark eyes and had the look of a country girl. Where was her family? How did she manage? Most customers didn't seem to consider for a moment that she was actually a person just like them. Whenever Murphy tried to engage her in conversation she seemed nervous as if he was an immigration official about to take her away. She seemed so gentle and so lost.

'Schull tomorrow I suggest,' Molloy asked the company after they had all started on another round of drinks.

'Count me out. I'm busy,' Kearney announced.

'That leaves us two,' the nymph said to Murphy, much to Kearney's amusement.

'Better not make it too early. I mean, you'll be wrapped around Sharon Stone in the morning,' Murphy told Molloy.

'You may miss the séance if you stay away,' Jane told Kearney.

'Well if there is a definite séance then let me know,' he said. 'That I wouldn't want to miss for anything.'

'Are you ever going to see Rose again?' she then asked Molloy.

'Not very likely,' Molloy sighed. 'The police told me to stay well clear. And anyway I'm not sure if she's still down there.'

'I wonder if Sadie will ever answer a text or a phone call again. Maybe I should try again just in case?' Murphy said.

'Good idea,' Molloy agreed. 'Maybe she's left William and is waiting for you?'

'Are you really interested in her?' Jane asked Murphy while the others were shooting the breeze about mass murdering Fred Astaire, Pseudocream, the Motleys and a list of other losers.

'Well she is very attractive but she's spoken for in any case and so what's the point?'

'You never know. Maybe she'll leave William for your charms?'

'Yeah right. And Molloy will join the Jesuits. And the Motleys will become polysyllabic.'

In any case he sent Sadie a short text saying they would be in Schull on the morrow. There was no immediate reply. He went to the counter to get a few drinks and there next to him was this Frusty he kept thinking was a nurse. He was even more impressed than before at her looks. She was wearing a slightly suggestive top which revealed a stunning pair of grade A celestial orbs. Would he or what! Pity about her attitude though - she was almost certainly goody goody material. They exchanged the usual few words and he went back with a second mental note made. He'd try to get into her favour one of these days as a prelude to tasting her orbs. The Romanian almost smiled at him but she seemed too distracted and sad to pay much more attention. When he got back Kearney was on one of his spiels about Gauguin and his adventures in Tahiti. He was impressed at the artist's ability to acquire nymphets (as well as his ability to paint).

'Very touchy topic these days don't you think?' Molloy said to them all.

'Western civilization had different ideas to those of the East and the South Seas, not to mind a lot of other places,' Kearney reminded Molloy.

'Not to mind Middle Earth and Newtown in particular,' Murphy added. 'The nymphs over there are a breed apart. Grown up at sixteen. All attitude and skimpy skirts. Saucy, coarse, low, trog-like, generally dim, tattooed, smoky, track suited, cheap - and available if you're down low on the evolutionary ladder.'

'Just like here?' Jane added.

People came and shot the breeze with the various rakes as they passed by and milled about. Molloy kept scanning for new victims. After a while Jane and Kearney got back to the conversation with

Murphy on his fellow rake's side but having a certain sympathy for the nymph's position.

'So what is soul exactly?' Kearney asked. 'So many people use the word without having a bloody clue what the word means.'

'Soul and mind are the same I think,' the nymph sermonised. 'The brain dies. It is obviously physical. But it produces non-physical things like ideas and thoughts. Our minds.'

'But when the brain dies so too does the mind,' Kearney pointed out.

'Well how do we know?' she persisted.

'It's obvious,' Kearney declared. 'The mind can only exist as long as there is a physical brain to sustain it.'

'Not necessarily,' the nymph stated obdurately. 'But there is a more important angle on all this. Don't you ever have an epiphany?'

'Course he does. Whenever he sees a ten,' Murphy interposed.

'Get lost,' the nymph reprimanded Murphy with a disdainful look.

'And what is your definition of an epiphany?' Kearney asked her patiently.

'A sudden spiritual manifestation of the numinous,' the nymph enthused.

'We're going round in circles,' Kearney said wearily. 'We'll be stuck in language all night and we still won't get anywhere. Seems it all comes down to individual experience. Why only some people have these epiphanies is another complicated question. They are either saving illusions or they really are what she says they are.'

'Yes but you willfully go out of your way to not even consider the possibility of a world beyond yours,' she scolded Kearney. 'Bet you had an unhappy childhood,'

'Terrible. It makes Oliver Twist's seem like a treat,' he informed her.

Murphy jumped a little. 'Frumpy and Motley alert. Now what's the opposite to an epiphany? Well whatever it is we're all about to have one.'

Kearney groaned. He was in no mood for another of these alerts. At least they were moving on to another bar in any case.

'Look. Bront's wearing leather trousers. Anyone got a camera. We could win a prize,' Murphy said to Jane with mock enthusiasm.

'You will all come to a bad end. Do I have to keep reminding ye?' she said plaintively.

'But all I said was something factual,' Murphy reminded her.

She hit him on the shoulder as they all headed for the door, Kearney going last and wearing one of his Heathcliff on the moors scowls. Outside there was a group of four thugs all lined up as if expecting someone they knew to emerge from the pub. It was the same group who had had a run in with Murphy the night before.

'Told you it was going to be one of those nights,' Murphy said to Molloy.

The rakes tried to ignore the posse of trash who were lined up against the wall of The Short Hill. When they started walking in the direction of Patrick's Bridge the posse followed them.

'Three rakes and a nymph followed by a taggle of rats,' Kearney said half aloud.

Murphy and Kearney both secretly undid their belts to use as weapons in the inevitable fray that was about to commence. The nymph was waiting for a chance to go and get help but she wasn't too happy about leaving her buddies outnumbered. The rats were getting nearer and nearer. The rakes were passing the big display windows of Brown and Thomas. Suddenly, in complete unison the three turned and ran at the rats before the rats could jump them. Molloy had been a karate black belt ages ago but was still fitter than the scumbags and he floored two of them before they could say boo, seriously putting in danger their ability to breed baby rats. The other two had surprised the remaining rodents with their belts and one of them ran away, his malformed skinhead bleeding profusely and muttering trog curses. The biggest rat who was left standing found himself facing a very irate Murphy and Kearney. Murphy was the weakest of the rakes in terms of physical strength but all his pent up anger and disgust at the trogs came together and he rushed at Big Rat and launched him through the window of the shop where they both fell against a few sexy looking mannequins. The nymph had by this stage phoned the police. As Big Rat tried to disentangle himself from the sexy lingerie Kearney gave him a satisfactory clatter and sent him back once more among the suspenders and frilly blouses.

The rakes and the nymph wasted serious drinking time giving statements to the police. They were lucky not to have been brought to the station as well but the rats were well known to the policemen and so they got to the festival club in the mood for a serious razzle.

'I'm going to find Ms USA,' Molloy announced as soon as they were in the lobby.

'I'll do a scan and meet ye in the ballroom,' Kearney told the other two.

'Don't you want to do your own scan?' the nymph asked Murphy.

'Let's get some vitamins first,' he suggested.

'All we needed tonight. I did say ye'll come to a bad end,' Jane said to Murphy as they savoured their drinks.

'They were lucky we were in a good mood,' he joked. 'The country is gone to pot. Even if they were to kill one of us they'd only get a few years. Life is getting cheaper by the day here.'

He gradually calmed down and when Kearney arrived he left the two of them and went walkabout. He needed to lose himself for a while. He was still having flashbacks to Schull though not with the same frequency. Sometimes some woman would remind him of Emily by her clothes or a turn of her head and then the shadow would come down. It still hit him again and again that he would never see her again. The word 'never' was really beyond comprehension.

Molloy meanwhile had indeed tracked down Ms USA but she was proving to be a far more formidable figure that she seemed on a first impression. She was not 'easy' as the Yanks put it. As well Molloy had rarely come across such an impressive intelligence and breadth of learning. Imagine. An American woman who read Chomsky, who knew who the French prime minister was, who was well up on literature and art. She even spoke French and Spanish. Very impressive for an American he could not help thinking. Her first impression of Molloy was changing as well.

'I thought you were just a philanderer?' she told him as they started their second round of drinks. Her plain Jane friends were scattered about the place.

'Me? Never?' he replied with lupine innocence.

As soon as she realised that he did actually have an intellect she relaxed a little. She was one of those very independent women who didn't like wasting her time. He asked her down to Schull after their third drink and she said she'd see. He didn't leave the table for the rest of the evening. He was just hoping that some of his local conquests like Isolde would not come along. In any case there was nothing he liked better than a challenge.

Murphy rejoined Kearney and the nymph. He said that there was one gorgeous sylph in one of the alcoves but she was surrounded by burly Russian mafia types.

'I hate that in a sylph,' Kearney said.

Overall the festival club was quieter than previous nights. At one stage Murphy saw the Romanian girl from The Short Hill in the distance and was about to go and talk to her when he noticed that she was with some people so he didn't bother doing the Good Samaritan. She still looked a bit forlorn but maybe she'd cheer up after a few glasses of vitamin M or whatever she was drinking. His phone buzzed and it was a short text from the elusive Sadie saying she would text again soon and not to contact her until then. 'All very enigmatic,' he mused.

'Look who's over there,' Kearney said with vexation. It was the ubiquitous Fred Astaire with his usual coven of women.

'Just forget about them. Why you even bother noticing him in the first place,' the nymph complained.

They moved on to talk about Molloy's prospects with the American.

'The trouble with him is that most of the women he has been with in the past have been so unintellectual and predictable,' Murphy expounded to the others. 'What he needs is someone who can challenge him - and I don't mean congressionally. Otherwise he will end up as a collection of sexual diseases in some old folks home.'

'Well one thing about Americans is that they are optimistic,' the nymph remarked. 'Ye both could do with one. Ye are so needlessly cynical and pessimistic ye'll never see the light.'

'Women are more optimistic than men in general,' Murphy mused. 'That's why they take it so badly when they break up after a serious relationship. Men, being more pessimistic, have fewer expectations.'

'Maybe women take relationships more seriously,' the nymph lectured. 'You two sleazebags spend so much of your time hunting and looking for meaningless liaisons you miss out on the right women.'

'Misguided sylph!' Kearney told her. 'It's easy for you to be more optimistic whizzing round Oxford and meeting the aristocracy of the intellect. We're here in prison surrounded by trogs and dogs. And anyway what exactly do you mean by the right woman?'

'Oh people like me I suppose,' she half-joked.

Kearney gave Murphy another of those 'I told you so' looks and then went off to get some drinks.

'We might as well be optimistic as pessimistic,' she went on.

'Easier said than done. You don't have the Dog after you all the time,' Murphy said.

'Sod the Dog!' she cried. 'I'm sure we can figure a way of getting him to go away. It is a *him* I take it?'

'Very funny,' Murphy laughed. 'As for women being more optimistic than men. I wonder. I suppose women have babies and there is an elementally positive thing in creating something, even a mewling sprog. They definitely can put up with suffering better than men it seems.'

While this banter was going on Kearney was at the counter getting drinks. Fred Astaire happened to arrive at about the same time. He was with a few good lookers as usual, much to Kearney's annoyance.

'Staring at my friends again,' Fred ranted at the rake. He was a bit drunk it seemed. He must have had at least two beers already.

'Why don't you go away you undersized fairy!' Kearney said cooly. He then intoned lines from a childhood poem:

Up the airy mountain/ Down the rushy glen
We daren't go a hunting/ For fear of little men.'

This drove Fred into a near frenzy of ire and he would have hit

Kearney except that the rake was far taller and more threatening.

'I'll get even with you yet,' the leprechaun threatened and went off in a huff.

Kearney just gave a Heathcliffian glower, then smiled and went back with the drinks. None of the company was in a great mood for circulating after all. The visit to Schull loomed over the nymph and Murphy while Kearney felt guilty for making an excuse not to go and face it all.

'Life is interesting if nothing else,' Murphy said to Jane. 'Here we are sharing some kind of common reality and you believe that Emily still exists while we think she is extinct.' 'Indeed,' she replied as if she was temporarily on their side of the argument. She looked tired and woebegone all of a sudden.

'I'll go and see what Molloy is up to. He may not be residing in the villa tonight,' Murphy said and went off to find the rake of rakes.

He found the Welsh tomcat having an in depth conversation with Ms USA about the Deep South. He told him they were all going shortly and Molloy said he'd be along later. So Murphy went back and sat down to finish his last vitamin M.

'Whatever about Samuel Beckett here,' the nymph said indicating Kearney, 'I just don't believe that you don't believe.'

'Well that's tough cos I'm a lapsed atheist,' Murphy told her.

By this time things were winding down and so they headed off to their respective bases. Kearney went off to get a taxi while Murphy walked along with the nymph. It was cold and a bit on the bleak side. When the time came for them to go in separate directions she didn't really say anything and so he asked her (more out of decorum than desire) if she wanted to come back for a night cap. She assented with surprising and uncharacteristic enthusiasm.

'Wuf, Wuf, we're home,' she half-shouted as they went into the hallway.

'Leave him alone or he might come and bite you,' Murphy joked. 'You're not drunk are you?'

This was a silly enough question as she could drink all of them under the table. They went into the front room and she looked through the music collection as he made two Irish coffees. She choose two CDs - an album entitled *Dead Can Dance* with a weird Hieronymous Bosch cover and Beethoven's Fourth Piano Concerto with Gilels as soloist.

'Which one?' she asked him as he came back with the Irish coffees. He had even sprinkled the tops with chocolate.

'You cheated,' she reminded him on her first taste. 'It's Scotch.'

Very impressive. He liked a nymph who knew her whisky. He looked at the two CDs and decided against the *Dead Can Dance* as he was not in that frame of mind.

'Looks like it's the Beethoven. We're not really going to listen to it all are we?'

'Why not? Are you tired or something? Better than reading yourself to sleep.'

The music had a kind of mystical glean to it. Near the end of the first movement the nymph had moved quite near to him on the long sofa and by the start of the enigmatic second movement she was lying against his shoulder. He was perplexed by all this and for once was at a loss in deciding how to react. In any case, she did seem to want to listen to the music and so he just closed his eyes and let the music float round the room. As the finale came to its radiant ending she moved away from him before he could consider his next move, whatever that was going to be.

'Well that's what a girl needs before going to sleep don't you think?' she said with an air of satisfaction.

'Indeed. What else?' he could only reply in a slightly confused state of mind.

Before anything else could be said or done the door outside was being opened and a slightly disconsolate Molloy came in, alone. He was surprised to see the nymph but she just bade them all goodnight and left.

'What have I walked into?' Molloy said wearily. 'Was my timing really bad?'

'Yes it was. I was just going to ravish her by the open window,' Murphy told him earnestly.

'A matter of time as Kearney says,' Molloy sighed.

He explained that the American woman had gone off with her friends but did give the Welsh wolf her phone number. He had that consolation at least. Another day without 'lopsy paw' - it was beginning to get to him. He'd have to start taking large doses of bromide tea. He would fade away if there wasn't a change of luck soon. There was a chance that she would come to Schull but she seemed to like keeping him in suspense. For the first time in ages he was not in control when it came to the fair sex and he was quite frustrated at this new experience. Maybe he should have told her more about the circumstances under which they were going to Schull but he didn't want to frighten her off completely. Tales of two murdered women in one Irish town was not exactly a great way of getting places with a formidable and dishy Yank. She certainly was different to the women he had been ravishing in recent times and was so fetching with her auburn hair and green eyes not to mind her curvy bod and fine intelligent face.

He went off to his room while Murphy waited a few minutes wondering what would have happened if Molloy had not come back so unexpectedly. He was usually very sure of himself with women but Jane confounded him. What did she really want? He certainly didn't fancy her in the way he had fancied Emily but he did really like her and feel at ease in her company. Surely this was not to be one of those friendships that waxed into romance? What they had gone through together had created a bond between them but that was hardly a basis for a romance. In any case, he was looking forward to seeing Sadie in the days to come. He finally went off to his room in a perplexed state but was so weary that for the first time in ages he fell quickly asleep.

Part Nine

REQUIEM FOR A CITY

She saw that events led nowhere, crisis was an illusion, and that passions of momentary violent reality were struck off like sparks from the spirit, only to die.

One could precipitate nothing. One is empowered to live fully: occasion does not offer...

Elizabeth Bowen
'The Disinherited' (from The Collected Stories)

Music heard so deeply

That it is not heard at all, but you are the music

While the music lasts...

T. S. Eliot 'Four Quartets'

Occasionally Murphy threw on a special breakfast for some of his circle. Everyone liked visiting his old house with its panoramic view of the city and spacious rooms lined with books, CDs and vinyl records. It was a kind of haven, an oasis in a desert of barbarians. Kearney turned up first and was not at all pleased. It seemed that his latest conquest, Nuala, was proving to be a version of Fatal Attraction *a la* Glenn Close. While she didn't exactly boil his bunny rabbit and throw acid on his limo she was becoming obsessive, possessive and an interference in his social life which was so free and fluid.

'Give me a break,' he said to Murphy with exasperation. 'She makes a Gestapo interrogation look like peanuts.'

It seemed he told her he might be going to Schull and she wanted to know with whom and a hundred other details, not to mind demanding an explanation as to why she wasn't invited.

'And on top of it all she's mean as hell,' he added with a sigh.

All of the company despised meanness in people and all had their own classic tales of frugal and miserly people they had banished from their lives for such an unappealing attribute. Murphy knew this doctor who was so mean that he used to go to the local library to read the daily newspaper. The frugal medico was also renowned for his dexterity in avoiding paying for his round in bars and had on occasion bought second hand dingy clothes in Oxfam to save a few shekels. He went to a funeral once in Scotland and was so appalled at the prospect of having to pay a ten pounds taxi fare to the cemetery he took his friend's bike instead and cycled the five miles in the freezing cold. He was invited to a seminar in Dublin on another occasion and his cruel dilemma was whether to fork out seven pounds for a hostel or sleep in his car and save the money.

The aroma of freshly ground coffee, the sun shining in the bay window and the surprise of new people were what most people relished about such mornings in Murphy's lair. Earl turned up a few minutes after Kearney and he wasn't very happy either. Ms Opera, it seemed, had more or less implied that his social standing was unsatisfactory and this got his gimp up at her petty snobbery and at her coterie of mirror gazing friends. Emma Larchfield then arrived with some quiet and utterly boring, rustic old maidish type. Murphy was not at all pleased with the presence of this old biddy as he had had a run in with her a few nights earlier. He had passed some remark about the scum bags who had come into The Shack selling the IRA rag *An Phoblacht* and she had attitude. He was going to tell her to go read a few tomes on Irish history but out of deference to Emma he just glared at the dry old spinster.

Corelli's *Concerti Grossi* could be heard in the background as Jane brought in fresh croissants from the kitchen while Murphy cleared the big table of books and music scores. The rakes and the nymph were considering a trip to Schull later in the day, despite Murphy's reservations. He was putting up a good show outwardly but was not at all that far away from complete despair. Walking on ice was fine until it cracked. People didn't notice until you were gone under and then it was all a bit too late.

Molloy was last to appear, having slept late. He was in a state of near shock having been without sexual congress for yet another night. He would certainly fade away in a matter of days if some wench didn't allow him to have his wicked way soon. However a few minutes later he had cheered up no end when he got a text from Ms USA. He returned the text by inviting her to turn up for a coffee and waited for her with new energy and purpose.

'So what's her name tomcat?' the nymph taunted Molloy jokingly.

'Kate O Reilly if you must know.'

'Oh you mean she's one of our own?'

'More or less. Now why don't you go off and bake an apple tart.'

Murphy had an old fashioned idea of hospitality which extended to those guests he didn't care for particularly. He tried to be civil to Emma's companion and offered her some warm croissants which she declined as if they were some kind of foreign, sinful object which could assail her virtue (which he was sure had never been assailed). 'Spare me,' he muttered as he walked away from her boring and inert presence.

Life was too short to tolerate bores. He had almost gone past the stage where he went out of his way to talk to people who just sat there expecting to be talked to, people with no ideas or thoughts of their own. The Shroud of Turin was tiresome enough but at least she wasn't a bad tempered shrew. And she had been known to smile, not like Emma's friend whose face seemed to be permanently set in iceberg mode. As he was going into the kitchen he got a surprise text from Sadie which said 'Please don't come to Schull before Wednesday. That includes all of your gang. Will explain later.' This was all very mysterious and Kearney's first reaction, when told was, 'Okay. Let's leave for Schull now.' Molloy was a bit nervous because of the McMicheal angle while Murphy and the nymph agreed that such a request from Sadie had to be honoured.

The door-bell rang. It was the American woman, alluringly dressed in a cream linen jacket and matching skirt. 'She certainly passes the daylight test,' Kearney mused as he looked through some books on science. Jane handed him one by the physicist Paul Davies - a tome called *God and the New Physics*.

'Why don't you look and see what he says,' the nymph lectured. 'That is if you could come off your high horse for a while.'

Kearney smiled and they both looked at the titles of the individual chapters. 'Mind and Soul', 'Did God create the Universe?', 'Accident or Design?'

'Okay. I'll read it just for you and then I'll tell you why it's all wrong,' he told her wryly.

His phone then buzzed with a text from Nuala which demanded to know where he was.

He ignored her message and sat down to look through the nymph's recommendation.

Meanwhile the American was impressing the rakes more and more. She had presence and style and had the most amazingly beautiful skin which made her seem far younger than she was. It was in fact almost impossible to believe she was American at all. There was an almost Mozartian lightness about her, a kind of ethereal grace. If the nymph was the Brahms *Double Concerto for Violin and Cello,* then she was Mozart's *Sinfonia Concertante for Violin and Viola.* As the morning lingered she got Molloy by himself in a sunny corner, having dazzled the company with a witty talk on the poetry of Richard Wilbur no less.

'What say you to a ten?' Murphy asked Kearney as they passed each other in the kitchen.

'No doubt. A class act,' Kearney enthused. 'Celestial being. I'm putting her on my list. We'll have to tell her about all Molloy's other conquests. And pronto, amigo.'

'Are you two talking about moi?' the nymph asked as she entered the kitchen.

'No. Not this time,' Murphy told her.

'But who's a ten here if not me?' she pressed, not without a certain degree of seriousness.

The rakes looked at each other and Kearney slinked off leaving Murphy to answer the question.

'We all gave you a ten ages ago. Okay?' Murphy assured her as he tossed her hair lightly.

Meanwhile the Welsh rake was not at all enjoying himself. His new American friend seemed to have read his file or got secret info on his antics from someone.

'So you are not involved with anyone at the moment?' she asked him almost coyly.

'Not at all. Of course not!' Molloy replied with false indignation. The mere thought of asking such a question.

'So what about Isolde?' she pressed.

Molloy was not at all amused. Cork was a small place but surely she couldn't possibly know of the Rhine maiden? He tried to pass off Isolde as an ex and an aberration but the American was not to be put off. It became clear that she knew about Rose as well and was convinced that Molloy had a few more wenches stacked away back in Middle Earth. He was losing the battle and maybe the war, much to the delight of his fellow rakes who were trying to listen without being intrusive in his 'execution'.

Molloy was crest fallen. There was little chance of her going to Schull now with him. She wandered off to talk to Emma and the old maid (Iceberg Face) while he just sat there gazing out the window. It was not long before the Renaissance nymph sat next to him. He expected another lecture on the meaninglessness of his life, the futility of his liaisons, the superficiality of his relationships, his disgraceful fickleness, his lack of a bottom line, his gross amorality, his unending conveyor belt of lies and half lies.

Instead the nymph just declared wryly, 'What goes round comes round.'

She wandered off as well and Molloy was not at all amused by such smug superiority in one so young.

'So does this mean that Kate is available?' Kearney asked him as he took an arm chair near the Welsh rake. Molloy had rarely been so seriously interested in a woman like the American but now it seemed he was paying for all his past indiscretions with interest. He swore that if he could 'win her back' he would give up all the philandering but of course no one would believe him, not even himself.

Meanwhile Murphy and the American shot the breeze about the Deep South. He loved the rare surprise of new people. After a while she noticed a copy of Rogier van der Weyden's 1460 *Portrait of a Lady* over the piano.

'My, my! So you must tell me why you choose that van der Weyden portrait?'

Murphy was even more impressed. What a Renaissance woman. What a relief to meet someone who actually appreciated art, not to mind being so knowledgeable about it.

'It's my favourite portrait in all art,' he enthused. 'It always just gets me. It's so ethereal. I love her finely crafted hands, far more beautiful than the Mona Lisa's, and her elegant, aristocratic looks. And that intelligence she radiates.'

'Indeed,' Ms USA replied, 'though I would have to go for one of the late Van Gough self-portraits myself if I had to name a favourite.'

The conversation modulated gradually into one about living in the city.

'So you must know a lot of people?' Murphy quizzed the shapely American.

'On the contrary. I know very few people here. As I said before it is a very cliquey and clannish place.'

'Indeed. Not the first time I've heard such remarks. But you must understand one important, indeed fundamental thing. It's not only outsiders think like this. Lots of people born here feel the same. It is certainly not the friendliest of places. There are so many here leading lives of quiet desperation and some of them are really interesting, creative people.'

In true American fashion however Kate did not like spending too much time on the negative and so they moved on to talk about Schull. Murphy for some unknown and inexplicable reason told her about recent events. She was one of those people who tuned in so quickly and her attractive brand of intelligence marked her out as a future confidante, that is if she were to stay in the city of types and trogs. She was a good listener and empathised with the rake as best she could. Murphy told her that she was welcome to come on their next trip though it was likely to be a bit on the iffy side. As this one to one was taking place Kearney was half-looking through the Paul Davies book while concentrating on mentally undressing the dishy American. She was quite a doll as they used to say in Butte Montana. He would have loved to seduce her slowly... he associated different women with different sexual positions but with her it was a case of the whole shebang. 'Would I or what!?' he sighed. She oozed sex appeal and he was fairly certain that she would be an exciting and imaginative lover. He loved having liaisons with sexually confident American women who were so good at the whole gamut. He was about to start an elaborate fantasy about her dressed in red and black lingerie when the other rakes called him over.

'We'll leave Schull until Wednesday,' Murphy told him and Molloy. They agreed though Kearney was quite willing to go against Sadie's request, being such an obdurate type. They were now all at a bit of a loss as they had planned on leaving for Schull that afternoon. Emma and Iceberg Face went off while the American waited a little longer before finally leaving as well. She made a date to meet them on the following night, giving Molloy a slightly ambivalent smile – half glare and half bemusement - and went off leaving an aura of near adoration behind among the rakes.

'Not another one?' the nymph asked them all as she got her coat and made for the door.

***

Murphy was alone. He was in a restless mood and the Dog was somewhere in the house and coming closer. The effort on even deciding to play a piece of music was great and almost impossible to put into practice. However, he poured a glass of Rioja reserve and eventually looked through his music collection. Outside as dusk fell there was a full moon framed by the window as if Chagall himself had fashioned it. He wavered between several works and finally decided to put on Kleiber's Beethoven's Seventh. This was a recording which had in past times charged him with enough spiritual energy to keep going for ages. He refilled his glass and settled down looking out at the city lights below and the moon above. He loved the way the symphony's architecture grew from the opening chord, played by the entire orchestra, followed by a sustained note from a single oboe. He got the impression of great primeval forces being created by some divine architect, like vast upward currents of air rising in some towering cumulus cloudscape. Such elemental sounds, such drama unfolding. His favourite movement was the last. Kleiber conducted the Vienna Philharmonic as if it was one instrument. It was a complete blast, full of an almost cosmic energy, so relentless in its drive, so blazing in grandeur. The thrilling final pages of the work, with the French horns of the Vienna Philharmonic especially prominent, filled him with a physical animation and spiritual glow. His heart always thumped with excitement after listening to this symphony and it thumped even more whenever it was Kleiber conducting. 'Yes!' was his only vocal reaction on this occasion. He had another glass of the Rioja and sat for a while just looking at the city lighting up as the moon shone down.

He had intended staying in but Molloy came back from one of his mysterious outings and wanted to go for a 'late one'. The Welsh libertine was not at all himself. Between the murder of Emily, his escapades with Rose (and escapes from McMicheal) and his brief encounter with Ms USA he was out of sorts and in one of his rare moods of rumination. They went into Murphy's local and found the snug empty. Molloy was going on and on about the American and about his past meaningless liaisons. Murphy listened to the usual Welsh rant and then said what he had always been saying:

'So what's the point? You are eternally known to say that you will reform on those all too often occasions when you say you have found the Right Woman. And then what happens? You stay faithful for about a month and the usual pattern starts all over again. Admit it - you are a serial womaniser without hope of a cure. A lupine Don Giovanni - and you know what happened to him?'

Molloy wasn't well up on opera so he ignored the allusion. He had no real defence as his fellow rake had facts on his side. It was indeed the fated pattern he had to confront.

'Okay,' he sighed. 'What if for once I am right? She could be the answer to my quest.'

'Your quest,' Murphy laughed. 'More like a self-defeating hunting expedition.'

The conversation went on and on without a conclusion as they both knew there wasn't any in prospect. Murphy wasn't really smitten by the American but at the same time he didn't want Molloy to end up with her either. And, in any case, no one knew how long she was going to be around for. They were just about to leave when the door opened and Emma arrived in with a couple she often hung around with. Murphy groaned when he saw them approaching the snug. Emma really picked them. She must have had a greater collection of losers, dipsticks, outcasts, pseudos, dimwits, half fools and bronts in her circle than the rest of the city combined. The present couple was no exception. The woman was one of those who spoke at rather than to people, and was so dazzled by her own reflection that she never even noticed if anyone was really listening. Hubbie was a big bulky type with thick glasses, straight out of a Hezbollah scenario. If anyone talked to Eskimo Nell (as Murphy has named her) for longer than five minutes he got nervous with jealousy. Murphy was in absolutely no mood for putting up with these types so he finished his drink and went off, leaving the Welsh rake to continue with the pleasantries and figure out that Eskimo Nell was not available.

Just as Murphy arrived back at the house the phone echoed in the hallway. He considered not answering it - it could be some awful relation looking for lodgings or Emma asking him to come back to the bar. However he decided against his better judgement to answer it. It was Sadie of all people. He was more than thrilled to hear her voice. She didn't seem at all like her usual self. The conversation didn't last long. She asked him how things were and questioned him about his trip to Schull.

'We'll wait until Wednesday, even though it's weird you can't tell us why you're putting us off.'

'Just trust me and everything will be clear later in the week,' she replied and then she was gone. 'All very strange,' he thought.

It was certain that he did have a special thing for Sadie though he always tried to repress it given her marital status. However he sometimes got the impression that she wasn't completely at one with the big W and he more than once wondered whether the way she looked at him was real or a figment of his oversexed imagination. He wandered off to bed and tried to read himself to sleep. He finally put out the light and had a vague half dream, half fantasy about her… she was on a bed somewhere and was wearing a black mini skirt with a revealing top. It was all very confusing and fleeting. He remembered her next in a car driving along somewhere in the country with no one about. She took his left hand as he drove along and put it on her knee… his last image was of a very erotic sensation of her guiding his hand up her leg to the top of her silk black stockings and taking away her skirt.

***

Next morning there was no sign of Molloy so Murphy assumed the Welsh rake would cater for himself or maybe see a priest about starting a new life of virtue and fidelity. He wasn't in the humour to get breakfast so he wandered off to the centre to have a coffee in one of his regular cafés. He bought *The Independent* (as in London) and went to The Woodbourne where he was served his regular coffee with cream by the usual friendly dark eyed brunette. One of life's better moments was indeed time spent having coffee in some bright and atmospheric café. It was a kind of retreat from the world and a place to meet people for colloquies without the influence of alcohol. If a woman showed interest at eleven o clock in the morning (and vice versa) then you were on to a good thing. There was nothing worse than being in some dimly lit bar with some wench all night and then at closing time the full lights would go on and reveal her to be some kind of coyote woman. Time passed. The sun shone in the windows as he surveyed all the news about the wreckage of the planet. He didn't really care anymore. He had given up on human nature a long time ago. The human race was non-league football. He didn't give a damn about the future of the environment or nuclear holocaust or whatever kind of future was due. People got what they deserved. Nothing was ever learned from history and the world was caught in an endless nightmare of injustice and cruelty perpetuated by the virus of populism.

He was distracted from such musings by the arrival of a female banker he knew to see for some time. She was formally dressed, quite dishy looking as well she knew it. She loved flaunting her looks and you could almost hear her say out loud, 'Look everyone how beautiful I am.' She wore a black top which showed just the merest hint of cleavage but it was no doubt all very deliberate. She was delightfully leggy. He couldn't be sure if she was in the Frosty category but she was a grade one poser indeed and probably a gold digger to boot. She had such a false smile which she must have used to effect with her (bank) customers he mused.

'Give me a break,' he said half aloud, forgetting where he was for a moment. He would have liked to have given her a once off table job despite her pretensions and airs and graces. 'She'd probably get on well with Ms Opera and that set,' he pondered.

***

Later, as Molloy wandered into the centre, Murphy ambled home. The Welsh rake seemed to be in crisis mode and was even more than annoyed than usual at the criticisms levelled against him by the company, especially as he knew they were all true. He was especially vexed at the American's knowledge of his antics. Time for a change it seemed before it really was too late. He, more than the other rakes, feared the prospect of ending up alone. He was the least independent of them when the chips were down - and now they were down indeed. He did the bookshops (all two of them) and then ended up in The High C for a coffee before heading back for high tea on a low table. The conveyor belt of women would have to stop he decided, especially when someone as intelligent and attractive as Ms Kate O Reilly, from Huron Drive, Claremont, Los Angeles came along. Things definitely needed to change when a twenty-five-year-old nymph (even if she was the Renaissance version) addressed him as a tomcat.

The bar was full of less interesting denizens. One Crusty was already comatose on the sofa and there was a trio of rough looking women in long cotton dresses dogging large pint bottles of cider in a corner. They all had very impressive orbs but they all were equally ugly apart from this attribute. They were like a collection of chieftains' daughters. Molloy didn't stay very long. He did one more walkabout on the off chance that he would come across the American. In any case, he had plenty of time to spare now that the trip to Schull was on hold.

Time passed. Murphy was in the kitchen doing some Argentinian steaks. He was feeling slightly better than usual and had even put on some Albinoni Violin Concertos while he was doing the dinner chores. The phone rang and it was the nymph.

'I'm going back to Oxford tomorrow,' she informed him. 'Got a phone call and I need to see some people asap.'

It was all very abrupt and a bit unreal. It didn't seem like she was coming back in the near future. More irresolution.

'So what about tonight?' Murphy asked her.

'I'll see. I'll text if I've got enough time,' she explained. 'This is all a bit unexpected but *c'est la vie* and all that,' she added and then she was gone. 'Just like that,' he mused. It seemed to him that the company was for her a passing source of diversion and no more. It was a phase she was going through. She would be having an Oxford romance within months he guessed.

In deference to the American Murphy and co had planned to meet in one of the city's hotel bars later that evening. Places like The High C were a novelty for her for a once off visit, but she was too classy an act to subject to the railings and medieval utterances of the clientele more than once. There were too many drunken brutes there who would have tried to paw her. Kearney arrived. There was no sign of Fatal Attraction or the nymph. Molloy for once was hoping that the litany of wenches he knew would not turn up. Kearney started humming *'I've grown accustomed to her face'* to annoy Murphy and was surprised at the nymph's sudden disappearance. She was indeed missed even though no one said anything.

On arriving at the hotel Murphy noticed Pearl with the Fred Astaire set and was more than annoyed to see them. Fred was becoming like one of those nefarious leprechauns who just wouldn't go away. It was becoming almost an axiom that Pseudocream would also turn up if Fred was around. Time passed and there was no sign of the American. It wasn't usual for Americans to be late. They weren't like local women who made a point of always being late in case they had to face the trauma of being alone in a bar or hotel lobby for a few minutes.

Molloy cheered up after a vitamin M and started on about Welsh rugby and The Valleys and the primeval nature of Pontypridd. Pseudocream came in and they all just looked through him. 'What a loser,' thought Kearney. It was rare indeed that they all took an extreme dislike to the same person but this was one of those occasions. No one knew where Earl was.

'Maybe he's planning vengeance on Ms Opera?' Molloy suggested.

'Like what? Sending her a set of Mozart operas?' Kearney said with unusual force.

'Charming talk and an American vision due to join us,' Murphy remonstrated.

A few female secretary types passed and the company admired their leggy shapes.

'Bet they have very good sex lives,' Murphy pondered.

'Maybe we should go to their bars some night?' Molloy suggested.

'I thought you were reformed, Don Giovanni?' Murphy reminded him.

Molloy winced and waited anxiously for the American to make an entrance. The evening lingered. They hadn't intended staying in the hotel all evening but as she was obviously delayed they got a table and had another round of drinks.

Kearney got a text from Fatal Attraction with the usual demand to know about his location. In return he did the usual thing and ignored her. Outside the door there was some to do between the bouncers and some drunken, oversized rustics who were completely ossified. A gang of trogs with bits and pieces of metal in their noses and mouths passed by and taunted the rustics. The rustics made off after the trogs and the bouncers phoned the police despite knowing how futile the phone call was. The bar began to fill up a little. A Chet Baker number played in the background.

'At least this is a Frumpy free bar,' Murphy reminded the others.

'Yes but it a serious Frosty haven don't forget,' Kearney retorted.

'I hate that in a bar,' Murphy could only respond.

As if fated to appear Susan the sexy coquette arrived in with another fairly stunning woman, all curves and geometry. Molloy was all antennae and interest. Murphy had his usual brief fantasy of having a table job with Susan as Kearney admired her 'would I or what!' friend.

'Give me a break,' Molloy complained. 'Why do they do it? There they are yet again, dressed to kill, oozing sex appeal and showing no interest in wolves.'

All this always got on Kearney's gimp. After some time the coquette and Ms Euclid were sitting down fairly close to the rakes. Susan had given Murphy her usual half coy smile which drove him into a state of sexual anticipation.

'Why don't you go over and work your charm on the two madonnas?' Murphy asked Molloy.

'I have to be good,' he told them a shade unconvincingly. I'm a new man. Ms USA is due here any minute.'

Murphy was more than interested in the psychology of the Susan type. Was she a mere gold digger? A small town snob? Just shy? What kind of sex life did she have? How highly sexed was she? Was the lingerie she wore as classy as her clothes? What made her tick? Did she like table jobs? Was she merely all glitter and pose? Was there anything at all beneath that sylph like charm? He decided to engage her in conversation on the way back from the toilets. She was always friendly enough towards him in an offhand kind of way, even though she always gave Kearney the cold shoulder.

Murphy eventually went off and on his way back asked her how things were. She introduced him to Ms Euclid and they shot the breeze with considerable ease for a few minutes. Typical Susan. She made all men feel as if she wanted them but Murphy knew better from experience. He noticed that Ms Euclid had a wedding ring on but she didn't seem at all married in the way she looked at him, not to mind the sexy pose she maintained throughout. Things were moving along nicely when Molloy came over out of the blue and told Murphy they all had to leave immediately.

'You'll have to excuse us a minute,' Molloy told the lookers and took Murphy back to the lupine table.

It seemed that he had phoned the American and a policeman had answered, telling Molloy that she had been attacked and was being taken to hospital as they spoke. It transpired that Kate O Reilly was indeed planning to be on time for her rendezvous with the rakes. However as she was walking along the Grand Parade she encountered a gang of three or four trogettes coming in the opposite direction. They seemed to be all about sixteen or seventeen years old. One of them stopped her and asked her for a light for her cigarette.

'I'm not a smoker,' the American told her.

'Do you know how to sew?' the biggest and ugliest of the trogettes then asked very aggressively. Before the beautiful American had time to respond to this weird question her interrogator put a razor towards her face and slashed her cheek in a downward direction.

'Well go home and sew that you bitch,' the trogette hissed and the gang ran off laughing.

The next hour was one of shock and incredulous horror for Kate as she was rushed off in a police car to the nearest hospital. The rakes couldn't do much for her. She had been sedated and would be kept in the hospital for a few days at least. The rakes ended up back in Murphy's house and had a stiff whiskey each.

'What the hell is going on?' Molloy raged. 'I buy a house in Schull and two women are savagely murdered there within a year. Then the scumbags do this to Kate. I came over here to get away from the Welsh trogs and this is all I encounter?'

They were all really angry and outraged. There was no doubt that if they had caught the piece of trash who had scarred Kate they would have thrown her in the river. No doubt if she were caught by the police she would end up getting a suspended sentence like so many other scumbags and orcs. Kearney wandered off and Molloy went to his room only able to sleep because of the whiskey. Murphy stayed in the front room staring out at the city lights.

The next morning was all hassle and grief. They went to the hospital to see about Kate but as they didn't really know her very well they only made inquiries and left her to her friends. She would be able to receive more visitors later and so they went off again. They sent her a bouquet of flowers and a card and planned to come back again soon. There was little else they could do. There would be no word on the long term nature of her wound for a few months.

By lunchtime the three rakes were once again in Murphy's place feeling a kaleidoscope of emotions ranging from a simmering anger to perplexity and disbelief. Molloy was in no mood for a trip to Schull. Murphy said he wanted to go and planned to leave in the early pm. Kearney was in two minds about what he wanted to do but sensed that it would have been better to leave Murphy off by himself to face the demons and whatever else there was to encounter down west.

***

Driving the Saab alone was always a bit therapeutic for Murphy. He headed off and as he drove along he put on some music to take his mind off the meaningless attack on the gorgeous American. Past Skibbereen the scenery began to get more rugged and in keeping with this he put on the Sibelius Fifth. By the time he reached Schull he was feeling very edgy with occasional flashbacks to the murder. He had no idea what to expect from Sadie. He did sense however that this was going to be more than an ordinary visit. He sent her a text and she replied by telling him to visit any time after four - so he planned to see her at four. He arrived in Schull about half an hour before the appointed time and so did a quick walkabout, visiting the bookshop and having a coffee in The Black Bull. There were a few locals about and, considering all the recent news, things seemed very normal. He didn't get much information from the owner of the bar who recognized him from recent visits. There were two solicitor types drinking coffee at the far end of the counter and there was an old maggie having an animated conversation with herself at a nearby table.

He went outside and could scent the sea air. It was a perfect spring day with a warm sun and a light breeze. *'Calm was the day and through the trembling air/Sweet Zephyrus did softly play,'* he half-murmured as he drove up towards Sadie's house. Life was interesting if nothing else he thought as he parked outside the big old fashioned door. She came out to meet him and gave him a kiss on the cheek. She was looking stressed and even haggard but was still very fetching and sexy. She was wearing a light cotton dress and a head band which made her look the real arty type.

'So where's William?' he asked innocently enough.

'It's a long story. You'd better sit down and prepare for a saga,' she advised him and went off to get coffee.

It transpired that William had become increasingly involved with local IRA thugs and Sadie had set him an ultimatum as she abhorred all that those retarded, psychopathic scumbags stood for. This really knocked the gimp out of Murphy and he tried hard not to show his delight at the prospect of a free and available Sadie. He was furious at

William and found it hard to believe that he was in league with such a set.

'I am just glad the whole thing is *finito* so I can go back to a normal life. I'm going to Italy very soon to stay with a friend for a few months,' she announced wearily and with a certain finality.

He didn't want to ask her any more details - he didn't want to hear her say that she was not coming back again. The afternoon waned. He gave her an update on life among the trogs and she was aghast at the news about Ms USA. He hadn't given the slightest thought about his plans for the rest of the day. He wasn't sure what she expected of him and he was completely drained of confidence. She suggested they go for a walk and they went up a boreen at the back of her house until they had a sweeping view of the surrounding mountains and sea down below.

'So what about Jane?' she asked with a certain amount of delicacy.

Murphy filled her in on all the details, including the world's attempt to match him with the nymph.

'And what is wrong with such a match?' Sadie pressed him.

'Here we go again,' he thought to himself. He told her what he had told everyone else, though with more patience and more persuasiveness. He was still really unsure what was going to happen. She was so alluring but not at all easy to figure out. He could hardly make a pass at her in her present state.

'You will stay for dinner?' she asked him. That seemed to mean dinner and nothing else he mused. He didn't want to spend another few hours being close to her and not being able to kiss her.

'No, I'll go back in a minute,' he replied.

She didn't object and this got to him. However he tried the patience card, for once. He thought again about being more direct but he decided that she was under enough pressure for the moment. She escorted him to the car and said she would see him again when she had got her bearings. As he was about to get into the Saab he gave her a kiss on the cheek but she pulled his face down towards her and gave him a really sensuous, grade A, lingering, deep throated kiss that rated in his top five ever. And that was that. At least for the time being. She said she'd see him in a few months and he left in a haze of emotions and drove back to the city still not knowing what she really thought. One more twist of the knife, one more point for the Dog.

He got back to the city to find Molloy about to leave for the local pub and so to keep his mind off the events of the day he went along with the Welsh rake for some vitamin M. Molloy had made a brief visit to Kate who was surprisingly upbeat considering her ordeal. They were not yet sure how scarred she would be in the long term.

'American women like her are the best. A class act or what?' Molloy asserted.

Kearney appeared a bit later. He was not at all in good humour. The scarring of the beautiful American was a kind of last straw for him. He was utterly fed up of the city and the trogs.

'Things fall apart indeed,' he exclaimed. 'An innocent woman slashed and scarred for life for absolutely no reason. What a dump of a one horse town of provincials and no nos.'

As if to confirm Kearney's assessment of Celtic Tiger Hibernia Molloy announced that he was selling the Schull house - there were too many shadows down there for him after his recent ordeals. Eskimo Nell and her Hezbollah hubbie came in with Emma Larchfield along with a few arty types with attitude. The rakes groaned collectively.

'Let's get out of here before they take hostages,' Murphy advised. They finished their drinks and left, having paid their respects to the downtrodden Emma.

***

Murphy was looking out over a sunlit Bantry Bay and the rugged mountains of the Beara Peninsula beyond from the steps of Bantry House. The summer music festival had come round once more - one of the calendar's social and cultural highlights. The spectacular setting formed an ideal backdrop to the series of concerts that ran for more than a week. It was a welcome break from the trogs and the tracksuit types that roamed the city. Unlike other festivals of such ilk it was truly informal with performers and audience mixing easily in a local hotel after concerts.

He met all kinds of extraordinary people not to mind some very classy women, and it was such a relief to be finally in the company of people with whom he could commune about composers from Machaut to Rubbra. He had earlier had an intriguing conversation with an elderly English gentleman of the old school who treated him to a string of diverting anecdotes about great conductors he had seen in performance. Another woman (who was in her seventies and had an Anglo-Irish accent) regaled him with stories of her meetings with Elizabeth Bowen in Kinsale. They spoke of the writer's resilience in both her life and in her fiction. Indeed he remembered her being interviewed on TV one time when she had cancer and was certainly dying. 'One must get on with it', was her attitude when pressed about her philosophy - he liked that in a woman. There were a few of the 'see and be seen, frightfully frightfully' set here and there but these were not so prominent for such an upmarket festival. The usual handful of obnoxious egomaniacs from the music world strutted about but these were more an object of amusement and parody than anything else.

Murphy was looking out at the scenery while he waited for an evening recital to begin. The divine Hélène Grimaud was to play the *Diabelli Variations* to a full house and people were milling about admiring the landscape and drinking wine. In recent months he had immersed himself in music as a way of dealing with the latest misfortunes. There seemed to be no end to the unrelenting series of painful happenings and disappointments. Fate indeed seemed to be malign and brutal. He had stopped going out socially and had spent hours listening to all the Mahler symphonies until he was familiar with every note of all ten. Without music he would probably have done away with himself or even become an alcoholic.

The gong sounded, beckoning people to the recital. Shafts of light lit up the distant Beara Peninsula. He felt a physical pain at the loss of Emily and departure of Sadie. Schull was so close and yet so far away. He turned from the sea and walked into the house. Ms USA was with some guy in the audience but he ignored them for the time being. He was relieved that she had recovered well from the trogette assault. He took his seat and looked out at the gardens in full bloom. Summer was indeed the height and fullness of living. There were some stunning women scattered here and there in the audience but most seemed to be matched off already. Another year had gone by and in some ways nothing had changed. It seemed that he had to endure despite himself, armed only with an innate resilience and a sense of humour. It wasn't good enough though, this mere survival.

So there it was. A highlight of another year about to unfold. Grimaud appeared dressed in her usual black and launched into Beethoven's last great piano work, a cosmos of sound, at times serene and otherworldly, composed in solitary silence. He liked her rapt way of playing. She made the work shimmer. He lost himself in the music and didn't open his eyes until just before she played the final notes. When she finished there was a lingering silence before the applause, as if time was suspended to allow a return from the world of pure spirit. He was happy that she had the good taste not to do an encore.

At the interval he did the usual walkabout with a glass of wine in his hands. He was not going back for the second part of the recital. He didn't want to hear any more music after the *Diabelli Variations*. Most people milled about outside as the weather was so clear and sunny. He said a few hellos to various people he knew to see. He walked towards the lawn which overlooked the sea. In the distance he caught a glimpse of a tall and curvy woman walking by herself. She had long wavy hair and was wearing black. 'Would I or what!' he said aloud as she half-turned to face him.

Available worldwide online and from all good bookstores

Michael Terence
Publishing

www.mtp.agency

www.facebook.com/mtp.agency

@mtp_agency

Lightning Source UK Ltd.
Milton Keynes UK
UKHW010735200122
397454UK00001B/12